DUMFORD BLOOD

DUMFORD BLOOD

S. K. EPPERSON

ST. MARTIN'S PRESS   NEW YORK

DUMFORD BLOOD. Copyright © 1991 by S. K. Epperson. All rights reserved. Printed in the United States of America. No part of this book may be used or reproduced in any manner whatsoever without written permission except in the case of brief quotations embodied in critical articles or reviews. For information, address St. Martin's Press, 175 Fifth Avenue, New York, N.Y. 10010.

Design by Glen M. Edelstein

Library of Congress Cataloging-in-Publication Data
Epperson, S. K.
    Dumford blood.
       p. cm.
    ISBN 0-312-06342-3
    I. Title.
    PS3555.P6187D8   1991   813'.54—dc20   91-21840

First Edition: November 1991

10 9 8 7 6 5 4 3 2 1

For Lynda, and for my father, J. W. Phipps.
He was a mountain of a man.

PART ONE

Dumford

The largest part of mankind are nowhere greater strangers than at home.
—S. T. Coleridge, Table Talk

Chapter One

Ben Portlock gazed at the lights of a distant helicopter in the night sky and wondered what the town of Dumford would look like from the air. Probably about the size of a Kennedy lawn, certainly not much bigger. His town was small and secluded, hidden away in Kansas foothills covered with lush bluestem grass. Beyond Dumford to the north and east lay the Flint Hills; to the south and west lay the city of Wichita, the Peerless Princess of the Plains. In comparison, a local newspaper had once called Dumford "the humorless hunchback of the hills." "Homely and poor," the article had said, "but full of character."

Dumford's community square boasted a drugstore, a food store, a Sears outlet, two clothing shops, two eateries, a hardware store, a bank, a post office, a police station, and a newly repainted town hall building. Scattered outside the square were three school buildings, two churches, a tavern, a liquor store, a mortuary alongside the hundred-year-old cemetery, and a long boxcarlike mausoleum with real marble steps. The Kennedys would be proud.

At the moment a party was in progress in the town

square. Tables covered with flimsy crepe tablecloths were lined up in a wide horseshoe around a crudely built bandstand, upon which an elderly band called Hubert and His Hoobers played songs that made teenagers cringe and old women cry. On the north side of the bandstand was a barbeque station, and on the south side was a table holding plastic cups and three floating kegs of Miller Lite beer. Women hovered around the food and used their napkins to swat at the last diehard flies of the season. Men hovered around the beer, taking quick chugs and swapping spit on a shared bottle of Jack Daniels.

Ben Portlock turned his back on the party and walked up the darkened main street to check out Luther's Food Store. Luther's parking lot was a favorite hangout for the younger teenagers, but on this night the area was deserted. Ben guessed most of the kids were either in the square stealing beer from the kegs or slyly spiking half-filled cups of Milly Bartok's all-occasion fruit punch. He'd done the same thing when he was a kid, and they hadn't come up with much of anything new that he could see. Kids were kids.

He kicked at a few broken beer bottles in the lot and retraced his steps in time to hear Hubert and His Hoobers strike up a tinny rendition of Spagoni's "Wedding Jubilee."

Ben groaned to himself and slowed his steps. As he neared the square his bored gaze caught a flash of red. He looked and saw Bryce McKee, a fellow police officer, leaning against a pickup truck and talking to a girl in a bright red dress. Ben walked closer and smiled as he heard his friend's teasing voice. Beneath Bryce's blue police uniform beat the heart of a frustrated stand-up comedian. Bryce's trouble was that he was too handsome to be considered funny. Women thought he was a smartass, a jerk, or a cynic, but few thought he was genuinely funny.

"It's true," he was saying to the girl in the red dress. "We don't let just anyone into Dumford. We check out everyone who comes into town. Even people like you, who claim to be visiting a cousin. We checked you out."

"I'm sure," the girl replied with a giggle. The light September breeze lifted the hem of her red dress enough to show black lace panties and a pair of long, skinny thighs. She appeared not to notice.

"I'm serious." Bryce drew a bottle of Wild Turkey from his hip pocket and took a long drink. "We're pretty clannish around here. This party here tonight? This party is sort of a town shower for Edie Jackson, wife of bank vice-president Portis P. Jackson."

"Portis?" the girl repeated. "Where'd he get a name like that?"

Bryce's grin was wide. His blue eyes gleamed beneath his dark brows. "Well, you see the Jacksons had this little retarded boy first. When Portis came along they decided to let the retard name his new baby brother. Now, all this kid knew was his mama teaching him how to say 'pease porridge hot, pease porridge cold,' so when the kid sees his brother for the first time he goes, 'Portis Pea!' That's how they named him."

"You're shitting me," the girl said.

Bryce held up a hand and crossed his chest. "Swear to God. That's how it happened."

Ben shook his head and eyed the bottle of Wild Turkey Bryce was holding.

"Okay," the girl said. "So what about this Edie? She's pregnant, right?"

"You bet. And Portis is throwing the party because Edie's baby will put the population of Dumford at one thousand. That's big time, sweetheart. You live in a town with a population of a thousand and people remember your name. They say, 'Why that's old Bryce McKee there, and I believe he lives in Dumford. Yessir, I'm almost certain of it. They got a thousand people in Dumford, you know. Lo, yes, a regular thrivin' metropolis is Dumford.' Trust me, honey. A thousand people is a landmark for a town like this. We might have reached that number a month ago, but

Joni Wilkson's new baby disappeared the day after she brought it home from the hospital."

"What happened to it?" the girl asked.

Before Bryce could answer, Ben stepped into view. He tipped his hat to the girl and smiled at Bryce. "How's it going, folks?"

"Hey, Ben," Bryce said. "Honey, this is my buddy and fellow officer, Ben Portlock. He's Edie's brother."

"Hi—" The girl jumped in surprise as the bottle of Wild Turkey abruptly found its way into her possession.

"I'd introduce you," Bryce said to her, "but I can't seem to remember your name, sugar."

The girl punched him in the shoulder and walked away, her red dress swirling around her skinny thighs. Bryce winked at Ben and went after her. "Hey, I was just kidding!"

In the square the music stopped and Hubert announced a short break. Ben glanced at his watch and saw that it was close to ten o'clock. Another hour and Hubert and His Hoobers would go home. By midnight the square would be left to the town strays. There would be plenty of leftovers available: chicken bones, dropped globs of baked beans and potato salad, and several dozen inedible homemade dinner rolls, courtesy of Maisie West, who some people said brought the same rolls every year and took them home again to put in the freezer for the next year. The fare was the same at every party, with the only variable being whether the chicken was fried, baked, or barbequed.

At a quarter after ten a wheezing, long-faced Calvin Horn approached the square and asked Ben where the chief of police could be found. Ben pointed to the keg station where George Legget was hurriedly putting away another swig of Jack Daniels.

"What's up, Calvin?" Ben asked.

The grizzled man stiffened his stubbled lip. "I got to tell the chief. This is bad, Ben. This is real bad."

Ben nodded and accompanied the stale-smelling Calvin,

sole owner of the town's trash-hauling business, over to the keg station.

George Legget wiped his mouth with a huge hand and looked at them with bloodshot eyes. He frowned and swayed as he addressed Ben. "I asked you to walk the perimeter. We've got to have some form of crowd control on display."

Ben gestured to the man beside him. "Calvin."

The garbage hauler whisked the cap off his head and held it before him. "Chief Legget, this is awful. I wouldn't have come now, during the do, but I figured it was my duty. I know how you like to get evidence fresh and all."

George looked past him in annoyance. "What evidence, Calvin? Why are you here?"

Calvin shifted his stance. "You know that bitch of mine that was gettin' ready to pup? Not the black one, but the red one. Kinda looked like she had some Airedale blood in her, but I never could find out for sure. I got some books with pictures and I—"

"Calvin," George growled.

"Okay. Yeah. Anyway, I've been takin' real good care of her, but tonight I come home to feed her and I find . . ." His voice lowered to a whisper that neither Ben nor George could hear.

"What?" George barked.

Calvin held his arms up and pretended to cradle thin air. Then he made a slashing motion. "Gone."

"For crissakes," George said. "Ben, will you please tell me what this idiot is trying to say?"

Ben looked at Calvin. "Somebody broke into your place and slit the dog's belly open?"

The trash hauler bobbed his head. "She's dead. The puppies are gone."

George put down his beer. "Good God, Calvin. You come out here for that?"

It was the wrong thing to say. Calvin's face crumpled. He burst into loud, braying sobs that made women's heads turn. Men looked up from their bottles. George looked heavenward and took the garbage man by the arm to lead him away from the keg station. "Okay. Okay, I'm sorry, Calvin. I know what your dogs mean to you. Have you got her here?"

Calvin looked horrified. "No! I wouldn't bring her to the party all stiff and everything. She's back home. And I didn't touch the knife, either. I came straight here."

George nodded. "You've got the knife. That's good. We'll come and have a look, Calvin. Wipe your nose, okay?"

Calvin used his sleeve. George turned to Ben. "Find Haden and tell him we're going out on a little run. Have him sober up Bryce and Mickey to help watch things here."

Ben nodded and made his way into the crowd. When he returned, he found the trash hauler sitting in the passenger seat of George's police car.

"You drive Calvin's truck," the chief said to Ben. "I want to ask him a few questions on the way."

"Thanks a lot, George." Ben took the keys and swore under his breath as he climbed into the reeking cab of the garbage truck.

Calvin lived five miles south of town in a tar-paper travesty built only yards away from the dump. Four dogs and ten cats were purported to share the one-bedroom house with him, but no one Ben knew had ever actually been inside Calvin Horn's place. No one had the nose for it, or the stomach, since Calvin was fond of telling people how his dogs cleaned the floor and his cats did the dishes.

Two weeks after the Wilkson baby disappeared, Calvin had made himself momentarily famous by finding the missing infant in a plastic garbage bag. The townspeople patted him on the back with relief and gratitude—until it was revealed that Calvin had stumbled across the corpse during a routine sorting of the town's garbage. The people of Dumford then became outraged. And paranoid. Many people began using their fireplaces and stoves early, though it was still hot and sweaty summer.

Ben had laughed at the smoking chimneys, but at the same time it made him wonder. The killer of the Wilkson baby had yet to be apprehended. For a time, Joni Wilkson herself was the favored suspect of the town gossips. Then it was Calvin, who had no business looking through trash and finding dead babies. The police department had no suspects in the case.

A cluster of tall elms hid Calvin's house and dump from the highway. Ben saw the taillights of the chief's car disappear in the turn onto the dirt road. He caught up in time to see the entire back end of the black-and-white car take a dip as the rear wheels encountered an axle-breaking rut. The chief's angry howl sliced through the night air and bounced off the rustling elms. Somewhere to the west, a coyote answered him.

The truck Ben was driving took the rut with only the slightest jolt. When Ben reached Calvin's drive he saw George's six-foot-five frame striding purposely toward the front door of the house.

"Don't you believe in lights, Calvin? I can't see a damn thing out here."

Calvin rushed ahead of him and fiddled with some keys in his hand.

Ben heard George's snort. "You keep this place locked? What the hell have you got that anyone would want to steal?"

George reached for the knob and Calvin batted his hand away. "I said I'll bring her out*side,* Chief."

Ben climbed down from the truck and slammed the door. He approached the house in time to see Calvin open the front door to a blinding flash of light.

As the blast rung in his ears, Ben instinctively hit the ground. For an awful, terrible moment, he thought he had seen Calvin Horn's head leave his shoulders. He told himself it was a trick of the light and scrambled onto all fours. Adrenaline pumping, he fumbled at his waist for his flashlight. When he pointed the bright beam he saw that George was on the ground, but on his back, not his stomach. Ben shifted the beam and winced as the light picked up Calvin's severed head on the ground beside his still twitching body. Blood poured from the jagged flesh above the collar of Calvin's only shirt.

Ben tore his stunned gaze away and forced himself to concentrate. A shotgun. A shotgun had done that. Someone was in the house with a gun.

"Ben!" George shouted.

"Here." Ben switched off his flashlight and moved across the ground to the chief. "Are you hit?"

George clutched at his chest. "Get my pills out of my pocket. I'm having a goddamn heart attack."

Ben reached for him and began to search his pockets. "Which one?"

"In my right . . . oh, God, this hurts."

"Try to be calm, George." While Ben searched the chief's clothes he darted glances over his shoulder to the house. The absence of yard lights and the tiny thumbnail moon in the sky assured them of adequate cover. It was too dark for them to be easy targets.

George began to groan. "Right, dammit. Look in the right shirt pocket."

Ben had already checked the pocket once. "No pills," he said. "Hang on, Chief. I'm going to call for an ambulance."

"Hurry, Ben!"

"I will. Be still and try to stay calm. I'll be back in a minute."

Hannah, the dispatcher, wasn't at her desk. Ben tried three times before giving up. The middle-aged maiden had probably read herself to sleep with one of her women's magazines. Ben swore into the mike, then he changed tactics.

"This is Officer Ben Portlock requesting assistance from anyone listening. I need an ambulance at Calvin Horn's place. This is an emergency. Anyone listening please respond. Over."

In seconds he heard a male voice. "This is Phil Taylor, Ben. I'll make the call for you."

"Phil? See if you can get some police assistance out here as well. Bryce and Mickey are at the party in the town square."

"Will do, Ben."

Ben sighed in relief and replaced the mike. Phil Taylor was a good kid. One of the few Taylors in town who didn't hold a grudge against him.

"Ben! Ben, did you get anyone?"

George's voice was weaker, more strained. Ben left the car and went back to him.

"I got Phil Taylor. He's going to call for help."

"Thank God for nosy pissants with police bands," George croaked. "What happened to Hannah?"

Ben turned to look at the house. "Try not to talk anymore, George. I'm going to have a look around."

"Rigged," George mumbled. "It was rigged. I saw the wire when the gun went off. The gun was rigged to the door."

"Damn." Ben sat back on his heels in surprise.

"Get in and check out the place," George said, and he made a motion with his hand.

Ben stood up and turned on his flashlight. In the distance he heard a siren begin. He looked at George.

"I'll be all right," the chief insisted. "Go on and check it out."

After a moment's hesitation, Ben turned and walked toward the door. He didn't want to, but the hand with the flashlight automatically picked out Calvin's headless body on the ground. Ben swallowed the bile in his throat and pulled a handkerchief out of his pocket as he stepped into the house. He didn't think he would need the handkerchief—anyone smart enough to rig a door would surely have thought to wear gloves—but he used it anyway.

A twelve-gauge shotgun was clamped to a small sewing table just inside the door. The wire attached to the triggers went around an old barber pole behind the table and ended in a twisted loop around the doorknob. Ben stepped on something that rolled beneath his foot. An unused shell. He picked it up and exhaled through his teeth. Three-inch magnum, double-aught buck.

Christ, he thought. Must've felt like being shot with a cannon.

He abandoned the shotgun and looked around in dismay. Calvin's living area bulged with plastic garbage bags, some full, some half full. Trash was everywhere, littering every inch of floor space. In one corner was a pile of men's magazines, most opened and carefully folded to the centerfold. Beside the television was a stack of videocassettes, and on the threadbare sofa sat an inflated doll with a round oh of a mouth. Her blond head was half bald; her left breast was patched with black electrical tape. Covering her hips was a pair of blue boxer shorts.

Ben shook his head and waded through the mess of the garbage man's home. Beneath a small table supported by two legs and four bricks, he found a bag seemingly singled out from the others. Using the end of his flashlight, he opened the top and peered inside. The bag was full of books. On impulse he pulled one out and saw a tiny metal lock on the cover. A diary?

"Couldn't be," he murmured to himself. Calvin Horn keeping a diary was unfathomable. He flipped open a page and immediately saw his mistake. Not Calvin's. Before he could investigate further he heard the ambulance siren cut off outside. He shoved the diary back into the bag, and without stopping to ask himself why, he looked for a place to hide his find. The kitchen looked good, since it held even more refuse than the living room. He tossed the plastic bag behind the grease-covered refrigerator and had to duck as the freezer door swung suddenly open. He closed the door, paused, then he opened it again. There was a green plastic garbage bag inside the freezer compartment.

Garbage in the freezer?

Ben opened the top of the bag, looked at the contents, then he left the kitchen in three swift strides.

Someone else could take the dog out.

Chapter Two

"Did you hear the way that reporter talked to George?" Hannah complained. "Little worm acted like he thought the chief's having a heart attack during a murder was funny. But I guess all those city folks act like that. Right, Ben?"

Ben put his newspaper away and gazed out the station window. "I don't know, Hannah."

"Well, you ought to know. You lived in the city for almost four years, didn't you?"

"Three. I was there for three years."

Hannah's ginger-colored brows rose. "Aren't you thirty-five?"

"I'm thirty-four. What does that have to do with how long I lived in the city?"

Hannah put her pencil in her stiff auburn hair and dug in her desk drawer. She came up with a blue memo book. "I keep track of these things. Oh, all right, I see now. Bryce lived there for four years and he's thirty-five. I always knew you boys would come back, you know. I told you about living there, didn't I?"

Ben fought a yawn. "Yes, you did."

"But you didn't listen. You had to go oat-sowing in the big city. Bryce should have joined the police force there like you did instead of—"

"Instead of what?" Bryce came out of the bathroom and picked up the paper Ben had discarded.

"Instead of marrying that girl who took your money and left you high and dry."

"Hey," Bryce said, "I left her. And it was her money to begin with, not mine."

Hannah pursed her lips. "I'm sure. Anyway, my point is that you both came home and gave me the supreme privilege of saying I told you so."

Bryce ignored her. "What's the sheriff say, Ben? His boys find anything out at Calvin's place?"

"Nothing to help. His lab people shook their heads and said adios when they saw the place. The shotgun belonged to Calvin. No one found the knife he was talking about."

"Did they say why the dog was in the freezer?" Hannah asked.

"No," Ben said. "I think they've written Calvin off as a nut who wanted an audience for his suicide."

Hannah adjusted her tortoise-shell framed glasses. "That's just ridiculous. Why on earth would Calvin Horn want to kill himself?"

"Probably got sick of watching the same old porn movies over and over," Bryce murmured behind his newspaper.

Hannah looked up. "Calvin had dirty movies?"

Bryce smiled. "A regular film library. You should sneak over to the evidence room at the sheriff's office and watch a couple, Hannah. I think you'd like the woman meets dog series."

Hannah's lip curled. "You're disgusting."

Bryce laughed and winked at her. "Not as disgusting as that German shepherd. Let's just say he was a fool for a snatch of hamburger."

As Hannah's cheeks flamed, Bryce turned to Ben.

15

"You going out?"

"Not for a while," Ben said. "My shift starts at two."

Hannah unscrewed her face and looked pointedly away from Bryce. "Ben, I think we should ask the sheriff for some help. With Cory still on vacation and George in the hospital, this town could go crazy and we couldn't do a thing to stop it."

"I love the way she says *we,*" Bryce said to Ben. "And we can always count on old Hannah to be at the radio when *we* need her, can't we?"

"I worked during the party as a favor," Hannah stiffly reminded him. "I wasn't used to being up so late."

Ben stood and put on his holster. "We appreciated the offer, Hannah. Someone had to stay here."

Hannah sniffed. "I go to the rest room for exactly ten minutes and someone happens to get his head blown off. That wasn't my fault. And just who is going to haul Dumford's garbage now?"

"I guess we know your priorities," Bryce said with a smirk.

Hannah rose and walked around her desk to Bryce. She poked a crooked finger in his chest and placed her heavily powdered nose on a level with his name tag. "Don't you talk to me like that, Bryce McKee. I've had it with your lip, mister. You were just as bad in school—young, smarty hooligan always upsetting the class with little pranks behind my back. You're still quite the clown, but it's no funnier now than it was then. You just keep your snide remarks and dirty talk to yourself."

Bryce gently removed her finger. "Hannah . . . Miss Winegarten . . . I realize this is not a gentlemanly thing to say, so I'll be blunt. Go get screwed. It's what you needed twenty-five years ago, and it's what you need right now. Trust me. I know what I'm talking about."

Hannah's cheeks went scarlet. *"What?"*

"You heard me. I've been dying to say that to you since the sixth grade and—how old are you now, fifty-two, fifty-three?" Bryce clucked his tongue. "It's never too late to start, Hannah."

Hannah raised a hand and struck him hard across the face. Bryce only smiled at her. "Wouldn't you rather use that old yardstick you used to carry?"

"Yes!" Hannah's face was purple as she jerked away from him. Bryce grinned and smoothed back his dark hair. His deep blue eyes sparkled with mirth.

"Damn, that felt good. I can't tell you how good that felt. I'm ready to fuck, fight, and hold the light, Ben."

Ben smiled and shook his head as Hannah clapped her hands over her ears.

"Filthy!" she seethed as the door closed behind Bryce. "Filthy, filthy, filthy! Is that what you boys learned in the city?"

"No," Ben said simply.

"He has no respect for women. No respect for *any*one for that matter. It's no wonder his poor mother died so young. A son like that would drive anyone to the grave before their time."

"His mother died of cancer, Hannah."

"See what I mean?"

Ben exhaled. "How's Kurt?"

"How do you think?" Hannah snapped. "He's rotting inside. We're all going to die of cancer. And don't ask if you can stop by, because my brother doesn't want to see anyone. He does have some pride, you know."

It was useless to try to appease her, Ben decided. Once Hannah became angry she tended to stay that way.

"Tell him I said hello then. I'm going now, Hannah. If the sheriff calls I want to know about it."

Her nod was curt. "Of course."

Ben picked up his hat and left her to the tiny six-desk office that served as their police station. The ten-cell jail behind the office held a drunk from last night's party, but was otherwise empty. Ben liked it that way. Greenwood County normally didn't have a high rate of crime, but he

17

thought Dumford's statistics were about to change that. The town was starting to remind him of what he'd left behind in the city.

In the whole of last year Dumford had seen four stolen bicycles, two shoplifters, five burglaries, and forty-six drunk and disorderlies. This year they had topped all previous statistics and made it to the big time on the regional news by adding one murdered infant and one possible suicide to the list.

Personally, Ben thought the suicide business was a crock of sheriffied shit. He got in his police car and drove to Calvin's place with the intention of picking up the diaries he had found and taking them home before his shift started. Aside from the obvious reasons, something about Calvin's keeping discarded diaries bothered him. He pictured the fuzzy, filthy old man digging through piles of trash and exclaiming with delight each time he found such a private treasure. Diaries usually meant secrets, and with so many diaries in his possession, Ben had to wonder if Calvin had stumbled onto something he shouldn't have.

A load of double-aught buck screaming through a rigged door said it was possible.

The sheriff's crime lab personnel didn't appear to have taken anything, with the exception of the doll and the videotapes. The bag with the diaries was still behind the greasy refrigerator, and today the kitchen itself was full of cats. A tiger-striped gray rubbed itself against Ben's legs and he stooped to give the lifted back a cursory pat. On a sudden thought he looked out the back door and saw three dogs chained to stakes in the ground. He found a bucket under the sink and filled it with water. The dogs wagged their tails at him when he approached, and the bucket was emptied by the thirsty dogs only seconds after he delivered it. Ben took it inside and filled it again, and he paused in the kitchen long enough to make a call to the county animal control office. After making arrangements for the animals, Ben found a bag of food and took it and the bucket outside and left food and water within reach of the three chained dogs.

Inside the house again, Ben retrieved the bag of diaries and went out through the front door. As he left the porch he wondered if the owner of the alleged knife had possibly come back to find his property. But if he'd found it, why rig up the shotgun?

"Suicide my ass," Ben muttered aloud. "Something's wrong here."

He tossed the bag of diaries in the backseat of his car and almost jumped as something brushed his leg. The gray cat meowed plaintively when he looked down at it.

"How did you get out?" he asked. Then he thought of the evening before and wondered why he hadn't seen any of the cats in the house then. He walked back to the shack and found what he was looking for on the south side of the house. The rubber flap of the pet door flapped open in the brisk breeze.

Okay, Ben thought. So that's why Calvin had put the dog in the freezer. He was afraid his starving dishwashers would mistake it for meat while he was gone.

As if reading his thoughts, the gray cat appeared at his side and meowed hungrily. Ben looked at the animal a moment, then he sighed and scooped it up into his arms to carry it to his car.

"Guess you're the only one who can read that sucker sign on my back."

The cat licked at his fingers with a rough tongue and planted itself in Ben's lap as he sat down behind the wheel. The animal didn't move during the ride back to town. Ben pulled into his drive and turned off the engine.

"Home," he said to the cat. He gathered it into his arms and carried it up to the door of the white bungalow he lived in. The house was the family home, bought by his mother and father in the late fifties. After his father's departure, Ben's mother had decided to lease the house and move to a smaller one-bedroom home next door to her tavern. When Ben left the city and returned to Dumford, his mother had politely booted out the tenants of the bungalow and handed the deed over to her son. Like Hannah, Stella Portlock claimed she had always known Ben would come back some day. It irritated the hell out of him that they were right. Still, the house was in decent shape and it was close to the station. He didn't need anything more.

He put the diaries in his bedroom and carried the cat into the kitchen, where he emptied a can of tuna onto a plate. As the animal buried its nose in the food, Ben lifted its tail and discovered that Spike, Butch, or other male names would not be applicable.

"Shit," he said. He picked up his hat and grinned as the cat proceeded to gorge herself. "Ten cats to choose from and I had to pick a probably pregnant female. Don't make any messes. I'll bring a box home later."

The cat concentrated on the tuna.

On his way out of the drive, Ben nearly backed into a familiar blue Camaro. Phil Taylor stopped the car in the middle of the road and waited for Ben to pull up next to him. An older woman sat in the seat beside the lanky eighteen year old. Ben didn't recognize her profile.

"Thanks for your help last night," Ben said to the boy. "I appreciate it."

Phil shrugged. "Glad to do it. Is Chief Legget going to be all right?"

"I think so. He's under observation and having a few tests done in El Dorado."

"That's a decent hospital," Phil said. "Isn't it, Lura?"

Ben's heart stopped as the woman finally turned her head. "Yes, I suppose it is."

"We've had Mom in there before," Phil said.

Ben didn't hear him. He realized he was staring, but he couldn't help it. The hair had thrown him. The long, raven black tresses he remembered so well were now shot through with bold strokes of gray.

"Lura?" he said.

20

Her eyes focused on him. The irises were still large and dark in their blueness. Her eyes hadn't changed.

"Hello, Ben."

His mouth felt suddenly dry. "Hello. When did you get . . . home?"

"About a month or so ago," Phil said. "She's been hiding in the house. Today I carried her out for some fresh air and a little sun." He turned to his sister. "You enjoyed yourself, didn't you?"

Lura's smile was weak. "Yes. Can we go now?"

"Sure. See you later, Ben."

Ben nodded and watched them drive away in his side mirror. They didn't have far to go; the Taylors lived only three houses down on the opposite side of the street. Ben knew he couldn't just sit there and watch her get out of the car, but he felt powerless to do anything else. For years he had wondered what his reaction would be at seeing her again. None of his imagined scenarios had quite matched this one.

His hands felt clammy on the wheel. He could see the passenger door of the Camaro opening.

Jesus, he couldn't get over her hair. She was only twenty-seven. Wait. No, that was right. Twenty-seven years old and gray hair down to her waist.

Her body looked fuller, more mature. He didn't remember her hips looking like that when she was nineteen.

The gray head turned his way for the briefest of seconds. Ben's first impulse was to mash the accelerator, but he forced his limbs to remain still. He watched her until she was inside the house and out of his sight. Only then did he look back to the road and drive on.

Chapter Three

"A month?" Edie Jackson stared at her older brother in surprise. "Lura's been home a whole month and nobody knew? You never saw her?"

"Never," Ben said.

His voice was low and quiet. Edie stood beside his chair and ran a sympathetic hand through his light brown hair. "Don't start brooding about her, Ben. I hate to see you brood. Your lips go into this straight line and make you look really mean."

When he said nothing she released his hair and moved her pregnant bulk to a chair facing him. "You knew she'd come home sometime, didn't you?"

Ben's gaze was far away. Edie sighed and brushed a few imaginary crumbs from the surface of her glass tabletop. She looked into her brother's eyes and thought of how they had always fascinated her. Her own eyes were a soft chocolate brown, like their mother's eyes; Ben's eyes were sometimes blue and sometimes green, depending on the color of his clothing. At the moment they appeared to be a muted mixture of both colors.

Edie reached for his hand and tried again. "How does she look, Ben? Has she changed much?"

Ben finally looked at his sister. "Her hair has gone gray."

"You're kidding," Edie said. "Like in old person gray?"

"Yes."

Edie made a face. "That's terrible." Then her brows lifted. "But come to think of it, her mother turned gray pretty young. It's probably something that runs in the family, don't you think?"

"I don't know," Ben said.

"I'll bet it makes her look really old, huh? And she's a year younger than I am."

Ben looked at Edie and exhaled. Addle-brained, their mother had always said of her little girl. Sometimes Ben was inclined to agree.

"Stop looking like that, Ben. I didn't mean anything. Did you talk to her? Did she say something mean to you?"

"No," Ben told his sister. "She barely spoke to me. Phil was in charge."

"Oh." A look of understanding passed over Edie's lightly made-up features. "Philip Napoleon is living up to his name."

"He's a nice kid," Ben said. "He takes good care of his mom."

"And now his sister," Edie added. "Lura Josephine and Philip Napoleon. Remember how we used to tease the Taylors? Call them frogs? Lura was always okay, but I never did like her cousins. I still don't. I know you don't want to hear it, but Michelle is the one I absolutely *hate*. She thinks she—"

"That's enough," Ben said.

"But she—"

"Edie."

"All right." Edie held up a hand and fell silent. As Ben's gaze slowly grew vacant again she held her swollen midsection and attempted to change the subject.

23

"Hey, did I tell you Mom received another offer from the Mortician?"

The corner of Ben's mouth twisted. "You shouldn't call him that, Edie."

"Why not? It's what he looks like. And I swear I can smell formaldehyde every time I see him."

"Does Mom like him?"

"Not enough to marry him. He has money, though."

Ben smiled. "Mom cares about that, I'm sure."

Abruptly he stood and bent over Edie to kiss her on the cheek. "I'm working a double shift while George is in the hospital. Is Portis going out of town again this weekend?"

"I don't know," Edie said. "Sometimes he doesn't tell me until the last minute."

"What's that on your neck?" Ben asked suddenly. He extended a hand to brush aside her collar, but Edie caught his fingers and pushed him away.

"It's nothing," she said with a tiny laugh. "Just a little hickey."

Ben's brows rose. He opened his mouth, then he gave up and shook his head. "I'll see you later. Call me if he's going out of town."

"I will," Edie promised. There was no way she was going to stay in the big house all by herself. Not with all the murdering going on lately.

When Ben was gone she wandered into the bathroom and looked at the thumbmark on her neck. She didn't know why she had lied, particularly when her brother knew she'd rather eat pig brains than have a hickey on her creamy white skin. But if Ben knew the truth he would beat her husband Portis to a pulp, and then Portis would retaliate and make things extremely unpleasant around Dumford for Ben.

Her husband could do things like that, Edie knew. Portis had pull in Dumford. He had one of the best jobs, he sat on all the committees, and he had his own computer down at the bank. He had once boasted to her of using his computer to run a greedy, conniving mechanic out of town. Portis claimed the man had overcharged him an outrageous amount for some ridiculously simple work on the BMW. When Portis refused to pay, the mechanic had threatened him with a lawsuit. Portis paid the bill and lay low for six months or more. Then one summer day the mechanic came in for a withdrawal. He was informed by a teller that he had exactly four dollars and seven cents in his account, and how did he want to pay for the seventeen bad checks he had written in the last two weeks?

Portis had done it with his computer. He had never said how, or explained any of the details to Edie, but he had pinched the mechanic where it hurt the most. And Portis had been in an excellent mood in the week thereafter. He hadn't put Edie in the closet, and he had actually encouraged her to listen while he talked about the wizardry of computers.

Afterward, Edie urged her brother to hold on to all of his deposit receipts. With the receipts, Ben was safe. But Portis could always think of something else to do to her brother. Portis put on a great show for the town: prominent businessman, concerned citizen, devoted husband. It was all a lie. His frequent business trips were actually short hops to Vegas with a secretary named Kayleen from the bank. Edie didn't mind, but she did wonder if Portis tied up his secretary with telephone cord and made her do the things he made Edie do. She didn't think so. The secretary might talk. Portis could fire Kayleen and zap her bank account, but short of cutting out her tongue, he couldn't do anything if the sleazeball decided to tattle on him.

Edie was thinking about this when she heard a car door slam outside. Seconds later Portis was in the house and guiding her toward a closet. She didn't bother to ask what she had done; it didn't matter. Sometimes she would hear the TV go on, according to which closet she was in, and after a while she would hear Portis making noises while he watched his pornographic tapes. Tonight she heard nothing.

After the first few times she had wised up and put a book light and a paperback in each closet. She had read all of Jean Auel's books in the closet near the den. Tonight she was in the linen closet with a new murder mystery. She was hoping it might give her some ideas about how to deal with Portis. She fished around between the sheets and finally found the book light. Before she could flick the tiny switch she heard approaching footsteps. Back went the book light.

Portis opened the door and glared at her. "Get your fat ass out of there and start dinner. The menu is on the kitchen counter."

Her sneer was inward. She made her way out of the closet and went straight to the kitchen. The menu was not on the kitchen counter, it was by the phone. She snatched it up and inadvertently knocked a stack of mail to the floor. She humphed as she bent down to pick up the envelopes. The first one, with an Oklahoma City postmark, was addressed to her. When she heard Portis turn on the shower she quickly ripped open the envelope. The small handwritten note inside was brief and disappointing:

Dear Mrs. Jackson:

I saw your ad in the personal column and regret to inform you that a Mr. Max Portlock was killed in a fight in my bar nearly two years ago. Don't know where he is buried. Please accept my sympathies.

Sincerely,
Mary Florence

Edie's eyes teared up and began to sting. There it was. Max, her father, had been her last hope. She didn't know what she was going to do now.

"What the hell is that?" Portis swooped down from behind her and snatched the paper out of Edie's hands. His wet skin dripped water onto the ceramic tile of the kitchen floor as his pale, colorless eyes skimmed the contents of the note. After a moment, he smiled. "Hell of a way to go.

What'd you do, put ads in every goddamn paper in Oklahoma?"

"I used my allowance," Edie said. She refused to look at her husband's nude body. His hairiness hadn't bothered her in the past, but now it made her want to throw up. His shoulders, back, even his butt was covered with thick, curly reddish-brown hair. It was ugly. He was ugly. He was fat and ugly and she hated him.

"Probably the way that redneck brother of yours will end up one of these days," Portis said with a snort.

"Ben isn't a redneck."

"No, he's just a gung-ho jerk with a badge who likes to use his fists," came the sarcastic reply.

Edie knew instinctively the occasion Portis was referring to. At a family dinner several years ago Ben had walked into the kitchen in time to hear Portis call Edie a stupid cunt. Without saying a word, Ben had taken the white-faced Portis and led him out the back door. When they returned, Portis had three loose teeth and a squashed and bloody nose.

"Ben's a good man," Edie murmured.

Portis laughed. "Oh, he's good all right. How many other guys would put their fiancée away rather than marry her? He's a fucking saint, Edie."

Edie cleared her throat. She didn't want to talk about Ben anymore. Portis hated her brother. He hated her absent father, too. She glanced at the crumpled note in his hand and wanted to cry. Her father would have come and killed Portis for her. Max had killed men in the Korean thing, and if he knew the horrible things her husband did to her, Max Portlock would waste no time in putting a bullet into that big, hairy chest.

One day Edie had bolstered her own courage enough to bake Portis a Drano cake, but she later chickened out and put it down the garbage disposal. She decided she didn't want to be sent away like Lura Taylor.

And asking Ben for help was out of the question. He

27

might put Portis in the hospital for a few weeks, but he wouldn't kill him, and that wouldn't do because Edie wouldn't receive any insurance money. No. She definitely wanted Portis dead and in the ground.

"Why did you get out of the shower?" she asked him suddenly.

He wadded up the note and dropped it to the floor. "I wanted to catch you snacking again. You look like a goddamn hippo."

Edie turned and picked up the menu. "I'm seven-and-a-half months pregnant," she muttered. "What am I supposed to look like?"

"What?" Portis barked.

"I said I know that's what I look like." She pointed to the menu he had written down for her. "Portis, we don't have any fettucini."

His face darkened. "I told you to add it to the list Saturday. Are you telling me you didn't?"

"I . . . forgot," Edie said.

"Well, I guess you'd better pull those elephant pants down then."

"I can go to the store."

"Get those pants down!"

Edie turned away and tugged at her maternity pants. She heard him open the drawer to take out his spoon.

"Where's the other one?"

"It had splinters in it," Edie told him. "I bought a new one."

His voice lowered and became menacing. "You wasted my money because of a few splinters? I guess you know you just earned another ten strokes."

Edie glanced over her shoulder and grimaced when she saw his erection. "You can't do anything, Portis. The doctor said no more rough s—"

A blow from the spoon on her bare skin silenced her.

"I can take care of myself, Edie girl. Don't you worry about that."

He grabbed himself with one hand and lifted the spoon with the other. Edie braced herself against the cabinets and breathed out through her teeth.

"You'd better hurry," she said as she glanced at the clock. "By the time I get to the store and back it'll be ten o'clock before we eat."

Portis grunted and went to work.

Chapter Four

"Mama, don't you want to watch TV?" Phil asked. Annette Taylor blinked and looked at her son. "What?"

"I asked if you wanted to watch TV. Your show is on tonight."

Annette touched her gray head in confusion. "Show? My show?"

" 'Knots Landing.' "

Her face lit up. *"Voulez-vous jouer aux cartes?"*

"Mama, speak English. You know I don't understand that stuff."

"She wants to play cards," Lura said from the hall. She walked into the kitchen and sat down at the table across from her mother. "Do we have a deck around here somewhere?"

"Sure. But she gets upset if she misses her show," Phil warned.

Lura turned to her mother. "Mama, your show is on. The one you watch every week. Do you want to play cards or watch television?"

"Is it time?" Annette looked at her son. "Has it started, Philip?"

Phil gave Lura an I-told-you-so look. "Just now, Mama. Can't you hear the music?"

Her mother moved quicker than Lura had imagined possible. Phil followed her charge into the living room and returned a moment later with a grin on his face. "If I don't watch her, she glues her face to the screen. Want a Pepsi?"

"Thanks," Lura said. She smiled as he handed it to her. She kept forgetting she could have one any time she felt like it.

Phil was watching her. "Remember Chocolate Soldiers?"

"Yes. Do you?"

"I remember you carrying me on your hip and sharing yours to keep me quiet."

Lura's smile faded. "How's school so far?"

"It's okay."

"Have you missed very much?"

Phil's blue eyes, a shade lighter than Lura's, narrowed a degree. "Why do you ask?"

"I'm just curious. In your letters you said Aunt Marie looked after Mama."

"She used to," Phil said. "When I was at school and later while I was at the garage she would come over and fix dinner and help clean up. Ben came over and helped when he could."

Lura ignored the last. "Why are you taking only morning classes this year?"

"That's all I need." His grin was proud. "I have enough credits to graduate. I could have graduated midterm this year if I'd wanted to take a full—hey, why haven't you asked me about this before?"

Her shrug was uncomfortable. "I didn't want you to feel like I was going to come home and take over."

"Not while I'm the breadwinner," Phil teased. "Mama's trust money ran out a long time ago." He paused and took a drink of Pepsi. Then he looked seriously at his sister.

"You need to get a job, Lura. I make good money for a guy my age, but I can't support the three of us on what I make at the garage."

Lura let her lashes shutter her eyes as she turned away. She looked at the stove and the ancient refrigerator, at the picture of strawberries in a cracked cup that her mother had owned for as long as she could remember. She imagined the yellow paint behind the frame would be a bright square on a faded, grungy wall if she took the picture down.

She hadn't expected things to look the same, but she wasn't prepared for the gray, frayed doilies on the tables, the old, virtually threadbare furniture, and the thin, worn carpet on the floor. Everything her mother had brought with her from France was gone—sold to cover medical bills, Phil had explained. The pearls, the rings, the fine silk dresses, all gone. Her mother had nothing from her past.

Did Aunt Marie still have her things? Lura wondered. She hadn't spoken to her aunt beyond a brief hello the day of her return. Marie resented Lura. In her eyes, Lura had plunged them all into long-lived notoriety. Lura knew it wasn't true. Her actions had simply added fuel to the eternal fire of gossip about her family, previously known around town as "those frogs."

The commotion started when Annette and Marie Mallett fell in love with the roguish American Taylor brothers during the girls' year-long visit to an uncle in Louisiana. Seventeen-year-old Marie had become pregnant by a Belgian of low reputation, and the wealthy Mallett family saved face as their ancestors did by simply sending the girl away. Her sixteen-year-old sister, Annette, accompanied her on the trip. At home in France, the family told friends that the girls were away for an educational experience. They had already been on the grand tour. America would be a lesson in what to avoid later in life.

Marie's baby was put up for adoption a day after its birth, and within six weeks Marie had forgotten the child's existence. With a little help from Jesse Taylor.

Legend had it that Jesse and Ordney Taylor became drunk one Friday evening and decided to leave Kansas and drive to Louisiana to spend the weekend eating shrimp and catching red snapper. Both men had served in the navy during the Korean War, and the long months on the water had instilled in them an unhealthy amount of wanderlust. The car they drove, their father's prized '55 Chevy, found its way to the trunk of a tree on swampy Mallett property. The two young girls thought the men were injured, when in fact they were stuporously drunk.

Lura had heard the story many times. When the uncle of the girls returned from a short business trip he found his nieces packing their things in preparation to leave. The marriages had already taken place under forged consent papers. To the Taylor brothers' keen dismay, however, their wealthy young wives were promptly disinherited by the family back in France. Jesse and Ordney soon found they had saddled themselves with two spoiled rich girls who had never seen a scouring pad in their lives and didn't know which side of a frying pan held the meat.

Sadly, the Mallett girls soon learned the wife's code of life in Dumford. A mere ten months after their arrival, Marie and Annette gave birth to baby girls, Lura and her cousin Michelle, born just days apart. Marie wasted no time in becoming pregnant again, and again, but it was nine years and two miscarriages before Annette produced Philip.

Now both Taylor men, Jesse and Ordney, were dead.

Marie had done all right for herself after Jesse wrapped his '83 Chevy around another tree. She invested the insurance money in municipal bonds and, according to Phil, she was now the owner of a big white Cadillac with frequent timing problems. He much preferred to work on Michelle's sporty little Datsun 280Z. It was an older model, but Phil loved it.

"Did you hear me?" her brother said loudly.

Lura started and looked at him. "I'm sorry. What were you saying?"

"A job, Lura. You need to get a job."

She looked at her hands. "Tomorrow I'll go to the bank and deposit my check in your account."

"Check? You mean you have more than the hundred dollars they gave you when you came out?"

"Yes. There was a mixup with the paperwork when I left. Yesterday I received my savings in the mail."

"Your savings? From what?"

"I worked in the kitchen after my classes," Lura explained. "I know it doesn't sound like much, but I made a dollar and five cents a day. Some of it I had to spend at the canteen for shampoo and things, but I did manage to save almost five hundred dollars."

Phil winced. "The kitchen. Why didn't you tell me that in your letters? I always wondered why you never asked me for any money. Jesus, Lura."

She frowned at his bitter tone. "It'll help. This place could use some work. A fresh coat of paint and maybe . . ." She paused and took a breath. "Phil, I need more time. I just . . . it's hard."

"You got a degree in there, didn't you? No one's going to sneer at that."

"I know," Lura said quietly. "It's the people. The way they talk and stare."

"You'll have to face it sooner or later," Phil responded. "In a week they'll find something else to talk about. You know how these idiots are. Right now they're buzzing over Calvin Horn having that plastic doll in his house, but two months from now they'll have forgotten Calvin and the doll both."

The conviction in his voice made Lura lift her gaze to study him. His height, breadth, and the dark stubble on his chin had amazed her the first time she saw him. Somehow, in all his letters, he had forgotten to tell her he had grown up.

"Phil," she said suddenly, "do you have a girlfriend?"

The change of subject threw him. "A girlfriend?"

"Yes. Do you date anyone?"

His mouth twisted. "I don't have time to date anyone. Most of my evenings and weekends belong to the garage."

Lura tried again. "There's no one you're especially fond of? A girl at school, perhaps?"

"Why are you asking me this?" he said flatly.

She shrugged and looked at her hands again. "I'm not sure. Guilt, I suppose. You have so much responsibility on your shoulders. Part of it's my fault."

Phil shook his dark head. "I'm not complaining, Lura. Let's get back to you. You can use your money to help with groceries or whatever you want to do with the house, but after that I'm taking you down to the school. Principal Wiley's secretary got a marriage offer from this guy in the city and Wiley's pissed because the school year just started and here she's leaving him high and dry. It's a good-paying job, Lura. If he sees your degree maybe he'll hire you on when she leaves."

Lura attempted a smile. "Have it all figured out, don't you?"

"I wish," Phil said. "She's supposed to be leaving in two weeks. In the meantime you could dye your hair and maybe buy yourself some new clothes."

"Dye my hair?" Lura reached for a strand and watched the black and gray separate around her fingers. The sixty-watt bulb above them turned the gray into silver.

"You don't want to?" Phil lifted his Pepsi, then lowered it as the police band on the counter gave a loud crackle.

"Most people your age listen to FM radio," Lura commented. She started to add something further, but when she heard Ben Portlock's voice come over the police radio she closed her mouth and stood up from the table.

"Where are you going?" Phil asked.

"To my room."

"Why? What on earth do you do when you're in there? You don't have to stay cooped up, you know."

"Maybe I'm used to it," Lura said.

She liked her room, though she had frowned when she came home to find it completely untouched in her absence. Billy Joel albums still lined the shelves by her dusty stereo, a photo of Ben still adorned the door of her closet, inside of which were a dozen pair of jeans that no longer hung loose on her hips. In drawers and on shelves she had found myriad secret, girlish treasures hidden from the prying eyes of parents and a pesky little brother.

"Hasn't anyone been in here?" she had asked Phil.

"Not a soul. I wanted to keep it the same for you."

Lura had breathed an annoyed sigh that later became one of relief. She spent her first week home rummaging through her childhood and adolescence with a ruthless determination. Some things were delivered to the charity box in the church, others were sentenced to the garbage cans.

Her bedroom walls were now bare, the dresser tops free of all feminine clutter. She felt more comfortable with the room's new spartan appearance.

But she didn't stay in her room all the time. She couldn't. Sometimes, when the house was quiet and her mother and brother were sleeping, Lura opened her window and enacted a fantasy she'd had every night for the last eight years. She escaped and went to Ben's house.

Ben rolled down the window of his patrol car and filled his lungs with the brisk night air. He loved nights like this one. The wind that ruffled his hair felt like gentle fingers, cool and somehow sensual. September was a good month. It was a month full of promise.

It hadn't felt that way in the city. In the city everything had been dry and abrasive . . . the months, the wind, the people. That's why he'd come back.

Right. Sure.

He pulled his head in the window and tightened his hands on the wheel as his thoughts went instinctively to her. He didn't want to think about Lura. She was the reason he had left Dumford. To forget her. He had wanted to do new things, meet new people, and maybe find someone else to love.

He had been a fool. A clear-cut case of a country french fry jumping out of the fat and into the fire. He was eager enough in the beginning, all right. But his first year out of the police academy had opened his eyes to the joys and perils of life in the city. The women were fine. There were girls who actually followed cops around like groupies tailing rock stars. The rest of it wasn't quite so amusing.

Teenage rapists attacking grade school children and twelve year olds selling dope, robbing stores, and carrying semi-automatic weapons were all new to Ben. He had never seen a Vietnamese person in his life until he saw one dead in a ramshackle duplex apartment, hacked to death by someone wielding a machete. He never grew accustomed to the smell of fear each time he and his partner were called to a family disturbance. Husbands beat wives, wives stabbed husbands, and all of them hated the cops who came to stop them.

City cops themselves were a different breed. They cried over a lost football bet, but didn't blink an eye at a car accident where bodies and parts of bodies were strewn for half a mile. To them it was just another shit detail in a janitorial job.

Ben compared the attitude to something Bryce had said in the station one day when Hannah asked if either of them had watched a movie the night before about the Holocaust. Bryce was flippant when he told her no, he didn't have to watch it because he knew what happened. He ignored her outraged expression and went on to say that umpteen other movies on the subject, each one more graphic than the last, had progressively desensitized him to the sight of cadaverous children and overflowing mass graves.

Such things didn't shock him anymore, he claimed. And that was dangerous, Bryce said. What television did was extremely dangerous, because the repetition made the atrocities lose their shock value, and if things like gas chambers and experimentation on humans didn't shock us anymore, we were all in big trouble.

Bryce McKee had his moments. But Ben privately thought it was a good thing his friend hadn't joined the police force in the city. Bryce would have become the kind of cop who thought it his duty to make sick jokes in already disgusting situations. The humor would be his way of dealing with what his psyche and all the religion in the world couldn't justify: the incredible ugliness of human behavior. Apathy was a must-have attitude for cops subjected to the pitiful side of reality. They had no alternative; they could insulate themselves or eat a bullet.

After three years Ben had used the ugliness as an excuse and turned in his badge.

Nothing at home had changed. The hypocrisy in Dumford was still enough to make the pope weep. The friendly ball games, the town picnics, the bazaars and the charity sales were all part of the mask that hid the humorless hunchback's true face.

The garbage at Calvin Horn's place was the real evidence. Calvin hadn't bought that doll or those pornographic movies—he had found them in the garbage. Dumford's garbage. It was hard to say who the tapes had belonged to. Did they belong to the saintly Mr. Luther at the food store? How about the seemingly innocuous Barney, at Barney's Steakhouse? Or perhaps Fred Gordon, the town's postmaster, had been the recipient of the mail-order inflatable doll. It was hard to say, though Ben did have to smile at the image of the farsighted Fred Gordon holding on to the doll. With his glasses off she probably looked real.

The rumbling sound of the train reached Ben's ears and made him shiver. Almost four in the morning. Every morning at the same time, *clackety, clackety, clackety.* The people on the north side of town slept right through the noise.

He drove as far as the old depot before he turned the car around. The memories brought by the sound of the train still made his gut tighten.

On impulse he decided to check out the vacant Parry house at the northernmost tip of the town limits. Frankie Parry and his friend Joseph had moved out three years ago and left the place open game for kids with six-packs and skinny little joints that smelled more like pencil shavings than marijuana.

Before AIDS gained national coverage, Frankie and his friend had simply been two middle-aged bachelors living together and sharing expenses. When AIDS made the television movie of the week, things were different. Small-town cruelty forced the friends—it was never proved they were lovers—to quit their jobs at the nearby cheese factory and leave town. The house was placed on the market, but the real estate office had yet to receive an offer. Common theory, and ignorance, held that the place might be infected.

It didn't bother the teenagers. During the summer it had become a weekend routine to roust them from the empty house. Since summer's end, however, the place had known some peace. Ben found no cars there tonight, but he thought he saw a light in the house as he approached the drive. A tiny flash, there and then gone. He stopped the car and was about to get out and investigate when Haden came on the radio and asked him to check out a report of a prowler. The location was Ben's own street. Ben sighed and sat back in his seat again. He drove away from the Parry house and glanced in the rearview. He saw the light again. A longer flash, a sustained beam.

"Next time," Ben promised. It was either a transient or some errant minors with a flashlight.

During his own adolescence the place to go had been the abandoned grain mill just north of the tracks. Until the summer of '72, anyway, when Bryce and a buddy accidentally set the building ablaze with a bottle of Everclear and a package of Black Cat firecrackers. Nothing was safe, be it a toad or a two-story building, when Bryce McKee had firecrackers in his possession.

Ben drove as swiftly and silently as possible back to his

part of town, and as he approached his street in the pre-dawn darkness he saw something that made him step reflexively on his brakes. Lura Taylor was walking down the street in a white nightgown. He knew it was her; his headlights had picked up the waist-length hair. No one else he knew had hair that long or that color.

The prowler was Lura.

What the hell was she doing? he wondered, his heart hammering in his chest. Before he could react, she stepped behind a row of hedges and disappeared. He turned slowly around and drove downtown to the station. He told Haden he had seen nothing but a stray on his street. Then he checked out and went home. After opening his front door he stood for a moment and looked across the street to Lura's house. She had to have seen his car, he decided. So why did she run away?

She didn't, he told himself. She walked. Lura had no idea when his shift ended, and she wasn't waiting for him. She was just out walking. At dawn. In her nightgown.

The tiger-striped cat darted between his legs suddenly, giving Ben a start. He watched it jump off the porch and disappear into the cluster of pines at the south side of the house. When it didn't show any signs of returning he went inside and closed the door.

There were three messages on his answering machine: the first from Edie telling him that yes, Portis would be leaving town Friday night; the second message was from his mother, shouting above the music in her tavern to give her a ring; and the third caller was Michelle Taylor, Lura's cousin. Michelle wanted to know if they were still on for Friday since Chief Legget was in the hospital.

"Good, okay, and no," Ben murmured to the three of them. He went to his bedroom, shrugged out of his uniform, then fell down on his bed.

It was harder to kid himself now. Now that she was back. He hadn't come home because being a cop in the city was difficult, or because he didn't like the way the wind blew. He came home because the guilt over Lura Taylor had driven him crazy. Phil was sworn to silence about the money Ben had given him to help out. Last year the boy had refused to accept any more cash. His job at the garage paid very well, thank you.

Fine. Find some other way to salve your conscience now, Ben.

And Michelle. No big surprise that Michelle had busted her tight little ass getting over to see Ben the day he came home. The surprise, Ben guessed, was that he had proved to be just enough of a lousy bastard to let her in. With the light low and her face turned just right, she looked a lot like Lura.

He frowned in the dimness and forced his eyes shut. It surprised him to feel like this. After eight long years of anticipation, he had been convinced he wouldn't feel anything when he finally saw her again. He was wrong. He felt plenty. He was consumed with thinking of her and wondering how she felt about seeing him again.

Eight years ago he had thought he knew how she felt. During the trial he had often found her looking at him with a strange yearning in her eyes, almost a sadness. But each time he attempted to see her, she sent him away without a word. Only once had she offered any words to him. He had gone to the jail to ask her forgiveness, to tell her he wouldn't have been able to live with himself, or her, if he had kept quiet about what he saw down by the tracks.

Lura had reached through the bars and touched his cheek with an unwavering hand. "I did what I had to do," she said. "So did you."

That was it. She wouldn't tell him anything more, or even look at him. It was over.

Until now, when eight years ago suddenly seemed like last week. Now, when the guilt, anger, and the longing were fresh, stinging, and begging for an overdue dose of something, anything, that would make the hurt go away.

Chapter Five

On the upper north side of town Hannah Winegarten sat up and turned off her radio alarm. She blinked and rubbed her burning eyes. She had been dreaming of Huntington Beach again. Her one brief trip away from home. The sunshine was so bright. So totally, glaringly, blindingly bright, even in her dream. Bronzed lifeguards reading Jean-Paul Sartre, giggling children chasing gulls and collecting shells from the powdery sand that clung to wet skin. Not pebbled and grainy like Kansas sand, but powdery, and warm.

Hannah hated winter. She knew it was coming soon; the dreams always told her. When she dreamed about the beach it meant winter was on its way. Although it was just September she liked to have a head start on hating and dreading winter. This year she had barely made it through August. It was the Christmas shopping ad on television. Some photographic place telling her to make her reservations for Christmas portraits now. Don't wait too late! Santa will be here before you know it!

You egg-sucking dogs, Hannah thought when she saw

the commercial. It gave her license to start hating winter earlier than she'd originally planned. Christmas was included in that package, since it occurred during winter. Same for New Year's and occasionally Easter, as well, depending on April's weatherly demeanor.

Spring was Hannah's season. Buds, flowers, warmth, the rebirth of sleeping beauties awakened by a kiss from the princely, charming sun.

But spring was a long way off. She had a whole six months of hating to get through before she saw spring again. She had to take warmth where she found it, mostly in her dreams, and try to—

"Hannah! Are you up?"

She kicked the sheets away and got out of bed.

"Hannah!"

"I'm coming!" she snapped. She jerked her robe from the closet and wrapped it around herself with familiar haste. By the time she reached his bedroom, Kurt was writhing around on the bed and lifting his bony legs away from the mattress beneath him.

"What on earth is wrong?" she asked him. And then the smell hit her nostrils.

"Number two," Kurt informed her.

"Lord have mercy," Hannah said. "Couldn't you have held it another minute?"

She yanked the top sheet away and found him nude from the waist down. "Kurt, where are your pajama bottoms?"

He wiped his nose with a palsied hand and pointed to the floor.

"What are they doing down there? Have you been playing with yourself again?"

Her forty-five-year-old brother nodded guiltlessly. A year ago, when the cancer was still in its first stages, he told her masturbation made him forget about the pain. Now, even with his pills, she caught him playing with himself constantly. In another month or so he would require morphine injections, the doctors told her. This worried Hannah. He would need to be given shots every four hours, and since Kurt wouldn't do it himself, she would have to ask a neighbor to help out while she was at the station. She could just imagine the talk if Kurt was caught flogging his penis every time Beverly Goodwin came over.

Hannah didn't know why he bothered anymore—the ugly little thing hadn't been hard in six months. And his testicles had begun to look like an old turkey wattle left out in the sun.

Disgusting. Men were so disgusting.

"Lift up," she commanded. "I can't pull the sheet off with you lying there like a sack of chunky dog food."

Kurt tried once, then he sagged back down again and gave her a strained smile. "Can't. Too weak."

Hannah's lip curled. He knew monosyllabic answers annoyed her. Sometimes she wondered if the cancer had left his colon and bypassed everything else to reach his brain. Incomplete sentences were an affront to her teacher's ears, and her brother knew it.

She went into the kitchen and came back with plastic gloves on her hands. She hated to lift him, but it was easier than it used to be. In a year he had lost fifty of his two hundred pounds. Still, it wasn't the weight she minded, it was the contact with his leathery, yellowish skin. Even with the gloves on it made her shudder to touch him.

"When will you go to the hospital?" she huffed as she lifted him from the bed and placed him in a chair.

"Never," he gasped.

"They can take better care of you, Kurt."

"No."

"Why not?" she asked, exasperated.

His features hardened. A single vein stood out in his forehead. "I didn't practice medicine for eighteen years to end up in a hospital bed with tubes up my nose and bills out the ass. I will die in my own goddamned house."

Typical, Hannah thought. Insult his own profession and

remind her that it was *his* house. She was only a boarder. A live-in nurse.

A bubble appeared at Kurt's nose. She grimaced and gave him a tissue from the nightstand as she mocked his speech. "Snot. Left nostril."

He sniffed. "I don't know what you're complaining about. Everything is going to you when I'm gone."

But you want to make me earn it, don't you? Hannah thought.

She left him in the chair and hastily stripped the bed. She wiped down the plastic mattress cover and put on fresh sheets. Within seconds after placing him on the bed, his head began to nod.

"I hope you sleep through every one of your soap operas," Hannah muttered.

She was struggling into her pantyhose when she heard him begin to moan. The varicose veins under her skin stood out in livid blue as she hopped up and down and pushed her fleshy thighs into the nylon. By the time she had straightened the cotton panty crotch seam, Kurt was baying like a blue tick on a coon.

Hannah stepped into her low-heeled pumps and tested her smile in her bedroom mirror before walking into her brother's room. "Ready for your pills?"

"Can't reach. Put the sonofabitching bottle where I can reach it, Hannah."

She glanced at the nightstand. The top was littered with pill bottles of every size. She closed her eyes, put out a hand, and closed her fingers around a bottle at random. "What do we have today?" she asked gaily. Then she opened her eyes. "Percodan. Does that sound all right for today, Kurt?"

His bald head moved around on the pillow.

"Good." Hannah shook out eight pills, popped two of them into his mouth and left the rest on the nightstand.

"Closer!" Kurt hissed.

She ignored him. She walked into the bathroom and filled

a glass with water. While there she checked her lipstick and eye makeup and cleaned her glasses. When she returned she handed Kurt the glass of water and moved the nightstand an inch closer to the bed.

Kurt drank the water in noisy gulps and gave her back the glass to place on the nightstand beside the pills.

"I'm going now," Hannah told him. "Be good today and try not to play with yourself."

"My television," he said.

"Is that all you can say?" she demanded. "How about telling me to have a nice day?"

"My television," he repeated.

Hannah stalked to the television and angrily punched the power button. She left the room without another glance.

When Kurt heard the front door close he defiantly grabbed two of the Percodans on the nightstand and shoved them into his mouth.

"Crazy bitch."

"I'm serious," Bryce said into the phone. "I really want to work for you Saturday, Ben." He shifted the phone to his other ear as Hannah made her field marshal's walk around the office.

"George is getting out of the hospital today," Bryce continued. Then, "Yeah, I'm surprised, too. He'll be in first thing in the morning. But, see, I made a date with this girl from the party. Yeah, the red dress. Let me tell you, this child is dumb. She works on one of the aircraft lines, but she couldn't tell you whether her ass has been punched or drilled."

Hannah cleared her throat loudly.

Bryce grinned. "You will? That's great. I really needed an excuse to get out of this. Okay. Sorry to wake you up, buddy. I'll see you at two."

He let the receiver fall to the hook with a loud clatter. When Hannah flinched, he smiled.

"And how are we this morning, Miss Winegarten?"

"I'm fine, thank you," she said stiffly.

"I must say, you certainly look fine. In fact, I don't believe I've ever seen you look so . . . so radiant. Yes, you look just positively radiant this morning, Hannah."

Hannah's carefully tweezed brows met in a confused frown. He was teasing her. He had to be.

"Good morning, Haden," she said as the sleepy-eyed, red-haired officer emerged from the jail. He nodded at her. "Morning, Hannah. The night's log is on your desk."

"I saw it," Hannah said. "Don't worry, Haden. Cory will be back soon and you can sleep nights again."

"Oh, Officer Preston," Bryce said loudly, and Haden looked at him. "Doesn't our Hannah look radiant today?"

Haden glanced at Hannah before picking up a report on top of his desk. "Just peachy."

"Peachy? Heavens, yes. I think you've hit the nail on the head. She looks just like a ripe, juicy peach just waiting to be fuh . . . plucked."

Haden snickered and ducked into the rest room. Bryce looked at Hannah's crimson cheeks and stood up suddenly. "I'll be back in a minute, my peachiness."

He couldn't stay in the same room and watch her open her desk drawer. When he strolled outside he glanced back through the plate glass and saw her filling the coffee machine. Ten minutes, tops. Fix the coffee, rearrange the desk tops, check her makeup, empty the wastebaskets. She was so predictable.

He decided to wander down to Milly's and buy a Danish while he waited. When he stepped out onto the sidewalk he saw something that made his eyes narrow. It was a white Oldsmobile with a stranger inside. The car was cruising down the main street at a leisurely speed, the driver keeping his eyes straight ahead. Bryce had seen the car and the man before, on the night of the party. One advantage to living in a town with less than a thousand people was that you could pick out those who didn't belong almost immediately. He stepped into the road and took his police pad from his shirt pocket to write down the tag number on the car. Time to find out who the man was and what he was doing in Dumford.

The early morning crowd at Milly's had already been in and out. Everyone at the cheese factory had to be at work by eight. It was now almost a quarter to nine, and only one booth in the tiny restaurant was occupied. When Bryce saw the person sitting opposite Michelle Taylor he gave a loud whoop. "My God, if it isn't Lura Jailbird Taylor!"

Her shoulders stiffened as she slowly turned to face her accuser. When she saw Bryce she relaxed.

"Hello, Bryce."

"Hello, Bryce? Is that all you can say? Stand up and give me a hug, for crissake."

Lura stood and let him hug her. A second later he pushed her back into the booth and sat down beside her.

"When did you get out?"

"Last month."

"August? You're kidding. Where have you been all this time?"

Lura's mouth curved. "Hiding."

"I can see why." Bryce was staring at her head. "What's with the hair?"

"It turned gray."

"No shit. Did the bulldykes come at you with fist-sized cucumbers or what?"

The laughter was out of her throat before she realized the sound was coming from her. It felt good to Lura. Bryce could always make her laugh.

Michelle yawned. "Premature graying. It happens in our family."

"But not to you, right Mishy?" Bryce elbowed Lura. "You could've sent her some of the stuff you use, Michelle. Miss Clairol number two hundred, right?"

Michelle's mouth tightened. "I don't dye my hair."

"Liar." Bryce ducked under the table and came back up.

"Just wanted to see if your pants were on fire. But while I was down there I thought of something else, Lura."

She looked at him. "What?"

He winked. "Your hair is actually kind of sexy. Did it happen all over?"

"What?"

He pointed to the zipper of her jeans. "You know."

Lura's cheeks warmed. "You haven't changed a bit, Bryce."

"Does that mean you're not going to tell me?" He clutched his chest in feigned agony. "You mean you'd actually let me lie awake nights wondering if your pubies are gray or not?"

Michelle reached across the table and smacked him hard on the arm. "Will you stop? Milly is looking at us."

"Let her look. What are you two doing here anyway?"

"I'm on vacation," Michelle said. "Phil asked me to take Lura to do some shopping. I didn't have anything better to do since Ben is working double shifts. I haven't seen him for nearly a month now. We've both been so busy we've rarely had time to see each other."

Lura flinched. Bryce felt her stunned gaze.

Shit, he thought. She didn't know yet. No one had told her. Michelle, you calculating bitch. He glared at the raven-haired cousin and gave Lura a nudge with his shoulder. The eyes she turned on him were carefully void of emotion.

"Michelle's been seeing Ben for some time now. She had to settle for second best when she couldn't get her hooks into me. I want you to know I stayed faithful while you were away, Lura. I only got married once."

Her smile was tentative. "Anyone I know?"

"Nah." Bryce looked at his watch then dug a five out of his wallet and dropped it onto the table. "Come on. Remember Miss Winegarten? I want you two to see something."

"What?" Michelle was suspicious.

"Come on or we'll miss it."

"Is this another one of your pranks?"

"Yep."

They followed him out of the restaurant and down the sidewalk to the police station. Bryce stopped just outside and told them to wait a minute. His handsome face was filled with excitement when he urged them to the window.

"Any second now. She's done with the wastebaskets."

Lura peered in the window in time to see the prim ex-schoolteacher open her desk drawer and let out a terrified screech.

"God," said Michelle. "What did you put in there? A tarantula?"

Bryce's voice trembled with laughter. "Something better. An old maid's dream."

Lura cupped her hands on the window and saw Hannah beckon wildly to Haden Preston. The tall, red-haired officer walked over to the desk and looked in the drawer. He spun away in a fit of laughter. Lura could hear the enraged Hannah screaming at him to take it out.

"What is it?" Michelle asked in exasperation.

Tears were streaming down Bryce's cheeks. He took a deep breath and pointed. "That."

Inside the station, Hannah reached into the drawer with two pencils and removed a large, pink, twelve-inch rubber penis.

"Pencils!" Bryce was nearly choking with laughter. "She can't even touch it! I paid good money for that and she's using pencils!"

Michelle began to chuckle. "Serves her right. The gossipy old bitch deserves everything she gets."

Lura stepped away from the window and looked at her watch. "I think the stores are opening, Michelle."

Michelle stopped laughing and looked at her. "Don't wait on me. You know your way around."

"Hey." Bryce immediately sobered. "Let's go out this weekend, Lura. I'll take you out to dinner."

Michelle stared at him in disbelief. "Dinner? Bryce, you never take girls out to dinner."

"That's right," he said. "I take ladies out to dinner. What do you say, Lura?"

She looked at her cousin's pinched face. "Uh, why don't you give me a call, Bryce. We'll talk about it."

"Great. I'll call you soon."

Michelle was still staring as Bryce disappeared into the station. Lura turned away and began walking up the sidewalk. Her cousin came after her.

"Are you really going out with him?"

Lura glanced at her. Even in the harsh light of early morning, Michelle could manage to look beautiful. Her skin, unlike Lura's, had the pampered appearance of a fashion model's. Her violet eyes were made up to perfection, the full mouth was lightly painted, and her cheeks had just the slightest hint of blush. Her dark hair was fashionably bobbed and showed no trace of gray. Lura felt awkward and ugly beside her with only a swift application of lip color and some coverup to hide the dark circles under her eyes.

"I don't know," she said to Michelle finally. "I won't know until he calls."

"He probably won't call," Michelle said. "Bryce is like that, you know. I'm sure he means well, but he's terribly irresponsible where women are concerned. Most good-looking men are."

"What about Ben?" Lura had to say it.

Michelle waved a red-nailed hand. "Ben isn't really handsome. At least not in comparison with Bryce. Ben's appeal is completely different. There's just something about him. You know what I mean, I'm sure."

Lura nodded. She felt sick to her stomach.

"His body is incredible, I'll give him that," Michelle added. She darted a look at her cousin and saw Lura's nostrils flare. "Oh, let's go in here first. This place just opened up last month and I've never been in. I usually do all my shopping in the city, you know."

Lura veered into the doorway with relief. An hour later she emerged with two sweaters, four blouses, and three skirts. When Michelle tried to push her into the next store she had to refuse.

"I can't buy any more clothes right now. I need to go to the hardware store for some paint."

"What are you going to paint?"

"The house needs some work," Lura told her.

Michelle's smile was knowing. "You're scared of going out, aren't you? You really should get a job, Lura. I hear you have a college degree."

"Phil offered to take me to the school. Principal Wiley's secretary is leaving soon."

"Oh no you don't," Michelle said quickly. "I was going to apply for that job. Phil knows how much I hate working at the drugstore. You can have my job. I'll even talk to Mr. Ailey for you."

Lura closed her eyes and sighed. She had the feeling that if she'd said Principal Wiley himself was leaving, Michelle would have laid claim to the job.

"Don't worry about it, Michelle," she said. "I'm sure I'll find something."

"I don't know, Lura. You might have to find work out of town."

Lura ignored the discouraging note in her cousin's voice and kept walking. When Michelle dropped her off at home Lura carried her purchases inside and stood by the door. A moment later she peered through the window curtain and saw the coppery brown Datsun 280Z pull into Ben's drive.

She wondered why Phil hadn't told her.

Chapter Six

Edie had been reading one murder mystery after another to find the perfect murder. Unfortunately, most of the methods she learned belonged in fiction. The villain who injected his victims with rabies was ingenious, but where was she going to find some rabies? They didn't exactly sell it in stores. Electrocution sounded good, but Portis always took showers rather than baths. Poison, guns, and knives were too uncertain; how much to give and how many times a blade or a bullet would have to pierce that blubber was unknowable and therefore unacceptable. One shot or one stab might save her cream-colored carpet from excessive staining, but it might not kill him—unless she had a shotgun like Calvin Horn's. And that would be an unholy mess to clean up. She wanted to save the carpet *and* the wallpaper if she could.

The thought of burying Portis alive was an appealing one. In her present condition, however, digging a deep enough grave was impossible—once she reached three feet she'd never be able to climb out herself. She wished she had the money to hire someone. She could save her allowance, but that might take months. And she didn't know the first place to look for a killer. Did they sit in nondescript cars parked on street corners, like on television? She could just imagine herself approaching a city man with her distended belly and—

"Excuse me, but I'm looking for someone to murder my husband. He's rich, you see, and I want him dead before I have this baby. He wasn't always the way he is now, you understand, but he did have a thing about closets when I married him. The rest of it started when I got pregnant, because it's not his baby. He knows it isn't because he made three girls pregnant the year he was nineteen, and his daddy shot him in the ass with some rock salt and accidentally hit his testicles, and since then he . . ."

No, that was saying too much. On television you just showed them a picture and gave them an advance or promised a cut of the insurance money or something.

She sighed and picked up her basket from the pantry. Her small backyard garden was in need of attention. While she wasted her time pondering the intricacies of murder, the last of her tomatoes were falling off the vines.

Vines. What about strangulation? she wondered, and as she wandered out to the yard she pictured his eyes bugging out and his tongue turning black.

It might be an improvement, she decided.

She settled herself in the garden and forced her mind away from the subject. There were at least a dozen tomatoes ready to be picked. She could give some to Ben and some to her mother. Ben had finally returned her call and told her he would stay the night with her on Saturday. He said they could go to their mother's tavern for a while and maybe rent a movie for later. Edie hoped it would be a suspense film, with at least one murder in it.

She thought she would take the letter from Oklahoma City along to the tavern. Ben and her mother had a right to know Max was dead, even if both of them liked to pretend they didn't care. It bothered Edie when they acted that way, but she supposed she didn't blame Ben. Max Portlock was a man's man, and he had raised Ben to be the same way, mostly with his fists and the toes of his boots.

Edie had been Max's blond-haired, brown-eyed little princess, and was treated accordingly. She could never understand the simmering animosity between her father and her brother. It had reached the boiling point on Ben's nineteenth birthday, when his lifelong pet, a collie named Paddy, was hit by a truck and killed. Edie would never forget the sight of her brother gathering that bloody, broken dog into his arms. It was the first time she had ever seen him cry. Max came out of the house and told Ben to put the dog down and blow his goddamn nose. Ben told him to go to hell. Max came off the porch and Ben put the dog down to meet him. When it was over, only Ben was left standing.

He buried Paddy in the backyard and cried the whole time. Then he packed his things and left the house. Max never said a word to him. A year later Max left Dumford and never came back. He sent Edie a postcard from Tulsa and told her he was working in an oil field. She was still his little girl, he wrote, and if she ever needed him she should just yell and he would hear her.

Edie plucked a tomato and thrust her head up to look at the sky.

"The one time I really need you and you're *dead,*" she said aloud. "What were you doing in a bar, Daddy? You were on the wagon last time I saw you. Ben knew you'd fall off. He knew. Things between you two would've been different if you hadn't kicked him around all the time. You had to mess everything up by trying to make him just like you. Meanie. Old, dead meanie. You deserted us."

She wiped her face and looked at the tomato in her hand. "I needed you for one little favor, Daddy. Just one little murder. And where are you?"

She squashed the tomato in her hand.

"That's where you are. And I—"

"Pardon me, ma'am," a male voice behind her interrupted.

Edie jumped and felt her bladder leak in her surprise. As she twisted to meet the intruder her face reddened in anger. "Don't ever do that again. You nearly scared the pee out of me."

Bryce laughed. "What the hell were you yelling about? I heard you all the way to the street. I come back here expecting to see a crime and all I find is a mad Edie with a squashed tomato."

"Go on," she mumbled.

"No." Bryce lowered himself to the ground beside her. His hand reached over to rub her round belly. "How's the baby today? Doing a lot of kicking?"

Edie pushed his hand away. "I said go on. I told you not to come by here anymore."

"Don't be like that, Edie. I wanted to see how you're getting along."

"I'm fine," she said coldly. "Now go on."

Bryce's mouth tightened. "All right." He stood and started away, then he angrily turned back. "You know, like most people I used to think you were a little dizzy, and I thought it was cute. Now I know better. You know exactly what you're doing. Underneath all that stupid blond fluff, you're a goddamned gold digger."

"And you're king of the swinging dicks," Edie retorted. "I hate your guts and I never want to see you over here again. Now get out of my yard!"

Bryce took a deep calming breath and exhaled. "You don't mean that, Edie. I know you don't. I came over to tell you I might be taking Lura Taylor out to dinner. Michelle's being a real shit about Ben."

"Michelle's a tramp," Edie muttered. Then her eyes rounded and she threw the squashed tomato at his legs. "You think I *care* who you take out to dinner? I don't! Just get out of here and leave me alone. I'm a married woman."

Bryce looked at the tomato juice dripping down his uniform. "Is this about the girl in the red dress at your party? I made a date with her but I broke it off. I told Ben I'd work for him tomorrow afternoon."

Edie plucked another tomato and struggled to her feet. Her face was scarlet. "I don't care! I wouldn't touch you if you were the last man on earth! Now get out of here, Bryce McKee, or I swear I'll put this one right in your face!"

He grinned. "Try it."

The tomato was already flying. It grazed his right ear and left him laughing at her. "You should see your face when you get mad. Where'd you learn to throw like—"

Another tomato whizzed past his head and made a loud splat behind him. Bryce ducked and headed for his car when she dipped into her basket and came out with more ammunition.

"I'm going, dammit!"

Edie dropped the tomatoes she held and planted her hands on her hips in satisfaction. When she heard his car door shut she dusted her palms and blew on her knuckles. "You taught me how to throw like that when I was twelve, you jerk."

As the roar of the patrol car's engine faded she picked up her basket and moved back to the tomatoes. Things might have been different if it was someone else. If Bryce himself were different. But that was wishful thinking. His name was on the tongue and in the heart of every female in town, and his reputation was known in three counties. He swore most of the tales were lies, but Edie didn't believe him.

Last February, Portis had gone on one of his trips and left Edie alone for the weekend. On the second night she had heard the sound of glass breaking in the house. She called the police, hoping Ben would come over, but only Bryce was available. He'd come out and found a broken Mason jar in her basement. Since it was near the end of his shift, he had stayed on for a cup of coffee. They wound up talking for hours, with Edie admitting to the terrible crush she'd had on him as a teenager. While they were playing a game of Scrabble, he leaned over and kissed her on the nose.

Edie knew he only did it to distract her, since she had just played the word "quibble" and added nearly fifty points to her score. But things took off from there, and his eyes had been so blue, his mouth so warm, and his hands so gentle that Edie had been swept away.

She never told him the baby was his. He just knew. In the first few months she had expected all of Dumford to know. It was a genuine surprise to her when Bryce kept quiet. One time he came over and asked her to leave Portis, but when Edie asked him why, he got angry with her and left. If he'd said he loved her or wanted to marry her, something romantic or even a tiny bit sincere, Edie thought she might have considered it.

Portis turned her butt black and blue, but he couldn't make Edie give him a name. The one time she defied him and tried to leave, Portis threatened to tell the whole town about his sterility and her adultery. That wouldn't do. Beatings with a wooden spoon were preferable to people knowing the baby was Bryce's and that Edie's name had been added to the list of his legendary conquests. Edie didn't consider herself religious, but she did believe adultery to be a sin. And adultery with Bryce McKee was a ticket to purgatory.

Hannah Winegarten had already figured it out, Edie was sure. It was the way Hannah looked at her. And all those stupid little notes she kept in the log about who went where and when. Hannah had probably counted up the days the minute she heard Edie was pregnant.

"Nosy old goat," Edie muttered. And if Bryce thought she would be impressed by his breaking a date with that slut in the red dress, he had another thing coming. She saw the way he danced with the skinny puss at her party. He probably slept with her later.

"I don't *care*," she told her small basket of tomatoes.

"And if he thinks he can come knocking on my door when Portis is dead, he's wrong. I know the score, my fine Mr. McKee. You sleep with anything that walks in heels, and don't think I'm foolish enough to—"

"Edie, who in the fuck are you talking to?"

Her bladder did give way this time. She dropped the basket in her hand and tried to keep the urine from spilling down her legs by wadding her dress up at the crotch.

Portis held open the back door and laughed. "Jesus Christ. I told you to start wearing those diaper things, didn't I? Didn't I tell you to wear a diaper?"

"I ran out," she mumbled. It was a lie. She didn't like to wear them because they turned Portis on.

"I've never seen such a weak bladder in my life," her husband swore. "Even before you were pregnant you pissed the bed once a month."

"I did not," she said under her breath.

"Well, what are you standing there for? Get your fat butt into the bathroom and clean yourself up. Have you got my things packed?"

"Your suitcase is on the bed," she said.

His hand shot out as she approached him. "Who were you talking to?"

"Myself. Do you see anybody else?"

His eyes were two gleaming bits of colorless glass set in a muddy clay pot. "I always knew you were a goddamn basket case. You and that brother of yours."

"I want my allowance before you go," Edie replied.

Portis lifted his brows. "Oh, you do, do you? And just what has Daddy's girl done to deserve it this week?"

Edie lifted her dress and turned to show him her bruised backside.

He smacked her on the cheek. "Get in the house and do that. You want the neighbors talking?"

They had no neighbors, Edie wanted to remind him. Their house was the only one on the street. The closest living presence was a roan horse in the field behind the house. The horse belonged to Bryce. He had leased the field last spring and he came out to ride at least twice a week. He always rode where Edie could see him.

"Did you pack my Rolaids?" Portis demanded.

"Beside the Mylanta."

"My new black socks?"

"Four pairs."

Portis grunted and nodded. "All right then. Put on a clean dress and get your butt in the closet."

Chapter Seven

Hannah dialed her number quickly. Chief Legget was talking to Ben about the sheriff's report on Calvin Horn and she didn't want to miss a word. She fluffed her short hair nervously while she listened to the phone ring. Five, six—what was Kurt doing?

When he answered, her brother was breathing heavily.

"What took you so long?" Hannah asked in annoyance.

Kurt grunted. "It was rather difficult getting to the phone with these handcuffs on."

"It's for your own good. And I only handcuffed your right hand. Your left is perfectly free."

"What do you want, Hannah? 'All My Children' is on."

"It's time for your medication," she reminded him. "Have you taken it yet?"

"Of course I took it. Stop treating me like some drooling retard."

"When you stop acting like one, I will."

Kurt coughed into the receiver. "I called my lawyer today. He's bringing two witnesses over so I can change my will. I've had enough of you, you crazy—"

Hannah hung up. It was an old threat. He was upset about the handcuffs, but that was just tough. His nasty old thing needed a rest, and cuffing his right hand to the bed frame was the only way to keep him from exercising his daily self-abuse. His left hand was virtually useless in the art of masturbation. She knew because she'd watched him try.

"Hannah, is there any more coffee?" George called.

"Coming up, Chief." She hurried to the pot and carried it over to refill his cup.

"I knew they wouldn't find anything useful," George went on. "That place was a forensic nightmare."

Ben waved Hannah away from his cup. "No thanks." To George he said, "Did they get around to examining the dog yet? I'd be interested to know what kind of blade was used."

"Why?" George asked. "Christ, Ben. If the sheriff wants to write this off as a suicide, who are we to argue? We don't have any evidence to the contrary."

"Suicides leave notes," Ben said.

George looked hard at him. "Don't start that city cop crap with me. Cite percentages if you want to, but show me where it says *every* suicide leaves a note."

Ben sat forward. "Do you think it was a suicide? Never mind what the sheriff's report says, just tell me what you think."

The chief shook his head. "I think I'm getting too old for this shit. And so do you, obviously. Stop trying to make it seem like I'm looking for easy answers. Don't you think I've had a few nightmares about what we saw that night at Calvin's place?"

"You still haven't told me what you think," Ben said.

"I think I want to retire in November. And that's all I think right now. If you want to play detective, then find the sonofabitch who killed that baby and left it in the garbage."

"The two could be related," Ben suggested.

George held up his hands. "Could be. Who knows? You ask me what I think? I think finding that baby was the last straw for old Calvin, and he made up his mind to go out with a bang. Like I said, who knows? He was a whacked-out old bastard any way you look at it."

Hannah cleared her throat and squeaked her chair to gain their attention. "Now that I've heard everything, I'm sure it was a suicide, Ben. And I think it was awfully nice of you to attend his service. Mr. Greenleaf said you and Reverend St. Clair were the only two people there."

Ben shrugged. He had attended Calvin's service in an official capacity, knowing that victim's funerals were often hard for killers to resist. He had kept his eyes open for any onlookers, but there were none. Calvin was sent off in a plain brown casket with three lilies and a reading of the twenty-third psalm.

"Do you know the town council hasn't had one nibble on the ad they placed in the weekly?" Hannah was saying. "You'd think people were afraid of finding another baby if they took the job. I'm telling you I never realized how important a garbage hauler is to a town. We might have to haul our own if someone doesn't apply soon."

Ben put on his hat. Hannah's voice was like the high-pitched whine of a dozen circling mosquitoes; it made Ben want to start swatting. He left his chair and looked up as Bryce slammed into the station. His dark-haired friend's usual bluster was replaced by a thunderous expression that grew even darker as the chief began to laugh.

"What the hell happened to you?" George pointed at what looked like tomato seeds on the legs of Bryce's uniform. "Get caught in a cafeteria crossfire?"

Bryce growled something under his breath and went to his desk. Hannah abruptly averted her face and pretended to be busy with her typewriter. She glanced up when Bryce opened his drawer, then she quickly looked down again.

His expression told her everything. She wanted to laugh out loud at the shock in his eyes.

She darted another glance from under her lashes and saw Bryce angrily wad up something in his hands. That would be the envelope with the question mark on it. He would keep the cigars hidden for now it seemed. One had a pink plastic wrapper with the words, *It's a Girl!* stamped on the outside. The second was blue, with, *It's a Boy!* for the other contingency.

Bryce was glaring at her now.

Payback is a you-know-what, she wanted to say. Instead she smiled sweetly at him. "There's coffee left if you'd like some, Bryce."

Ben watched them and knew something was going on. Hannah had had it in for Bryce as long as Ben could remember, and Bryce was always up for a prank. Ben had heard about the rubber penis gag from Haden and had fully expected war to be declared. Hannah's pleasant smile for Bryce was a surprise. Ben picked up his keys and walked over to the other man's desk. Bryce quickly slammed his drawer shut.

"Still working for me tomorrow?" Ben asked.

Bryce nodded. "Yeah." Then he grinned. "You get a whole Saturday off, you lucky bastard. Made any big plans?"

Ben looked at the drawer and shrugged. "Thought I'd spend some time with Edie. Maybe take her out to Mom's place for a while."

"Sounds like fun," Bryce said. "In fact, I might run into you at Stella's. Your old flame has agreed to go out with me tomorrow night."

"Lura?"

Bryce nodded. Before he could open his mouth, Hannah was there shaking her finger. "Don't let that sister of yours drink anything, Ben Portlock. I've read stories of what alcohol can do to unborn babies. Remember Annette Taylor being forced to have a caesarean with young Philip? She drank like a fish, and everyone knows that's why she couldn't have him normal."

She paused and looked at Bryce. "Lord knows Edie has a time as it is without adding to the burden. She's not the brightest child in the world. Not a brain in her pretty little head. In my class she was always looking out the windows and—"

"Hannah, why don't you shut the shit up?" George said from his desk.

Hannah sucked in her breath. Ben and Bryce were still eyeing each other, neither paying attention to the former schoolteacher.

"Where did you see Lura?" Ben asked.

"Shopping with Michelle. I stopped by the house this morning and talked to her for a minute. She was wearing a pair of Phil's overalls and had paint all over her face. Man, that hair of hers is something. You ask me, she's still got Mishy beat hands down in looks. Uh, no offense intended, of course."

Ben's voice was flat. "None taken."

He turned his back on the smiling Bryce and looked at George. "I'll see you Sunday."

"Are you off now?" Hannah asked in disappointment.

Ben nodded and walked out of the station. He drove straight home and forced himself to keep his eyes directly ahead as he left the car. It was useless. The urge to look at her house was overwhelming. He gave in by inches as he fumbled for his house key.

The Debrecht's house was first, with its lopsided mimosa tree and plastic pink squirrels on the lawn. Mr. and Mrs. Debrecht were in Paraguay at the moment, on one of their Christian missions to save the ignorant. At the next house, Mrs. Pendleton still had yellow mums blooming in her yard. Her hedges needed trimming, and the bricks in her chimney looked ready to crumble. Mickey Pendleton, the fourth officer of the Dumford Police Department, was her son, but he had been too busy with work to help his mother.

Ben's eyes leaped the last measure and saw the Taylor's door standing wide open. The curtains were gone from the large picture window in the living room. Inside, he caught a glimpse of Lura using a paint roller on the south wall. Her hair was covered by a bright red scarf, and yes, she did have on a pair of overalls.

Okay, Ben told himself, so Bryce was telling the truth. The bastard.

He caught himself then. No, not fair. Bryce wasn't any more of a bastard than—anyway, if Lura wanted to go out with him, that was her business.

He thrust his key into the lock and looked down to see the tiger-striped cat waiting patiently at his feet.

"It's about time you showed up," he said to it. "When I bring a girl home to live with me I expect a little loyalty."

The cat lifted her tail and looked pointedly at the door. Ben pushed it open and followed the animal through the house and into the kitchen. He opened a can of cat food onto a plate, then he took a beer for himself out of the refrigerator and sat down at the table to watch the cat eat. After a moment he decided that her plump belly was not his imagination. "Not only are you disloyal," he murmured into his beer, "but you neglected to tell me you slept around before you met me."

The cat's tail twitched and she changed position at the plate, putting her back to Ben.

He smiled and carried his beer into the bedroom, where he retrieved the bag of diaries and opened it up. Closed case or not, it wouldn't hurt to examine his find. See what Calvin saw. He stuck a hand in the bag and pulled a diary out at random. The fake blue leather was cracked; the tiny lock was broken. He turned it over in his hand, then he took it into the living room.

When he plopped down on his couch he found himself looking at his own walls and thinking of paint. He hadn't done much to the place since moving in. What furniture he had was left by his mother and her previous tenants. It was all old and all junk by anyone's standards. The one improvement he had made was to put in a central air unit the previous year. He didn't care about buying a matching loveseat and sofa, or having wall-to-wall carpet installed.

Edie's ivory-colored furniture and plush white carpet were nice, but she had married Portis Jackson so she could have those things. She denied it, of course, but Ben knew his sister. It had begun in the sixth grade when she was playing jump rope at school one day and a boy she would have died for laughed and told everyone she had a hole in her undies. Edie had come home crying buckets, and from that day on, the money to buy new things had taken priority in her mind.

It was ridiculous, but that was Edie. One isolated, seemingly innocuous event had had traumatic impact on his sister, and Ben couldn't help but wonder how Edie would have turned out if the event had never occurred.

He sighed and made himself more comfortable on the couch. He flipped open the diary in his hands and saw a date written in ink on the inside cover. *June 1st, 1965.* He looked for a name and found none. The words *My Journal* were written at the top of the first page, which appeared to be a continuation of a book that had come before this one. Ben sighed and riffled the pages with a finger. Someone had attempted to burn it, evidenced by the black, charred edges of much of the paper. He went back to the first page and began to read.

An hour and two beers later, Ben had gained some insight into Hannah Winegarten. In 1965 she had been twenty-seven, about to turn twenty-eight, and was still a virgin. There was a man in her life, someone she frequently referred to as, "my love," though she had not yet named him. She and Kurt had been reared by their strict Baptist father, who was forever reminding Hannah of the uncleanliness of women, and of the sin involved in the act that men and women performed together. Kurt, she wrote, paid their father no attention whatsoever. He did as he pleased. But Hannah took him quite seriously, often chiding herself for her impure thoughts about her lover. The rest of the world, according to Hannah, was made up of hippies and sex maniacs and drug-crazed city people. She alone was chaste and would do her best to remain that way in the face of all temptation.

Still she secretly thrilled at the very look and lightest touch of her love. She knew it was wrong. Even looking at him was wrong. But she couldn't help it. He was the most charming, magnetic man she had ever met, and when he looked at her, she knew the feelings in her breast had to be inspired by God. He wouldn't let her fall in love with the wrong man. He simply wouldn't.

Ben stopped reading and put the book down on his chest while he thought. He had been eight years old in 1965, and he remembered thinking of Hannah as an old maid even then. How strange it was to read her romantic thoughts. Strange and somehow distasteful.

His doorbell rang then, causing Ben to rise and stuff the diary under a cushion of the couch before going to answer it. Michelle glowered at him in greeting.

"I thought you were working tonight?"

He kept his hand on the knob. "George decided to show up."

"I see." Michelle glanced over her shoulder once, then she turned back to him. "Well, can I come in?"

Ben looked and saw Lura in her driveway. Her back was to them as she soaped down her mother's faded yellow Toyota.

"Yeah, I guess." Ben stood aside and opened the door.

Michelle stayed put. "You guess?"

"Do you want to come in or not, Michelle?"

"Not if you use that tone of—oh, never mind." She swept past him and tossed her purse on the nearest chair. "Lura's quite the busy little bee lately, isn't she? Cleaning, painting, and washing everything in sight. A month ago she wouldn't come out of her room."

Ben grunted and returned to the couch and his beer.

"Do you have any wine?" Michelle asked.

"No."

"Bourbon?"

He looked at her. "I have Budweiser."

"You know I can't stand beer," she replied. Suddenly her eyes rounded. "What in God's name is that?"

Ben followed her pointing finger. "It's a cat."

"In the house? What if it has fleas?"

"Then I guess I will too."

Michelle made a noise of disgust and came to sit beside him on the couch. "Why didn't you call me when you found out George would be working?"

"I didn't think about it," Ben said. It was the truth.

"Oh. You probably thought I'd already made other plans, right?"

Ben rubbed his eyes. "I'm tired, Michelle."

"You look tired," she said. She placed a hand on his thigh and began to rub. Ben leaned back and sighed.

"I mean it. I'm tired."

The hand was jerked away. Michelle's mouth contorted in a search for the right words, then she finally gave up and left the couch. At the door she turned to look at him.

"I'm not stupid, you know."

"I know," Ben said.

When the echoes from the slammed door quieted, he reached beneath the cushion and took out Hannah's diary. He read all about the building of the new school—the school now twenty-five years old—and how Hannah had been involved in selecting a site and planning the construction and even in choosing the colors for the finished building.

He fell asleep with the diary in his hands and was awakened by a rough tongue on his eyelid. He rolled off the couch with a start and saw the cat run to the front door. He looked at his watch and saw that it was half past midnight. When he let the cat outside, she made for the same pines on the south side of the house. Ben watched her disappear, and he was ready to close the door when he caught a glimpse of fluttering white in the glow of Mrs. Pendleton's porchlight.

Lura moved across the lawn and stepped noiselessly through a break in the hedges. The fabric of her nightgown whipped around her legs and outlined the curves of her hips as she walked against the cool breeze. Her hair floated behind her in long, dancing wisps.

Ben's first impulse was to run after her and ask her just what in the hell she was doing. His second impulse was to follow her and see where she went. His third was to relieve his bladder.

With a long exhalation, he closed the door and walked into the bathroom.

Chapter Eight

"You're right," Phil said knowingly. "The conniving bitch didn't even know about the job until you told her."

"Philip, don't talk that way about your cousin," Annette chided.

Lura glanced at her mother. Annette's pale, lined features seemed unusually attentive this morning. Had she been following the conversation? It was hard to tell.

"How do you like the new paint, Mama?" she asked.

Annette shrugged. "I don't care for white."

"It's not white. They call this color Mission Ivory."

"It looks white to me. Does it look white to you, Philip?"

He frowned. "Not really. Lura, you don't owe her any free space just because she claimed dibs to the job. I want you to apply for it anyway. Principal Wiley can decide who's better qualified."

Lura bit her lower lip. "No . . . I don't think so, Phil. You know what a volatile temper Michelle has. She hates competition."

"She always did," Annette said. "She's got inverted nipples, you know."

Philip and Lura looked at each other. *What?*

"How do you know that?" Phil asked, grinning.

"Because Marie once asked me if I thought she should have them operated on. She thought they were giving Michelle an inferiority complex."

Phil burst out laughing. Lura covered her mouth and could only shake her head when her mother asked what was wrong. Annette finally stood and went to the stove. "Who wants eggs this morning?"

Lura stopped laughing. "Mama, we just ate."

"We did?" She looked at the dishes on the table with surprise. "What did I have?"

"Eggs," Phil said. "Cartoons are on now. You want to watch Scooby-Doo?"

"No. No, I think I'll do the dishes."

Phil left his chair. "We can't afford for you to do the dishes. Last time you broke every plate you touched. How about the radio? Do you want to sit and listen to some music for a while?"

Annette curled a finger around her long, gray braid and looked at Lura. *"Je ne sais que faire."*

"Faites comme vous voudrez," Lura replied.

"Stop that," Phil said sharply. "You know I can't stand it when you talk in French."

Lura frowned. "We didn't say anything important. She just said she didn't know what to do."

"And what did you say?"

"I told her to do as she liked. Honestly, Phil, what did you think we said?"

He picked up his plate and dumped it in the sink with a loud clatter. "I don't know. I just don't like you talking without me knowing what you're saying. It's rude."

"I'm sorry," Lura said.

Phil exhaled, then the corners of his mouth slowly began to curl. "Me too. It just makes me feel stupid. I had a chance to take French in school and I didn't. Guess I thought auto shop was more—Mama, no!"

72

Lura whirled in time to see her mother stab herself in the wrist with a fork. The tines went deep, deep enough to let the fork stand on its own when Annette took her hand away. Phil grabbed her arm and twisted the hand behind her back. The three tiny holes filled with dark red blood when he yanked the fork out.

"Lura, get me the alcohol and some bandages out of the bathroom."

Lura's feet wouldn't move. The blood flowing down her mother's wrist paralyzed her. Her mother looked at her and smiled a beatific smile.

"Lura!" Phil snapped.

Lura blinked. "Why . . . why did she do that?"

Phil cursed and shoved his mother's bleeding arm over the sink. "We just mopped this floor yesterday, Mama. See the mess you've made? Lura, would you please get the goddamn alcohol and some bandages? You want it to get infected?"

The exasperation in her brother's voice penetrated her shock. He was used to this. He was actually used to things like this happening. Lura stumbled out of the kitchen and made her way down the hall to the bathroom.

"I can't go," Lura said later. "It's not right."

Phil looked away from the television. "You're going. You need to get out of the house. Besides, she's doing just fine now. Aren't you, Mama?"

"What? Did you say something to me? I just hate these circus of the stars programs. Is there something else on?"

"I'll look," Phil told her. To Lura he said, "Go on and get ready. Bryce will be here any minute."

Lura glanced at the bandage on her mother's wrist. Was the slightly irritated expression marring her brow some kind of signal? What would she do if she didn't like the highwire act—cut her throat?

"Phil, how do you know she won't . . . ?"

"I know," he said patiently. "Trust me. I've been around

73

her a lot more than you have. It's when she acts perfectly sane that you have to worry. It's like the few brain cells she has left all wake up at once and . . . anyway, you'd better hurry. It's almost eight."

Lura took a last defeated look at her mother. "I just don't understand. Everything was fine."

"I don't understand, either," Phil responded. "But I've learned to live with it. Now *go on.*"

Bryce arrived at exactly eight o'clock. Lura walked into the living room to find him engaged in an animated conversation with her mother. His eyes flickered to the bandage again and again, but he made no mention of it. He stood up when Lura entered the room. His smile was huge.

"This is the Lura I remember," he said. He looked her up and down and clicked his tongue. "Still a knockout. Those legs are legend in Dumford, you know. Lura Taylor in a skirt is on the list of things to see around here."

Phil groaned and Bryce made as if to cuff him on the head. "I'll have her home after midnight, so don't bother to wait up." He turned to Lura and made a sweeping motion with his hand. "Shall we?"

Bryce made a joke about the Debrecht's pink squirrels on the way to the car, and by the time they reached Barney's Steakhouse, Lura's sides ached from laughing so much. As they entered the restaurant, Bryce suddenly stopped and looked at a white car on the street. His expression made Lura inquire what was wrong.

"Nothing," he said. "I just realized I forgot to check someone out. It can wait."

He led her inside the restaurant, and from that moment on she was his captive audience, forced to sit and listen to one joke after another. After dinner he suggested they go to Stella's Tavern for a drink, and Lura nervously agreed. Stella's would be crowded, probably too crowded for comfort on a Saturday night. But, as Phil said, she had to go out and face the Dumford public sooner or later.

Stella dropped her bar towel and came around the bar

when Bryce and Lura stepped inside the small tavern. She took Lura into a lung-squeezing hug, then rebuked her in a stern voice for not coming to see her earlier.

"I hear you've been home a month! What on earth have you been doing all this time?"

"This and that," Lura said. Ben's mother looked the same. Her bleached hair and job-hardened features had made the leap of years with no visible changes. Only her soft brown eyes had succumbed to time: she now wore glasses.

"Are Ben and Edie here?" Bryce asked.

Lura looked at him in alarm. He smiled and put an arm around her. "It's okay."

"They're on the dance floor," Stella said. "Can I get you two something to drink?"

Bryce looked at Lura. "Beer?"

"That's fine."

"Two Buds, Stella. We'll be down at the end of the bar."

The end of the bar marked the beginning of the dance floor. Bryce took her hand and pulled Lura behind him as he navigated through the packed bodies in the bar. Familiar faces looked her way with a start, followed by blinks of recognition. A wave of unintelligible remarks filled the space behind them as they moved steadily toward the dance floor. Lura felt her insides begin to quiver.

"Bryce . . . I . . ."

"Fuck 'em," he said harshly.

She swallowed and kept moving. When they reached the end of the bar, Bryce placed her back against it and stood in front of her. "You okay?"

Lura didn't know. The unfriendly eyes were boring into her flesh. The music throbbed against her eardrums and refused to resemble any kind of rhythm. The smoke and the blue haze of the neon light above them made her eyes sting.

"Lura?" Bryce's voice was anxious.

"Nervous," she finally got out. "I'm not used to all the . . . I'm just nervous, Bryce."

"I know." He touched her arm. "I'm sorry. We don't have to stay here. Do you want to leave?"

Yes.

"No," she said. "I'll be all right."

"Good." Bryce smiled. "I knew you were tough."

"Two Buds," Stella said from behind the bar.

Lura turned and saw her reflection in the mirror on the wall behind the bar. She looked like a blue-skinned phantom with two black holes for eyes. While she was looking, another blue face appeared behind hers. Their glances met in the mirror. Her stomach muscles tightened as she turned around to face him.

"Hello, Ben. Edie."

"Hi, Lura," Edie said brightly. "How are you? I love that skirt. Did you see us dancing? My belly kept getting in the way, but Ben's such a good dancer no one even noticed." She glanced at Bryce before turning to Ben. "I'm not tired yet. Can we dance some more?"

Bryce winked at Lura. "I'll give Ben a rest. Come on, Edie, dance this one with me."

"No," Edie said bluntly.

Ben and Lura looked at her, surprised by the abrupt change in her voice. Edie darted a glance at her brother and quickly changed her tone.

"All right. Just one dance, though. I *am* a married woman, you know."

Bryce's smile was tight. "I know."

Lura took a quick sip of beer as she watched the two head for the dance floor. She dared not look around herself too much; everywhere she looked, people stared back. Even Ben was staring at her.

"It must be hard," he said after a moment.

She let herself look at him. This close to him she could see the changes that stolen peeks through a window at night denied her. His face and body were leaner than she remembered. The lines in the corners of his eyes had deepened, and up close she could see a tiny moon-shaped scar above his right eyebrow.

"It is hard," she said. "Your mother should have sold tickets tonight. Lura Taylor's return."

Ben forced a smile. "It won't last long. They'll find a new attraction soon and you'll be old news."

Lura gazed at the dance floor. "That's what Phil says."

They were silent a moment, both of them watching the dancers on the floor. Finally, Ben took her arm in a firm grip and led her out to the floor. Lura resisted, but when he showed no signs of releasing her, she gave up and allowed him to steer her to a free space. When his arms came around her she held her breath and closed her eyes.

"Relax," Ben told her. "Just open your eyes and talk to me."

Meeting his gaze was impossible. She felt a line of perspiration trickle down her scalp and become lost in the heavy weight of her hair.

"What about?" she said.

"You can start with why you take walks at night."

Lura looked at him in surprise.

"I've seen you twice now," he continued. "Both times you were barefoot and in your nightgown. Where do you go?"

Her eyes drifted to the buttons on his shirt and the tiny growth of hair springing from his collar. She didn't remember his being so tall.

"Sometimes I go to your house," she said quietly, and she felt his muscles jump beneath her fingers.

"Why?" he asked.

"I don't know. I've never asked myself why."

Ben closed his eyes and sighed. "You're still honest as hell. What do you—"

"This must be where I sign up," Michelle said loudly. "It *is* take pity on Lura Taylor night, isn't it? First Bryce takes her to dinner, and now the old lover deigns to dance with her. Maybe I should commit a murder and improve my own social life. Have any tips for me, Lura?"

Lura's mouth went dry. Her spine stiffened and her legs became wooden supports with unbending joints. The stares were on her again, some amused, some scornful. She couldn't look at Ben. His arms were still around her, but they had stopped dancing.

"First she wants my job and now she wants my man," Michelle went on in a high, drunken voice. "Not that I *blame* her, though. After humping with bulldykes for eight years I think I'd be ready for a man, too."

"Why don't you shut up," Edie hissed at her as Bryce moved them closer.

"My God," Michelle laughed. "Who let the cow in here?" She blinked then and pretended surprise. "Edie, is that you?"

Ben abruptly released Lura and moved toward Michelle. He grabbed her roughly by the arm and propelled her to the rear exit, leaving Lura standing alone on the dance floor. Silent, watchful faces awaited her reaction. She inhaled once, then headed for the nearest retreat.

"Go after her," Edie urged Bryce.

"I can't. She went into the ladies room."

"I'll go then."

Bryce held on to her. "Let her have a few minutes, Edie. Lura's tougher than you think."

"A cow," Edie muttered. "Michelle called me a cow."

"She looked pretty out of it, sweetheart. If a wino drank her piss tonight he'd swear it was chablis."

Edie smiled and relaxed in his arms. Then she stiffened. "How do you know what she drinks?"

"I don't. It was a joke."

"I'm sure."

Bryce pulled her closer. "Just be quiet and dance with me, Edie."

"I said one dance, Bryce. This is the second song. There

are people here who know Portis. More than one dance looks suspicious."

"Edie, you're making me crazy," Bryce said in annoyance. "You want to see suspicious? I'll show you what looks suspicious."

Before she realized what he was going to do, he had caught her face between his hands and kissed her full on the mouth. Edie endured it for a stunned second—until she remembered what her hands were for in a situation like this. When he released her she slapped him hard across the face.

He grinned. "Lightweight. You throw tomatoes harder than you throw a punch."

Edie shrieked through her teeth at him and pivoted on her heel. The dancers closest to them began to applaud, and Bryce raised his arms and took a bow before leaving the floor. He went straight to the ladies room and thrust open the door.

"Lura? You ready to blow this joint?"

There was no answer.

Bryce stuck his head inside the tiny room and looked around. "Lura?"

The window above the toilet was open. The room was empty.

"Shit," Bryce said to himself. Maybe she wasn't so tough after all.

Chapter Nine

"Where's Ben?" Stella asked as she finished totaling out the register.

Edie sighed and fingered a broken pretzel. "Still outside with Michelle. She's been crying and screaming for two hours now."

Stella clucked her tongue. "Michelle hates it when someone else gets a little attention. Has to be the main attraction everywhere she goes. I pray to God that Ben isn't serious about her."

"Are you kidding?" Edie laughed. "She's tried every bait and snare in the manual with no luck. Last year she even told Ben she was pregnant—did I tell you about that? Ben marched her butt right down to Dr. McMurphy's office and sat there with her while they took blood. The next day he hauled her in there again to find out the results. You could've cooked bacon on Michelle's face when they came out of there. She was supremely embarrassed. Ben's no dummy, Mom. And did you see the way he looked at Lura? I know him."

"And I know you," Stella said suddenly. She whisked off

her bar apron and looked seriously at her daughter. "What's going on with you and Bryce McKee? I haven't seen you shiver and quiver like that since—"

"I hate him," Edie interrupted in a sharp voice. "He's such a . . . what do you call it? A philanderer."

Edie swiveled on her barstool to escape her mother's penetrating look. "You know, Mom, this place always looks different without people. It's strange, but it seems so much smaller when it's empty. You can see the rips in the booth cushions, and the holes in the walls, and . . . well, the dumpiness, I guess."

"Thanks," Stella said in a dry voice. "I had plans to renovate, but it seems a certain bank vice-president turned down my application for a loan."

Edie swiveled back in surprise. "Portis? Portis turned you down?"

"He did," Stella confirmed. "But that's all right. I've got enough saved to repair the old stuff. I'll start with the booths, since you mentioned them first."

"I'm sorry, Mom," Edie said softly. "Why didn't you tell me you applied?"

"What difference would it have made? I'm sure your husband doesn't consult you on bank matters."

"No," Edie said. On the purchase of wooden spoons, maybe. But not on bank matters.

She wished she could tell her mother everything. Just spill her guts on the bar and let Stella make sense out of the steaming mess. Her mother was accustomed to dealing with other people's problems. She became a barmaid at the age of eighteen, when her father died and left her the twelve-stool, ten-booth, twenty-table joint called Happy Harry's. At twenty she married a college dropout named Max Portlock. He talked her into changing the name and removing six tables to put in a dance floor and a Wurlitzer jukebox with Hank Snow records. When Ben was born, business was booming.

Max wanted to stop with Ben, but Stella eventually won out. By the time Edie was born, the tavern was in a slump again. A fiery Baptist preacher had Dumford under his thumb, and all but the most hopeless sinners shunned the local booze-drinking and belly-rubbing establishment. The blight lasted fourteen years, until the preacher was caught diddling a thirteen year old in the choir box one evening. Some said it was Michelle Taylor, but the rumor was never substantiated.

Though business soon picked up again, it was too late to save the Portlock's marriage. Max had already driven Ben away, and things between he and Stella were hopelessly sour. Edie could still remember the morning Max left—6:00 A.M. on a sultry Monday in July. The air conditioner was in a coma, and shiny sweat rolled off the tip of Max's long nose as he yelled over the phone at someone at the daily paper in Wichita.

"Do you know what time it is? It's nearly six o'clock, and I don't see a paper in my driveway. Yesterday it came at a quarter after six, and let me tell you I didn't subscribe to a goddamned evening paper. After I shit, shower, and shave in the morning I like to read the news while it's fresh—what do you mean, don't talk to you like that? I pay this fucking phone bill every month and I can talk any goddamned way I like. Now I expect that paper to be in my drive no later than five-thirty, or I'll take my subscription to the goddamned *Kansas City Star* and—"

Seconds later the phone was slammed down and Max was gone. To Kansas City, he said.

Ben returned to the family home to help Stella for a few years, and bit by bit the tavern regained the ground lost during the biblical oppression.

Edie knew Ben still helped their mother on occasion. Stella had given him the family home, but he refused to accept the deed. Several times Edie had seen him slip a handful of twenties into the register when Stella wasn't looking. That way Stella couldn't refuse the money. Edie thought it was nice of her brother, but she didn't know how Ben could stand to be without money. Not that he ever bought anything for himself anyway. He drove the patrol car provided by the police department while he was on duty, but his own vehicle was an old rusted-out Jeep with the most horribly uncomfortable seats. Edie hated to ride in the thing. It made her feel poor again.

When Portis was dead she would buy Ben a new car, something flashy like Michelle's Datsun, only newer. And she would help her mother renovate the bar. Maybe she would hire one of those decorators from the city. He would come in, shake his coiffed head in disgust, and talk about how desperately decadent the place was. Then he would put fake palms in all the corners and replace the ripped red booth cushions with shiny chrome chairs and smoked-glass tables. A nice painting would hang over the—no, a portrait! An honest to goodness portrait of Stella, painted by some famous artist, with a little gold plaque at the bottom that had her name engraved on—

"We're closed," Stella said loudly. Then, "Oh, it's you. We're still closed, Bryce."

Edie swiveled around on her barstool to view the enemy's approach. He ran an agitated hand through his dark hair and didn't even look at her.

"Have you seen Lura?" he asked Stella. "I've looked all over for her."

Stella lifted her brows. "You lost her?"

"She lost me. She climbed out the bathroom window while I was dancing with Edie."

"Lord," Stella said. "Did you try her house?"

"I just came from there. Felt like a fool, too. Phil is pretty upset with me."

"He has every right to be," said Edie. "You should have let me go after her."

Bryce ignored her. "I've driven all over town. I don't know where else to look."

"Go home," Stella told him. "Lura's a grown woman, Bryce. She can take care of herself."

He opened his mouth to speak, then he turned and left

without saying a word. Edie looked after him with a thoughtful frown. Not one wisecrack. Not even a joking voice. Was he genuinely worried? He had to be. He hadn't even said good-bye to her.

"Was that Bryce leaving?" Ben asked a moment later.

Stella gave Edie a warning glance. "Yes. He thought he lost something, but then he remembered where it was. How's Michelle?"

"Sober enough to drive. You'll have to hose down the parking lot in the morning. She was sick."

His mother grimaced. "That's the one part of this business I hate. You kids leaving now?"

"Not yet," Edie said quickly. "I have something to show you guys."

She opened her purse and dug out the envelope with the Oklahoma City postmark. She handed it to Ben first. He took the letter, read it, then passed it to his mother. With only the faintest flicker of emotion in his eyes, Ben asked, "Why were you looking for him, Edie?"

She shrugged. "I wanted to see him again. He is our father, you know."

Ben said nothing.

Stella took the letter to the register and turned on the lamp beside it. She adjusted her glasses to read and was silent for a moment. Then she began to laugh.

"Mom?" Edie stared at her in amazement.

Her mother lifted a hand to her mouth to stifle the outburst. When she could breathe normally, she held up the letter. "You poor little thing. How long have you been agonizing over this?"

"What do you mean?" Edie's mouth began to tremble. "Shouldn't I feel sorry about his death?"

"Yes," Stella said with a chuckle. "But save it for when it happens. This is Max's handwriting."

Edie left the stool and went around the bar to snatch the letter away from her mother. "How do you know it is?"

84

"Believe me," Stella said. "I was married to him long enough to know his handwriting when I see it."

The trembling became a pout as tears filled Edie's eyes. "That bastard! Why would he do something like this to me?"

Stella sighed and patted her daughter's soft blond hair. "I stopped questioning the whys and wherefores of his actions a long time ago. Don't fret over it, honey. I'm sure he felt he had a good reason. But he obviously didn't count on my having such a sharp memory."

Ben rubbed his jaw with a weary hand. "Let's go, Edie. I have to be up early."

Edie wiped her nose with the back of her hand. "I'm coming. I just can't believe he would do this to me." Her eyes rounded suddenly and she looked at Ben. "Do you think he's rich? Do you think he's married to a woman with money and she doesn't know about us? Maybe that's why he wants us to think he's dead."

"I don't think about him at all," Ben said. He stepped behind the bar and gave his mother's cheek a swift kiss. "We'll see you later."

"Be careful," she said. "And stop worrying about that old man, Edie. It's not good for the baby. Hear me?"

Edie nodded. "Bye, Mom."

When Edie was squeezed into the passenger side of Ben's Jeep, she looked at her brother with a concerned frown.

"You don't look so good, Ben. Did you get sick watching Michelle get sick?"

He turned in his seat. "Edie, tell me why you really want to find Max. Why now, I mean. Is it because of the baby?"

"Partly, yes." Edie didn't want to say anymore.

Ben's pupils were large and dark as he searched her face. The neon sign above the tavern entrance filtered through the windshield and bathed his features in a red glow. "Why do I have the feeling you're hiding something from me?"

"I don't know," she said innocently. "I wouldn't hide

anything important from you." Edie smiled then. "Did you get Michelle straightened out? I swear I'll never forgive her for the cow business. I don't care if she *was* drunk. It hurt."

Ben started the Jeep's engine. "Michelle was hurt, too. That's why she said those things."

Edie made a noise of exasperation. "Why are you making excuses for her? What she did was vicious and mean, drunk or sober. I felt so sorry for Lura. She looked like a little deer frozen by a truck's headlights."

"I know," Ben said.

"And you've never promised Michelle anything. She doesn't own you."

Ben stared through the windshield. "Michelle said she would slit her wrists if I dumped her."

"You're kidding."

"No."

Edie laughed. "Now *that's* original. Come on, Ben, don't be such a sucker. Michelle loves herself too much."

"Maybe," he said.

"Oh, I see. You're thinking of Annette Taylor. Well, they do say suicide runs in families. But I don't think Lura's mother was actually serious about killing herself. I mean most people who really want to die find something more effective than a motorcycle in a garage. She probably knew they would find her in time. Now, if it had been a car, I'd say she was serious. But a motorcycle?"

When Ben didn't say anything, she went on. "Okay, I might have forgotten about the bottle of Amytal she took before she went into the garage, but like I said, Annette probably knew someone would find her in time."

"They didn't," Ben said.

"Of course they did. She might be something of a zombie now, but at least she's still alive. I think Phil and Lura are—"

"Edie, just shut up now, would you?"

"But—"

"I said shut up. You're starting to sound like that babbling, bitching, gossiping Hannah."

The shock went deep. Edie's brother had never told her to shut up before. Ever.

"Ben?" she said cautiously.

He reached for her hand, but his jaw was still taut. "I'm sorry. I didn't mean to snap at you. Just do me a favor and don't talk anymore, all right?"

She nodded and squeezed his hand. She had intended to tell him the truth about who Bryce was looking for, but she guessed she wouldn't. Not now.

Lura sat on the wooden steps of the old train depot and thought of how he had smelled. His smell was something she had never forgotten: clean skin in a wear-softened leather jacket, woodsy after-shave on smooth cheeks, a freshly laundered shirt with a faint hint of bleach. It was the rest of him that had changed. Ben and Michelle. Lura still couldn't believe it. The Ben she had known would never have touched someone like Michelle. Not in a million years. Lura closed her eyes and sighed. She guessed she was the only one who hadn't changed. Being with him, dancing with him and touching him had told her that much.

She hugged her knees to her chest and began to rock. The nights were growing cooler; she could feel the skin of her bare legs prickling. She should go now. She should start walking home.

The creak of floorboards behind her made her drop her knees and spring to her feet.

"I thought I might find you here," Phil said.

Lura exhaled in relief and clasped her arms together. "Bryce came by?"

"Yeah." Phil leaned against the railing and took out a cigarette. The match flame illuminated his face for the briefest of seconds. He looked older than eighteen.

"I didn't know you smoked," Lura said.

87

"I don't."

"Oh?"

"Not really."

She smiled. "Let me have one."

"Do you smoke?"

"Not really."

Phil chuckled and lit a cigarette for her. As she took it from his fingers she heard him sigh.

"Bryce told me what happened at Stella's. Is that why you came here?"

Lura inhaled the cigarette before answering. The menthol smoke burned her lungs and stung her nasal passages.

"I don't know," she said. "I guess I wanted to see if I would feel anything."

"Do you?"

She shook her head. "No. Everything came to the surface my first day back in Dumford."

"It's a shitty little town with shitty little people," Phil said bitterly. "I hate this town, Lura."

"It's home," she replied. "Is Mama sleeping?"

"Yeah. She sacked out pretty early."

"Did Bryce wake you?"

"No, I was still up." He flicked the cigarette and watched the glowing coal spiral away through the darkness. "What are you going to do about Michelle?"

"Nothing."

Phil came away from the railing and took her arm in a warm clasp. "You're a better person than I am. Let's walk a little. Are you cold?"

"Not uncomfortably so."

Phil grinned. "I love the way you talk now. You slip back into the Dumford twang every now and then, but most of the time you sound like an English teacher."

"Is that good or bad?" Lura asked.

When he didn't answer she fell silent and thought of how nice it was to walk with him. It didn't bother her to look at the tracks or to hear the gravel crunching under her feet. The train would make the difference, she supposed.

"Why haven't you ever talked about it?" Phil asked suddenly.

She tensed. "About what?"

"About being in prison. What it was like. Are the women there really the way you see in movies?"

Lura's pulse returned to normal. "Oh, I don't know. Movies exaggerate quite a bit, but some of the women act as tough as men. There were some weightlifters who actually looked like men."

"Huh," Phil said. "Do they fight a lot?"

Lura laughed. "Put more than five women in a room and you're bound to have a fight. Some were serious, but most were just squabbles between gangs. Like in school, there are gangs, or cliques, and your personality decides which one you join."

"Which one did you join?" Phil asked.

"None of them. And I paid for it. There were three main factions, and each of them took a turn at me."

"You mean they attacked you?"

"Yes."

"Did you fight back?"

"At first I did, then I realized it was pointless. After they learned I wasn't going to fight back, and that I wasn't afraid, the thrill was gone. They left me alone. Most of them did, anyway."

Phil looked at her. "Most of them?"

"There was a woman named Carla. She was a member, but her actions for the most part were unsupported by her gang. She was quite ugly, with a face like a pustulant pumpkin pie—"

"A what?" Phil laughed.

"—and she hated everything about me. She cut off my hair twice and even tried to get a job in the kitchen so she could brutalize me at will. I managed to outwit her most of the time. My aim for a degree was largely to escape her."

"Why did she hate you so much?" Phil asked. "Did she ever do anything to hurt you?"

Lura glanced at him. "She hated me because I shunned her. She wanted my affection and I couldn't give it. And because I was smaller and weaker and easy prey, she took advantage." She paused. "Do you really want to hear the rest?"

"Yes. I feel like I need to. I want to understand what you went through."

Lura nodded. "All right. Carla raped me three times, two of which occurred when she cut off my hair. The last time was two years before my release."

Phil swallowed. After a moment he said, "What . . . uh, what did she use?"

"Vegetables, mostly." Bryce hadn't been far off in his quip about the cucumbers. "She had to be careful, though. Any woman caught with a carrot, a cucumber, or a corn cob was put on report or sent to solitary."

Phil was staring at her. "You're serious. What did you do, Lura?"

"The first two times I reported her. Nothing ever came of it, so the last time I took my own revenge. I worked in the kitchen, remember, and I started saving scraps of food. I hid them until—"

"Food poisoning," Phil interjected. "You poisoned the bitch."

"She was sick for three weeks," Lura confirmed.

Phil's laugh was a short, vengeful bark. "And she left you alone after that?"

"They moved her to another cellblock, where she transferred her attentions to someone else—someone who could give her what she wanted."

"I'll bet you were glad." Phil reached out and ran a hand through the thickness of his sister's hair. "She must not have cut very much off."

"Sawed is a better word," Lura said. "She used a short metal strip that wouldn't cut butter. She did manage to make a mess of it, but it grows fast."

Phil let the heavy length slip through his fingers. "Now I know why it turned gray. Why haven't you dyed it yet?"

Lura lifted a shoulder. "It doesn't really bother me. In fact, I think of it almost as a trophy. As a symbol of my survival."

Her brother's sob took her by surprise. It was a ragged sound, like the tearing of fabric. In the next second his arms were around her.

"I'm sorry, Lura. I'm so sorry for what happened to you. She used that metal strip on you, didn't she? To rape you. She must've hurt you really bad."

"No, Phil. No, she didn't." Lura held on to him and chided herself for her mistake. She shouldn't have told him anything. Though he looked, sounded, and acted like a man, he was in reality still a boy, with none of the emotional experiences and defenses of a grown man.

"I shouldn't have told you," she said.

"No. I'm glad you did." His arms tightened around her. "It wasn't fair. None of it was fair."

Her hands paused in soothing him. A tiny frown creased her brow. *None of it was fair.* Was he talking about Carla and the prison, or something else? Lura decided it was time to find out just how much her brother remembered.

"Phil," she said softly. "Let's talk about Mama."

He lifted his head and rubbed awkwardly at his eyes and nose. "What about her?"

"Does she often try to hurt herself?"

"No, not often. I just have to watch her."

Lura held her breath. "What about you, Phil? Has she ever tried to hurt you?"

"Me?" He snorted and stepped back. "I've got seventy pounds on her."

"You know what I mean," Lura pressed.

"No, I don't know what you mean." He turned toward

the depot and blew his nose with a handkerchief from his back pocket. "You've been away a long time, Lura. Maybe you've forgotten just how tight our bonds are. We have no one but each other, and Mama would never hurt either of us. You of all people should know that." He straightened then. "Speaking of Mama, we need to be getting home. She'll be up in a few hours."

Lura watched him start away from her with defiant steps. His spine was stiff, his head at a rigid angle. He remembered, all right. She was sure of it.

Chapter Ten

"I'll never eat steak again," Bryce swore.

Ben looked at the colorful insides of the dead cow on the ground before them and silently agreed. Brown, purple, and puce intestines littered the surrounding grass and released a powerful odor. The belly of the Black Angus cow was a stringy red maw crawling with flies and other insects. Several rodents had made their mark on the carcass during the night: one eye was missing, and one knobby black foreleg had been gnawed through to white bone.

The rest of the herd huddled against the east fence of the forty-acre pasture. Their bovine stares were more alert than usual, somehow wary of the three men standing above their fallen sister. Only the bull grazed, his broad back displaying a studied indifference to the presence of the men.

Ben forced his gaze away from the carnage to look at the owner of the cow. Julius Hinshaw was a short, sixtyish, bowlegged widower with a crew-cut head and a brown, creased face. He had been raising cattle outside of Dumford as long as Ben could remember, and at one time his herd had numbered in the thousands. When people stopped eating beef and started eating poultry, Julius slowly phased out of the beef market. He still sold the occasional steer, but most of his income now came from the chicken houses he had installed five years ago. Even from the pasture Ben could hear the scratch-peck-cluck activity of the fowls in the matchbox dwellings just beyond the barn.

"Well?" Julius asked, and Ben winced as he saw the man send a stream of tobacco juice into the dead cow's empty eye socket. When the shot struck its mark, Julius chuckled and said, "Cow's eye. Get it?"

"Jesus," Bryce said.

Ben took his pad and pencil from his shirt pocket. "What time did you say your dogs started barking?"

" 'Bout a quarter to eleven. I got up and couldn't see nothin', so I figured it was a coyote."

"And what time did you find the cow this morning?"

"An hour ago. Nine, I guess. I thought I'd better get right in and call you boys. I woulda called the sheriff, but they tell me I'm in the town limits. You gonna call him in?"

"For a dead cow?" Bryce said.

"For a mutilated cow," Julius corrected. "I've heard about this stuff before. I saw a show on 'Geraldo' about these black cults that slice up animals for sacrifice. I can't see no circles or altar marks in the grass, but it's a possibility. And then you got your UFO cover-ups. Don't tell me you boys ain't received a few reported sightings, 'cause I know you have. Aliens use a little more surgical precision in operations like this here, though. Lasers, I heard."

Bryce's face hurt from trying not to smile. "Are you writing this down, Ben?"

Ben lifted his eyes heavenward as Julius Hinshaw went on. "You ask me, them Miller folks out by the graveyard are mighty suspicious. I didn't know it, but just last week Hannah Winegarten was telling me about them two. Hell, I thought they was black, you know? Turns out they're both Haitians, and how in God's America they ever came up with a name like Miller is beyond me, but Hannah says they have some pretty peculiar habits."

"Such as?" Bryce asked.

"Goats," Julius said knowingly. "They keep three goats on the place all the time, but Hannah swears they're never the same three goats. And they buy chickens from me like crazy, so you tell me what you think. I say we either got devil lovers or voodooers makin' mischief here. What other sort of person would slit open the belly of a cow and take the calf and everythin' else out?"

"Wait," Ben said. "This cow was getting ready to calve?"

"Next two weeks, I figured. What I can't figure out is what happened to the calf."

"You've looked?"

"Before I called you I looked. I can't find it. Do you see it layin' around here anywhere?"

Ben and Bryce exchanged a glance.

"Did you look over the rest of your property?" Ben asked.

Julius spat tobacco juice again. "I ain't got time for that shit. Why d'ya think I called you boys out here? Now what are you gonna do about this?"

"We'll begin an investigation," Ben told him.

"Investigate my ass," Julius said. "You go down to that Miller place and see if they ain't dancin' around naked and eatin' premature calf for lunch."

Bryce groaned. "Mr. Hinshaw, do you know what xenophobia is?"

Julius peered at him from beneath heavy brows. "Can't say as I do. Is it contagious?"

"Very," Bryce said. "And you're obviously infected."

The old man's eyes narrowed. "How can you tell? Does it come from chickens?"

"Something like that." Bryce turned to Ben. "It's all yours, buddy. I'll get on the horn and find someone to take care of the carcass."

95

Julius mumbled something about a medical dictionary and started after him. Ben watched the two depart, then he turned and walked to the nearest line of trees. He kicked through the leaves and the tall grass for several hundred yards before making his way back to the patrol car. He approached in time to hear a familiar female voice come over the radio. He froze and stared at Bryce's broad back.

"What channel should I use?" he heard Lura ask in a hesitant voice.

"How about the age you lost your virginity?" Bryce said with a chuckle. "No, wait. Hannah probably has that written down somewhere. Let's see. Do you remember the number of the dinner you had at Barney's last night?"

"Yes," she said.

"Okay, let's go to that channel."

A moment later Lura asked, "What makes you think *you* know when I lost my virginity?"

"It was a joke for Hannah's big ears," Bryce replied. "Where the hell did you go last night?"

Lura's answer was long in coming. Bryce listened to the hiss of the radio and waited. Ben shifted his feet and wished Bryce would turn around and see him.

Finally she said, "I went to the old depot. I'm sorry I ran out on you."

"I understand your reasons," he said. "You had me worried though. I drove all over the place looking for you, and now this morning we have a mutilated cow at Julius Hinshaw's place. I remembered how much you enjoyed your steak last night and I wondered if you decided to come out here and help yourself."

"No," Lura said in an amused voice. "I prefer mine on a plate, thank you. Are you serious about the cow?"

"Yeah," Bryce said. "It's a good thing you said you were at the depot, otherwise I might have to come and arrest you for bovinicide or something. Listen, I'm sorry for deserting you to dance with Edie last night. None of that mess would have happened if—"

"Don't apologize," Lura broke in. "We've known each other too long."

Bryce sighed. "You're right. Okay, then. I'll call you later this week and we'll go ride my horse or something, okay?"

"Fine. Thanks for . . . radioing."

"You bet."

When Bryce turned from the car Ben was three feet away and staring hard at him.

"What happened after I took Michelle outside last night?" he asked.

Bryce held the chilly gaze and considered his options. Finally he said, "I'd say you heard enough to guess. If you require further elucidation, I suggest you ask Lura herself, though she may tell you, and rightly so, that what she does is none of your business."

Ben's fingers curled against his palm. "What do you want from her, Bryce? Why the sudden display of interest?"

"Come on," Bryce said with a coy smile. "That's *my* business."

His fists still clenched, Ben took a deep breath and walked away.

Seven hours later he held his desk phone between his shoulder and chin as he struggled to write down the information the county coroner was rapidly repeating for him. "Sweep point blade, just under five inches. Very sharp. In fact, I'd say it was sharpened just before the cow killing, thus the sliver I found. I'd say it has blood grooves, too."

"A hunting knife," Ben said.

"You got it. Have many deer hunters in Dumford?"

"Only every male over sixteen."

"Good luck then. But I'll tell you, Ben, this is the lousiest field dressing I've ever seen. This person isn't experienced with the knife."

"What do you mean?"

"I mean the hand that wielded the blade was shaking and wavering all over the place on both the cow and the dog.

The point of entry was a strong thrust, but after that the gutting was a messy job, as if the person lacked the strength to pull the blade through all that muscle and tissue without stopping for rest."

"How do you explain that?" Ben asked.

"I don't," came the pointed reply.

"Okay," Ben said with a smile. "Listen, I really appreciate the favor.

"No problem. There's been a lull in human corpses. Don't worry about the chief or the sheriff. This phone call never took place as far as I'm concerned. I'm just sorry I couldn't let you see the paperwork."

"That's all right. I don't have the proper authorization," Ben admitted.

"And the people who do have the proper authorization are a little too complacent, is that it?"

"You might say that," Ben said. "Again, thank you for the information."

"You're welcome, Ben. Take care."

Ben hung up and leaned over his desk to study his notes. What the coroner had related about the person who wielded the knife was interesting, but what did it tell him? That their perpetrator had a weak arm?

Hannah left her desk and slowly began to drift his way. Ben quickly shoved his notebook in his pocket and stood up. Since beginning her diary, Ben found it difficult to be in the same room with Hannah. He knew things about her that she herself had probably forgotten, and looking at her now, knowing what he did, he was uncomfortable. He wished he had never opened her diary. But he was powerless to stop reading it.

"Does the Miller family still live on Ninth Street, Hannah?" he asked.

She nodded. "Out past the graveyard. Are you going out there?"

"Yes," Ben said.

"By yourself?"

"Yes. Why are you whispering?"

"Am I?" Hannah blinked. "I didn't mean to. They're strange people, that's all. Very strange. Was I really whispering?"

Ben nodded. "I'll see you tomorrow."

"Wait," she said quickly. "You're off duty now. Why not have Mickey or Haden go out there?"

"I'm just going for a visit," Ben replied. "Don't try to turn it into anything else."

Hannah's painted mouth tightened. "And just what is that supposed to mean? What's happened to your manners, Ben? It's Bryce, isn't it? Mr. Rubber Dick is turning you all—" She clapped her hands over her mouth in horror at the words she had spoken.

Ben left her that way.

Berniece Miller was a tall woman with a big frame that suited the wife of a truck farmer. Her long, lightly muscled arm seemed to go on forever as it held the screen door open for him. When she smiled he caught a flash of gold on one bicuspid.

"Come in, Officer Portlock."

Her dark hair was pulled back and tied with a blue silk bandanna that matched the starched blue of her blouse. He looked past her grinning face and snapping dark eyes and was surprised to see an immaculate room with furnishings that would have made Edie green with envy. Fuchsia, gray, and pink pillows lined a virgin white sectional sofa that stretched the length of one wall and ended in front of a three-foot sculpture of a woman holding a baby at each stone breast. The large oriental rugs were lint free, the hardwood floors gleamed. The room reminded Ben of a picture in one of his sister's decorating magazines.

"Very nice," he said with genuine appreciation. "You have a beautiful home, Mrs. Miller."

The golden tooth appeared. "I work like a dog to keep it that way. Can I get you a beer, or is this an official visit?"

"A beer would be great, thanks."

"Sit down anywhere you want," she told him. "Most people who come in are afraid to mess something up."

Ben sat down on the nearest end of the sofa and decided he would definitely have to look into truck farming. The Miller's crops were known throughout the county, but he had no idea they had done so well financially.

"Nope," she said as she handed him the beer.

Ben lifted a brow. "Pardon me?"

"We didn't get the money for these things from our truck farming," she clarified.

He stared at her. "I take it that's a fairly common misconception?"

"It's what you were thinking, wasn't it?"

"Yes," he admitted reluctantly.

"And now you're wondering where we did get the money if it wasn't from the truck farming. Right?"

Ben frowned thoughtfully and took a drink of beer before answering. "I think I know now. You must be the anonymous psychic who advertises in the weekly."

Mrs. Miller beamed. "Not just another dumb country boy, are you? And you're a lot better looking than I heard. A man put together like you ought to have sired at least four children by now. What's the hold up?"

He smiled at her frankness. "I didn't come here to talk about me, Mrs. Miller."

"I know that," she said tersely. "But it don't mean you shouldn't. You got a mess on your hands right now and that's for sure. You cut that black-haired bitch loose before someone gets hurt."

The smile fell away from Ben's face. "I came here to warn you, Mrs. Miller. You and your family."

"I know all about it," she told him. "Since I was born in Haiti, people think I chop the heads off goats and drink their blood. Ignorant bunch of shitheads. Is everyone born in Nevada a gambler? Does everyone from Washington eat

Jonathan apples? Hell, no. I have a gift, yes, but *voudou* has no claim to it. It's a God-given talent and I'm not ashamed of it. I don't have to hide myself away like some sixteenth-century hag with a mole on her tit."

"I'm not asking you to change anything in the way you live," Ben explained. "I'm only asking you to be careful. One woman in particular is behind the rumors, and for some unknowable reason, people listen to her."

"Hannah Winegarten," his hostess said with a rueful smile. "She tries to camouflage the stench of her own miserable soul by bathing herself in the misery of others."

Hannah in an eloquent nutshell, Ben thought.

"But it's you who ought to be worrying," Mrs. Miller said meaningfully.

Ben looked at her. "Why?"

"There's a knife. A big one. Bone handle with initials carved into it. Can't see them clear, so don't bother with asking me what they are. Your fingers are in the way. It's you holding it, Ben Portlock."

He cleared his throat and looked uncomfortably around himself. "Okay. What am I doing with it?"

"I don't know. Can't tell you that now." She leaned forward then. "Something else, too."

In spite of his sudden discomfort, his eyes lifted to meet her black, probing gaze. "What?"

"Tainted blood. For this one, the line between right and wrong is perforated like a store coupon."

Ben sat back. "What?"

"Look between the black and white, Ben. Your guts'll twist a little, but keep looking. There's a sickness in the blood. Look and you'll see it."

"I'm sorry," he said with a tone somewhere between disbelief and amusement. "I don't understand."

Berniece Miller blinked suddenly. "I don't either. When it comes out it always sounds nutty as hell. But it usually means something. Me and Jeanne Dixon. Ask any—well, you can't do that because I keep my client list confidential. You'd be surprised how many of my customers are afraid of ridicule."

"I can imagine." Ben looked for a place to put his beer bottle. She saved him the trouble by rising from her seat and taking it out of his hand.

"No, I don't want your money," she said. "I like to help folks who need it."

He sighed and dropped the hand that had reached for his wallet. "You must be difficult to live with."

The gold tooth appeared in a mischievous grin. "It's a bitch, Harv says. He can't have a backward thought that I don't know about, and I'll swear he's the most faithful man that ever walked. Of course I don't pick his brain all the time. But he don't know when I am and when I'm not."

Ben followed the chuckling woman to the door, where she turned suddenly and placed a gentle brown hand on his arm.

"You're a good man coming out here to warn me like this. Don't you worry about a thing. I can usually see trouble coming before it picks up the keys and leaves the house. Because we drink goat's milk and eat chicken I guess we're cause for suspicion, but I could tell you thoughts in Hannah Winegarten's pea-and-pearl-onion brain that would make your hair stand on end."

Ben knew exactly what she was talking about. Before she could read the thought, he said, "I'll bet you could, Mrs. Miller."

Something flickered in her eyes, as if she had caught the thought anyway, and Ben smiled impulsively. He liked the candid Mrs. Miller. He offered his hand to her.

She took it and chuckled. "I like you, too. Don't be a stranger now, hear?"

Ben shook his head and left her laughing in the doorway. As he climbed into his car he found himself thinking Harvey Miller was either the luckiest or the unluckiest sonofabitch in the county.

As for himself, Ben didn't know what to make of her talk. The perforated coupon bit was definitely something he would have to think about. Not to mention the vision of him holding a knife with an initialed bone handle. That part worried him. It worried him because he had the feeling Mrs. Miller hadn't told him everything she could have.

When he reached home he glanced across the street and saw Lura struggling to replace the screen on her bedroom window. The blue softball jersey she wore brought back many memories for Ben. He had pitched the Dumford Devils to the state tournament three years in a row and made it to the nationals twice. He could still see his biggest fan sitting in the bleachers, her dark hair whipping around her face as she laughed and teased him about a lousy 39¢ hamburger pitch.

On impulse he got out of the car and walked across the street.

"Need any help?"

She flipped her gray ponytail and barely glanced at him. "I can manage, thanks."

Ben looked at the stiffness of her shoulders and stood back. "I'm surprised you still have that jersey. Looks good as new."

The screen slipped to the ground. The dark-lashed eyes that met his were cool and distant.

"What are you doing, Ben?"

"Offering my help."

"I've turned it down," she said.

He shifted his stance. "Look, I want to apologize for what happened at Mom's place last night."

Lura turned away from him. "You don't have to. I shouldn't have danced with you."

"Why?" he asked.

She picked up the screen again and didn't answer.

"Why?" he repeated. "Tell me."

She ignored him to line up the screen with the window. The metal made a grating noise as she missed the slots on

103

the first try. Ben reached forward impatiently and jerked the screen out of her hands. He fitted it to the window within five seconds and turned to see her glaring at him. He had forgotten how dark the blue in her eyes became when she was angry. Like winter storm clouds.

"Will you answer me now?"

She crossed her arms over her breasts and refused to look at him.

"What the hell is wrong with you?" Ben asked. Then suddenly he knew. "Did Michelle call you today?"

"Go home, Ben."

"She did, didn't she?"

Lura's gaze shifted to a point beyond him. "Ask her. She just pulled into your drive."

Ben didn't turn. "You don't make it easy for me, Lura. I don't know how to talk to you, or what to—"

"Don't say anything," she interjected. "My moonlight strolls have stopped, so you can sleep easy tonight. Now please go home and leave me alone."

His eyes caught hers and held them. "I don't think I can do that."

"You've done it before," she said.

A muscle in Ben's cheek began to twitch. "If you need me for anything, call. Anything at all."

Lura lifted a hand to massage the nape of her neck. At the same time, a frown appeared between her fine brows.

"That's really generous of you, Ben, but I think you've done enough already. When I get a job I'll start repaying the money you loaned Phil. I understand he hasn't made any payments to you yet."

"Jesus," Ben murmured. "Is that it? Is that what you're so upset about? It wasn't a loan, Lura, and I don't expect to be paid back."

"So it was charity? Well, I certainly hope you made the proper deductions on your taxes."

Ben looked at her in amazement. "I can't believe this.

The first conversation we have in almost eight years is an argument about goddamned money."

"What did you expect to talk about, Ben? The good old days? Did you think I would wet myself like a puppy at hearing how you looked after my family?"

"You weren't supposed to *know,* dammit. Phil promised he wouldn't tell you."

"Lura?" Annette stepped onto the porch and put a cautioning finger to her mouth. "The two of you really shouldn't be out here yelling at each other in front of the neighbors. And Ben, you have company in your drive. I think it's young Michelle, though I don't see as well as I used to."

Ben ran a tired hand through his hair. "Hello, Annette. How are you today?"

"The apple pie smells good," she replied. "You shouldn't keep Michelle waiting, you know. She's very insecure about her nipples."

"Mama," Lura said sharply. She glanced at Ben and was surprised to see his mouth give a threatening twitch. Her own mouth wanted to curve but she held it straight.

"Ben's just leaving, Mama. You and I need to go in the house and see about starting some supper. Maybe we can bake an apple pie."

"Can Ben come and have some? That would be nice, wouldn't it? Just like when you were younger."

Lura grimaced. "He has company, remember? And we really don't want to take up any more of his time."

She directed a meaningful look at Ben, and as she passed him he reached out to take her arm.

"Let go," Lura said.

Her eyes refused to meet his. After a moment he released her and watched as she hurriedly escorted her mother into the house.

Chapter Eleven

"It's fascinating, isn't it?" Annette said as she flipped channels with the television remote.

Lura yawned. "What is?"

"The human body. Philip says it's like a machine. He does very well in biology, you know, and I think it's because he's a good mechanic. Heart, lungs, liver, and kidneys—everything under the hood has a function."

Lura sat up in her chair. Her mother was making semi-sense, so it was time to be wary.

"What made you think of that, Mama?"

She shrugged and drew her fingers through her unbound hair. Lura watched her and thought how alike their hair was now. From behind, they would appear identical.

"Watching you and Ben," Annette murmured. "The two of you were like overheated engines. I could feel the heat coming off your bodies. For a moment I imagined I could see it. You still worship the man."

It wasn't a question.

Lura swallowed. "No, Mama. I don't."

"He has the strangest eyes, doesn't he? Sometimes blue,

sometimes green, never the same when you look at him twice. And he's so . . . strong. Yes, that's a good word to describe Ben. He'll keep all his hair, too."

"I suppose." Lura scanned the area around her mother. There were no sharp instruments in sight, nothing but a *TV Guide* and a plastic tumbler full of milk.

"And Bryce McKee is *le diable* himself. I hear him on that radio taking pokes at Hannah Winegarten. She hates the ground that boy walks on, doesn't she?"

"Bryce is a prankster," Lura responded.

Annette giggled and stuffed a handful of her gray hair into her mouth. "That's not why she hates him."

The words were muffled, but Lura heard them.

"Why, then?"

"Because of his father, that's why. He was a painter, and he met Hannah when he contracted to paint the new school. She fell in love with him, and he made her think he was in love with her. He told Hannah he was going to leave Bryce's mother to be with her."

Lura frowned. "No, Mama. You have it wrong. Bryce's father ran off with that woman from the flower shop."

"Faites attention a ce que je vous dis!"

"I am paying attention, Mama. And speak English, please. Now, you just said Bryce's father told Hannah he was going to run off with her."

"And he did," Annette said. "They went out to Huntington Beach in California. Hannah paid for everything with her own money. Once there, Bryce's father left her. He had arranged to meet the flower shop woman in Los Angeles, but he needed Hannah's money to get there."

Lura grew worried. "Mama . . . you're not going to hurt yourself again, are you?"

"Poor Hannah crept back into town and tried to keep the whole thing quiet. But that's impossible in a town as small as this one. Her father had a stroke and died shortly thereafter. What happened was no secret to him, I'm sure."

"Mama, please answer me."

"We've managed to keep our secret though, haven't we, daughter?"

The clarity of her mother's gaze made Lura's skin crawl with sudden fear.

"Are you ready for bed yet, Mama? I have an interview at the weekly in the morning."

Lura knew her voice was trembling, but she couldn't stop it. Phil was due home from the garage any minute and she prayed for him to hurry.

"He hated apple pie, you know. Your father wanted cherry or nothing else. I made him eclairs and he threw them out the window for the neighbor's dogs to eat. One dog in particular loved my eclairs. That big dog Ben used to have—what was its name?"

"Paddy. His name was Paddy."

"My Papa used to beat that horse like you wouldn't believe. It made me cry the way he treated that animal. Oats and carrots were Paddy's favorite foods, and he wouldn't let anyone but me get close enough to give them to him. Have you ever had a horse, Lura?"

"No, Mama."

"I'd like to have one again. I think Ben would buy one for me if I asked him."

"Don't you dare ask him for anything," Lura said to her in a stern voice.

"I'd ask for a chandelier before I'd ask for anything," Annette replied. "I don't know why those people always start off by choosing stereos and things. I think the game shows are rigged, don't you?"

Lura's nerves were frayed. When the front door opened she nearly leaped out of her chair. Phil laughed at the whiteness of her features and stuck his nose in the air.

"My God, is that apple pie I smell?"

"Did you want cherry pie?" Annette asked.

Lura put her hands over her ears and headed for her bedroom. She closed the door behind her and threw herself onto the bed. Phil gave her exactly three minutes before he came and knocked. "Lura? Can I come in?"

"Yes," she said into her pillow.

He opened the door and flicked on the light. Lura turned over and blinked against the glare.

"Bad night?" Phil asked.

"The worst. There was nothing to watch on television."

"So she started rambling?"

Lura sat up. "It scared me to death, Phil. She sounded so rational I found myself looking for possible weapons."

Her brother laughed. "I probably made it sound worse than it is. She's only hurt herself a couple times, Lura. You don't have to be on the lookout every time she connects three logical sentences."

"I think she knows more than she lets on," Lura said seriously. "At one point her eyes were so clear I knew she was fully aware of what she was saying."

"Oh?" Phil said with interest. "And just what did she say?"

"Nothing important," Lura assured him. "It was simply the way she said it."

Phil smirked and reached for the door again. "Don't let her fool you. And don't let her rambling make you crazy. Just nod every once in a while and she's happy."

Lura sighed. "Today has been one confrontation after another. First Michelle, then Ben, and now Mama and her eclairs."

Phil's hand dropped away from the doorknob. "What happened with Michelle?"

"The usual. She talked, I listened. I have been duly warned to stay away from other people's property."

"Meaning Ben Portlock. And I assume you had to run right over and tell him you knew about the money he gave me."

Lura frowned at her brother. "I did no such thing. He came over here and offered his help. I explained that he's already done enough, and that I'll repay him as soon as possible. If you didn't have the foresight to know what my reaction would be then you shouldn't have broken your promise to him."

"You're right," Phil said in a flat voice. "Impetuous adolescent that I am, I mistakenly believed it would curb any bitterness you might be feeling because of his relationship with Michelle. I thought if you knew how much he cared, it would make you feel better."

Lura's face grew warm with anger. "That money was to salve his conscience, Phil. It wasn't because he cared, it was because he felt guilty."

"He wanted to help," Phil replied shortly. "And he did help us, Lura. Without Ben's money, Mama and I would have had to throw ourselves on Marie's mercy a long time ago. Or maybe you'd rather we starved for your stupid pride?"

Lura turned her back on him and stared at the wall above her bed. "I won't deny that pride is involved. But so is principle."

She heard the doorknob turn. Phil's voice was suddenly tired. "Do me a favor, Lura. When I leave, ask yourself just what it is you want to pay Ben back for."

The door closed. Lura squeezed her eyes shut and waited for the sting of his words to pass. Was he right? Did she have more than money in mind when it came to repaying Ben?

How did Phil get so smart? she asked herself suddenly. He was only eighteen. At eighteen he should've been out drinking beer with the boys or sweet-talking girls into his backseat. He wasn't supposed to be at home babysitting a brain-damaged mother and lecturing a gray-haired sister. It wasn't right. Surely he knew that. Surely he knew he was missing something.

Phil had been eleven when they put Lura in jail. Eleven, with a suicidal parent and a mountain of hospital bills. But he had somehow managed to maintain control and keep Marie from taking over.

How had he done it? Lura wondered. How had the boy convinced their aunt to let he and his mother remain together in their home? Marie had visited daily, of course, but the bulk of the responsibility had rested with Philip.

Jesse Taylor had doubtlessly figured in the decision. His brother Ordney's death had been a terrible shock to him. Not only because he'd lost his best hunting, fishing, and drinking buddy, but because Ordney had made his wife, Annette, the beneficiary on his insurance policy after swearing he had filled in his brother's name. Lura knew her uncle had attempted to get control of the money, but the judge had taken pity on Annette and Philip and set up a trust instead.

Normally, in a town with less than a thousand people, the locals would have pitched in and done everything possible for a young boy and his sick mother. Circumstances, and Dumford, made this particular instance a different story. The Taylors were crazy. They were wild and thick as thieves with each other and not decent to be around. If the boys had married local girls instead of bringing home those uppity frogs from Lousiana, things would have been different.

Very few families felt any sympathy for young Philip's plight. Those that did kept it hidden. Like Ben. He had returned after three years in the city and found the tall fourteen year old quietly struggling, Lura imagined. She still found it hard to believe that Phil, who had a healthy amount of pride himself, had ever accepted a dime from the man whose testimony had put Lura behind bars. But Phil had always liked Ben. And perhaps accepting money from him was easier than begging it from the prissy Marie. All things considered, Lura decided her brother was to be admired.

A noise from her window made her sit up suddenly and stare with rounded eyes at her curtains. She watched and waited for several moments, but nothing further happened. Quietly she slid off the bed and went to peer through the curtains. The screen from her window was hanging at an angle across the frame. On the ground below she could see the broken metal slot fixture that the screen had been attached to. "Great," she muttered as she opened the window. She pulled on the screen until it came free from the window, then she tossed it onto the ground below. The rotting frame was too weak to hold yet another set of screws and slots, and there was no money to repair the frame.

Lura sighed and returned to her bed. It was definitely time to find a job. She no longer had a choice.

Chapter Twelve

Edie replaced the receiver of her white kitchen phone and automatically ran a rag over the surface to wipe off her fingerprints. The TWA airline counter in Wichita apparently didn't believe in answering their phones after midnight—that or someone was on an extremely long potty break. In New York there would have been an answer, Edie told herself. L.A., too. Half-annoyed and half-overjoyed, she couldn't decide what to do next. Portis was always home by eight o'clock on the Sunday after a weekend spree. Here it was, half past twelve, and no Portis yet.

His being dead was too much to hope for. Some cop would have opened his wallet and seen her name on the emergency card Portis carried with him. His parents were first on the list of numbers, but they surely would have called her from the city if bad news had been received.

Unless he had perished in a flaming car accident and his wallet had burned with him.

Edie shivered at the morbid fantasy and opened the refrigerator. Her chocolate-covered peanuts were hidden in the mustard container. She unscrewed the lid and allowed herself a smile as she grabbed a handful.

Maybe it would be days before they identified him. The police would have to use his teeth and that silly horseshoe diamond pinky ring he wore.

The secretary. What about her?

Edie shoved the peanuts into her mouth and groped in the cabinet for Dumford's fifty-page phone book. A moment later she hung up the phone and wiped the chocolate from the receiver. No answer.

Had the secretary burned up, too?

Serve them both right, she thought viciously. Though in truth she bore no real malice toward the slutty Kayleen.

The M&Ms buried in the flour tin were next. She tore open the package and shook a few of the brightly colored candies into her palm.

Suppose he didn't show up for work tomorrow? Was she expected to call in Portis and his secretary as sick?

Her jaws moved rhythmically as she chewed the candy. When the package was empty she put it in the sink and set fire to it with a match. She rinsed the ashes down the drain and moved toward the caramels hidden in the Bisquick box in the cupboard above the stove.

As she unwrapped her fifth caramel the phone rang, causing her to give a startled squeak. When she couldn't swallow the chewy wad fast enough, she took it out of her mouth and held it between two fingers as she picked up the phone. "Portis, is that you?"

"I didn't think he was home," Bryce said. "Where the hell is the fat toad?"

"That's none of your business," Edie told him. "What are you doing calling me this late at night?"

"I drove by and didn't see his car. I thought I'd see if you and Junior were okay."

Edie looked at the glob of caramel between her fingers and sighed. "Would you please stop calling it Junior? What if it's a girl?"

"Fine by me," he replied. "What are your thoughts about names?"

"What makes you think I would—"

"Personally," Bryce inserted, "I favor Patrick for a boy and Analise for a girl."

Edie's frown dissipated and her brown eyes lit up with interest. "Analise? That's a pretty name. Where did you hear it?"

"What do you think about Patrick? Those were my grandparents' names. Patrick and Analise McKee."

"I remember them," Edie said. "They raised you after your mom died, didn't they? I never knew their first names though. Remember how they always put out those huge jack-o'-lanterns full of Brach's candies at Halloween? We used to race each other to Old Man McKee's house."

Bryce laughed. "Remember the time me and Mike Wells ambushed the chirruping little bunch of you? You had on that Snow White outfit and—"

"It was Cinderella," Edie said caustically. "And you tripped Cathy Dale and took her Almond Joy candy bars."

"It wasn't me," Bryce swore. "I only wanted to scare you. It was Mike's idea to rob the booty. If you remember, it was me who helped you up and dusted off your little dress."

"You only did that because you were afraid Ben would beat you up," Edie said.

"Bullshit. I'm a year older than him, remember?"

"So? You fought each other once. It was after that football game when you deliberately let him get sacked."

"I don't remember that," Bryce said.

"You were out of it."

"Drunk?"

"On the field," Edie confirmed.

"Damn," Bryce said. "I really don't remember that. We might go for it again sometime soon. Ben caught me talking to Lura on the radio today, and if looks could kill I'd be rigor mortified right now."

Edie licked at the melting caramel glob between her fingers. "Why were you talking to Lura?"

"I was worried after last night. So were you."

"Are you going out with her again?"

Bryce's chuckle was low. "Are you jealous?"

"No," Edie said in exasperation.

"Why not?"

"Because I think you're doing it just to make Ben mad, that's why."

"What?" Bryce laughed. "My sweet little heart, what terrible things you think of me. But I suppose I should be grateful that you think of me at all."

"I don't," Edie said.

"Never? Never ever?"

"Never."

"Little liar. You enjoyed dancing with me last night, and you opened your mouth when I kissed you. Tell me what that means."

"I did not open my mouth."

"Bull," Bryce said. "One second more and you'd have offered up your tongue."

Edie nearly spat into the phone. "Now who's the liar? I can't believe you, Bryce. What does it take to get through to you? I have a *hus*band."

"Portis the Tortoise? Don't give me that shit. Has he ever made love to you the way I did? I counted three that night, sweetheart."

"Three what?" Edie snapped.

"Orgasms. My back is scarred for life. Was that the first time you've ever had one?"

"No," Edie said smartly. "It's the first time I've ever had to settle for just three."

There was silence for a long moment, then Bryce gave an uncomfortable laugh.

"You're lying again, you mean little shit. I'd like to come over there right now and prove it. Just dancing with you last night was enough to—"

Edie hung up on him. She didn't hang up because of what he was saying, but because she heard the lock on the front door turning. With furtive movements she buried the caramel and the wrappers in the middle of the wastebasket and wiped down the phone again. By the time she was done she heard him dropping his suitcases in the foyer and asking her what the hell every light in the house was doing on at this hour. She ran a quick finger over her teeth and hurried out to meet him.

"I was nervous, Portis. Why are you so late? I was getting worried."

"I'm sure," he said with a snort.

"Well, what happened?" she pressed. "Did you miss your plane?"

He threw his overcoat at her. "What happened is none of your goddamned business. Unpack my stuff and take the suits to the cleaners tomorrow. And sleep in the spare bedroom tonight."

"Why?" Edie asked cautiously.

Portis's voice was blessedly tired. "Because I have just six hours to sleep and I don't want to listen to you snore. Is that all right with you, little miss—" His nose lifted and his red-rimmed eyes rounded. "Do I smell caramel?"

Edie's mind raced. She twisted her lips and tried to look annoyed.

"I knew they had to have switched labels. It's that simmering potpourri stuff that makes the house smell good. See, you put it on the stove in a pot and let it simmer. I bought the Frosty Maple, but it doesn't smell anything like it sounds, does it?"

Portis grunted something under his breath about wasting good electricity and moved off toward the stairs. Edie waited until he was out of earshot before allowing herself a sigh of relief. The simmering potpourri was a good story. She might even use it again sometime.

After unpacking Portis's things and readying his suits for the cleaners she retired to the spare bedroom and let herself

117

fall fully clothed onto the bed. Her hands went instinctively to her rounded abdomen, and after a moment she felt a tiny jab. She lifted her blouse and watched for movement under the flesh.

There, a small rolling flutter to the left. Was it an arm? A leg perhaps? She placed her hand over the spot and felt a tiny shifting underneath.

"I hope you're not as vain as your daddy," she said to it in a whisper. "He really thinks he's something. And okay, I never had a you-know-what before him, but God's gift to the gender with tits doesn't have to know that."

Another shift bumped her fingertips and she smiled into the darkness.

"We can't think about him right now, can we? We have to worry about saving you from the hairy old boogeyman down the hall. Mommy's got to think of an accident very soon now. Something fatal."

The hairy old boogeyman down the hall stared at the red, veiny squiggles on his inner eyelids and wondered just how big of a fool women took him for. The unfaithful little twat in the spare bedroom wasn't the worst, by any means. Portis had Edie's number, all right, and he could tighten or loosen the reins at will. She was so fucking transparent sometimes it made him want to laugh. Standing there with caramel in the corners of her lying mouth and expecting him to be stupid enough to believe that simmering potpourri bullshit. She was lucky he was so tired tonight. Maybe when he had some time he'd go through the house and find her little stash.

Right now he had more important things to worry about. Like Kayleen. The blond bitch was actually going to blackmail him. Oh, she hadn't come right out and said it, but her request-demand for money had been loaded with unspoken implications.

Who did she think she was dealing with? Portis asked himself angrily. The videotape had been her idea to begin with, and if she hadn't misplaced it, none of this mess would have happened.

All right. It was his own damn fault for giving in to her. He didn't know what he was thinking about at the time. But then again, that was the problem. When those long legs of hers were over his shoulders, he didn't do a whole hell of a lot of thinking. Kayleen had every piece of kinksex equipment ever invented, and next to Miss Michelle Tightass Taylor, Kayleen had the roundest, most perfect little behind he'd ever seen.

Her face wasn't so great. In fact she was ugly as shit in a paper bag when it came right down to it. But hey . . .

He could still remember the day it started, the first Saturday in April and that last Vegas trip for the month. Both he and Kayleen had been lying naked on a rock-hard motel bed and wiping the Vaseline from their hands while they watched a few boring lust-in-leather vignettes on the bolted-down TV in the corner. Kayleen had turned down the volume to perform her own sound effects, but she'd suddenly stopped and turned to Portis.

"Wouldn't it be fun to make a video of ourselves? Think of it, Portis. Me and you, playing our bondage game. We could rent a camera, costumes, everything. You could take it home to watch on the VCR any time you wanted to."

Okay, it had sounded fun. And yeah, it was a fucking blast getting dressed up in a Colonel Khadaffi uniform and beating the literal piss out of the horse-faced bitch. But why he had been stupid enough to let her have the tape was beyond him. Who else but a woman could actually lose a videocassette? It was packed in her suitcase with her crotchless panties and her nippleless bras and the rest of her Frederick's kinkwear. He had seen it go under the vibrators and Kayleen's rainbow-colored collection of French ticklers with his very own eyes.

How the tape ended up in the garbage was anyone's guess.

Kayleen's big blue eyes had been red, puffy slits the day

she stepped into his office at the bank and told him she thought it might have gotten thrown away, and what were they going to do if someone found it and played it?

As the Reverend St. Clair's younger sister, she worried about such things. Her brother was the town's spiritual leader, the perennial winner of the people's choice award for purity, and a self-proclaimed celibate who had no idea that his baby sister was a flagellation freak.

Portis, of course, was worried for reasons of his own. His father had retired on the promise that Portis would behave himself and do good things for the bank. The old man moved to the city and bought a house with an indoor pool while still retaining the title of bank president in Dumford. He said Portis could have the seat of head honcho when he proved himself worthy, and not a moment before.

The situation sucked. Portis did all the work while his father played golf at Crestview Country Club and drank martinis with judges and commissioners. Still, the old fart was boss. One mistake, like a little playacting on a videotape, could ruin everything if Daddy Jackson got wind of it. Something had to be done.

And something was done. He and Kayleen had donned black clothing and yellow Playtex gloves and gone searching through the garbage in the dump for almost a week. It wasn't easy at night, and Calvin Horn had nearly caught them twice because of their flashlights. Kayleen shrieked at every rat she saw, and more than once Portis had to restrain himself from grabbing her by the neck and strangling her. Getting caught in a dump with his hands full of trash was not on his list of scheduled events. Finding the tape was.

When the dump-sifting turned up nothing but disgust and nightly nausea, Kayleen decided to have a look at Calvin. Against Portis's wishes, she had crept up to the shack and peered in one of the windows. What she saw there nearly made her shriek again. Portis joined her at the window and nearly roared himself at seeing Calvin with his bald-headed doll. Both Portis and Kayleen sobered immediately when they saw what was playing on Calvin's television. Portis had discarded that particular videocassette over a month ago. (He hated to throw away tapes, but he had the unfortunate habit of hitting the pause button on scenes he particularly liked. After stopping the tape in a certain area several dozen times, a glitch appeared. The glitch ruined the scene and, ultimately, the entire tape.)

A careful scan of Calvin's filthy living room found their own tape on top of a stack beside the television. A new question presented itself. Had Calvin watched it? And if so, had he recognized Portis or Kayleen in their costumes? Better yet, had he told anyone?

After a quick whispered discussion, they decided he had not told anyone. And even if he did tell, who would believe a guy who porked a bald, inflatable doll?

"We can't take any chances," Kayleen had said, and when Portis asked her what she meant, the good Reverend St. Clair's sister had looked scornfully at him and said, "We have to dust the idiot, you idiot."

Brothers and sisters were strange, Portis often thought. His own sibling had been retarded from birth, so Portis had always considered himself an only child. He was glad he didn't have any sisters, of course, but he would never understand how two people raised in the same house by the same people could know so little about one another. Besides the Reverend and kinky Kayleen, Edie and Ben Portlock were two perfect examples of sibling ignorance. How Edie could idolize the chilly, hard-nosed sonofabitch was an enduring mystery to Portis. Her brother was a loser in every department that mattered. He had no money, no vehicle to speak of, and he couldn't even call the house he lived in his own. He was worthless as a man.

As a cop he wasn't too shabby though, Portis had to remind himself. Everyone in town seemed to take it for granted that Ben would be chief when George Legget retired. Portis had done his best to sway the town's loyalty to someone else, someone he could buy, but he'd had little luck. Ben was going to be in, and that could mean trouble for Portis if he wasn't careful.

He had to be careful with Kayleen as well. Their argument tonight had been a violent one. She had screamed about money all the way home from the airport—until Portis pulled the car over and slapped the shit out of her. Her response had been to throw open the door and hit the asphalt at a run. Portis followed and knocked her off the highway shoulder and into the bordering field, where she had kicked, clawed, and pummeled him into a monstrous erection. By the time he'd gotten his pants down the greedy slut was urging him to hurry.

Kayleen had been a rare find in Dumford. But she was still a woman, and a cunning one. He had to think of some way to implicate her before she implicated him—and Portis was sure it would come to that. He wasn't about to give her a dime when the shotgun and everything else had been her idea to begin with. She was the one who had staked out Calvin's house. She was the one who had come running to Portis at dusk the day of Edie's party to tell him she had just seen someone in a ski mask gutting one of Calvin's dogs. When the trash man left his precious dump later that night to come to the party, Kayleen, eyes flashing with anticipation, had signaled to Portis that it was time for him to move. Portis had slipped away from the square for a mere twenty minutes and rigged the door just the way he had practiced in his den at home. No one at the party, not even Edie, had noticed his absence.

As far as Portis was concerned, his pantry was in good shape. The only bug in the flour was getting that cursed tape away from Kayleen, since the light-fingered bitch had somehow managed to steal it from Portis's car after he had returned to the party. Once he had the tape again he could start cooking with no worries. Just for kicks, he thought he might send the good Reverend a few photographs he had taken of Kayleen in Las Vegas. That might breathe some life into his sermons and leave a dose of hellfire and damnation on his own saintly doorstep. All Kayleen had on Portis was the tape. Portis had never allowed any photographs to be taken of himself.

After the business with Kayleen was over he could devote his attention to his loving wife. He couldn't do anything to her this week because she had an appointment with her physician, and the crotchety Dr. McMurphy might ask her about her purple-welted butt. It was depressing to think that soon her doctor appointments would be scheduled weekly. Portis supposed he'd just have to paddle her armpits until she had the little bastard. He looked forward to that day. He had toyed with the idea of holding dear Stella's bank loan over Edie's head to learn the identity of the father, but Edie was too much a daddy's girl, dead though the worthless sonofabitch might be. Since Portis couldn't beat the prick's name out of her, he decided he would have to wait until the baby was born to figure out the father. The man would pay, Portis promised himself. Either through sudden bankruptcy, or the barrel of another shotgun, the man would pay.

He still couldn't believe his sweet little Edie had done this to him. From day one he had given her everything she wanted. Except a baby, of course. But she had always sworn children were too expensive and impossible to have in a house with fashionable furnishings. What made her adultery even more unbelievable was the fact that she had been a virgin when he married her. Portis knew she was, because being checked by a doctor had been a condition of his marrying her at all. His mother and father had found it hard to believe that Edie Portlock was the only virgin in town, but she was the best Portis could come up with when they told him it was time to find a wife.

No one else would go out with him after Michelle Taylor spread her little tale about what a weirdo he was. The fact that Edie hated Michelle had worked in Portis's favor.

When he asked the sweet Miss Portlock for a date, she had jumped in his old Jaguar and looked at him with cartoon dollar signs in her eyes. He knew he had her hooked the day he bought her a dress and took her to a fancy restaurant in the city. She practically drooled when she saw the absence of prices on the menu. By the third course she was bought and paid for.

Portis thought he would have to teach her the proper behavior for the wife of a banker, but Edie had surprised him by knowing more rules of etiquette and social behavior than his own mother. His mother realized this the day she chose to wear white shoes to a board luncheon. Portis hadn't seen anything wrong with white shoes, but Edie showed him his mother's error by taking a small card-sized calendar from her purse and pointing out the date.

"So?" Portis had said.

"It's a week after Labor Day, Portis. Many people no longer observe the rules, but those of the upper crust know that wearing white shoes before Memorial Day or after Labor Day is a fashion taboo."

"You tell her," Portis said with a smirk.

Edie did, and since that luncheon no more than ten words had passed between his wife and his mother. When Portis told them Edie was pregnant, the old lady dismissed his lie about a genius semen implant with a knowing smile.

"My son, the sperm banker. I believe your father destroyed half your brain when he hit your testicles."

Portis had gone home and parlayed his smarting anger into a raging spoon session with Edie. He had been paddling her ever since. For a while he worried she would tell Ben, but he soon realized just how greedy his wife was. Edie would take physical abuse over penury any day.

The birth of her baby might change things, however. She was already mouthing off and getting uppity with him, acting protective and telling him what he could and couldn't do. Perhaps the best way to handle her would be to make sure this baby disappeared like the other one. If the nut who took the first kid got away with it, Portis was certain he could. In fact it would be a cinch. He was, after all, the child's *doting* father.

PART TWO

Blood

The blood is the life.

—*Deuteronomy 12:23*

Chapter Thirteen

Fall in Dumford typified fall in Kansas. Cottonwoods, maples, oaks, and elms filled the yards and sprinkled the streets with colorful refuse. The wind picked up the refuse and scattered it against fences with tossed-away school papers and the odd cellophane wrapper. Blackbirds clustered in fields and treetops to observe the fall planting, while brown squirrels devoted frantic attention to storing their winter food. Busy first graders scanned the ground for the perfect leaf, which they would cover with butcher paper and use to make their first crayon rubbing. Third graders drew cornucopias and wheat shocks and ate paste, while yawning sixth graders watched the clock for recess time and blinked sleepily over a Robert Frost poem about a lost foal.

The older kids buzzed over coming rock concerts in Kansas City, varsity football, and who was going to the pep rally after school. They flaunted their new clothes and complained about the loss of summer tans, the stupidity of their teachers, and the incredible ignorance of parents when it came to understanding why it was sometimes necessary to stay out past ten o'clock on a school night.

The parents, and most other responsible adults, concerned themselves with changing filters on furnaces, planting bulbs, reseeding lawns, and performing the proper hibernation maintenance on the lawnmower. The electric bills were lower, the gas bills were still reasonable, and the charge cards were in good shape until the holidays. Fall was a time to relax and enjoy the passage between the Scylla of summer and the Charybdis of winter.

Hannah Winegarten stood at the window of the police station. The dazzling array of color and the crisp, clean air made her slightly ill and sharply contemptuous of the general cheerfulness others seemed prone to display. Fall, with its deceptive beauty, was only the raging fever before the chilly, barren death of all things warm and green. Didn't people see that? Didn't they know things were *dying* in the fall? Everything. Everything was dying.

Everything but Kurt.

Her brother was the last stubborn leaf on the tree. And lately he had become quite vociferous about his wants and needs, not to mention acrimonious and irascible toward Hannah. His weight had remained stable for so long she feared he might be—God forbid—going into remission. But that was impossible at this stage, the doctor had assured her. Weeks from now, maybe only days, Kurt would slip into a coma. When that happened, it was suggested that Hannah bring her brother to the hospital, where he could be hooked up to a state-of-the-art life-support system.

No can do, Hannah thought to herself. Kurt had indeed called in a lawyer and changed his will. If one tube, tape, or IV needle touched his skin, Hannah would receive nothing. The house and everything in it, as well as the bank accounts, would go to the local diehard chapter of the Wheel of Fortune Fan Club.

This was no surprise to Hannah, as Kurt's favorite whack-off period was during the game show's time slot. On numerous occasions she had scurried into the bedroom believing his hoarse cries were for her, when in fact he had been calling out for Vanna.

He was so disgusting.

She no longer bothered trying to stop him. Instead, she turned her head and looked away as she changed the sheets and delivered his meals. More often than not, his yellow skin and his veiny limbs robbed her of her own appetite. Still, she remained as cheerful and polite as possible to keep her place in his grace.

To take her mind off her problems she often fantasized of ways to deal with Bryce McKee and the other troublemakers in town. Bryce knew the truth about her, Hannah thought. There was no other explanation for his attitude toward her. He knew the wicked, horrible truth about her virtue, and how his own chicken-thieving hound of a father had been responsible for her deflowering a mere hour before his escape to the arms of a guttersnipe with a green thumb. That was why Bryce showed so little respect and treated her the way he—

Her painful thoughts came to a halt as she caught a glimpse of Lura Taylor striding down the sidewalk in front of the station.

Now there was a walking cause for concern. The girl's harlotry in the tavern with Ben Portlock was a shameful business, thought Hannah. Michelle was a whore, true, but at least she wasn't a murderess. Lura had no right to come waltzing home with that gray hair and start causing problems. Just that morning Hannah had heard Mickey Pendleton's mother telling Milly at the restaurant that she had seen Lura out walking in the dark last night. Doing what? Hannah wanted to know. It was downright spooky.

She glanced away from the window and looked at the chief lounging in a chair. His long legs were stretched out before him and crossed at the ankles. His head was nodding.

"George?" Hannah said. "George, are you feeling all right?"

He snuffled and snorted and opened his eyes with a start. "What? Did you say something?"

"You frightened me," Hannah told him. "I thought you might be ill. I've heard of people who die sitting up in their chairs, you know."

The chief rubbed his face with his large hands and grimaced at her. "Is that right? You're just a never-ending source of enlightenment, aren't you?"

Hannah smiled modestly. "If you say so, George. I just saw Lura Taylor walk by outside. I don't know why she doesn't do something with that hair of hers. You'd think she was proud of it the way she lets it hang loose. I hear she's been looking for a job for two weeks straight and hasn't had a bit of luck. You can't blame folks, really. These are respectable people with respectable businesses.

"Do you know she even had the gall to apply for a proofreading job at the weekly? Word has it that Joseph Prill came out, took the pen out of her hand, and tore up her application. He told her he wasn't interested in hiring any convicted felons at the moment. And the manager at the cheese factory laughed right in her face. He was good friends with Jesse and Ordney, remember. It's a wonder he didn't have her tossed out on her backside."

George rubbed his eyes and yawned.

"Seems to me," Hannah went on, "that she would do the intelligent thing and look for a job where no one knows her. I know at least twelve people who drive into the city to work. It's a long trip, certainly, but a Taylor can't be choosy. The farther she gets from Dumford, the better off all of us will be. Ben Portlock in particular. He used to be the sweetest, most cordial young man in town, but lately he's been short-tempered and quite as rude as another young officer I can think of.

"And has anyone put it together that Miss Lura was home when that baby disappeared? I hear she was back a month before she ever showed her face. It's funny that Mickey Pendleton's mother sees her out walking last night in the dark like some . . . George?"

His eyelids were drooping. "Huh? What?"

"I said it's funny about all the strange things that have happened since Lura Taylor came home. First the baby, then Calvin and his dog, and Julius Hinshaw's cow."

George's eyes opened wide. "Good *Christ*," he spat. "Haven't you got anything better to do than stir up trouble for that girl?"

Hannah's face flushed. "Don't be silly. I'm not—"

"The hell you aren't," George said loudly. He twisted in his chair as the station door opened. Bryce and Mickey came inside. George turned back to Hannah. "You've been at it a long time, Hannah. The happiest moment in your life was when you heard that Parry fellow lived with another man. You weren't satisfied until you ran both of them out of town with your AIDS bullshit."

The color in Hannah's cheeks was deepening. Silently she begged him not to go on. Not in front of Bryce McKee.

"George, I really don't think—"

"That's right, by God, you *don't*. You had the missing baby to keep you going for a while, then it was Calvin Horn. He was dead, so you curled your pit viper's tongue around the Miller family. When you couldn't make all the trouble you wanted there, you looked elsewhere. Now you want to pick on Lura Taylor, and my guess is that half the people who've turned her down for a job had your flapping mouth in their ear before she even applied."

Hannah's lips trembled. She looked beyond the chief and saw Bryce smiling happily. The thin, blond Mickey was wide-eyed.

"You can't talk to me like this, George," she whispered. "I want an apology. I don't know what I've done to deserve this humiliation."

"Then you're not listening, dammit!" George slapped his palm down hard on his desk. "What the fuck is wrong with you, Hannah? Don't you know people talk about *you* the minute you walk away from a gossip session about somebody else? Do you honestly think you're above anyone in this town?"

"I never said I was." Hannah rose from her chair on trembling legs. "Is this your way of telling me I'm fired?"

George groaned. "For Christ's sake. Did I say that? I'm not firing you, Hannah. I'm only trying to tell you to keep your mouth shut and mind your own goddamned business. If you find that too difficult, then you can walk out of here and I won't stop you. Hell, I can send Bryce down the street after Lura and hire her to take your place in five minutes. It's up to you."

Out of the corner of her eye, Hannah saw Bryce pick up his hat.

"You'd do that?" she asked in a thin voice. "You would actually hire a convicted murderess to work in a police station? Doing my job?"

George snapped his fingers. "Like that. I hear she doesn't say much, and I've always been fond of quiet women."

Hannah had to sit down before her legs gave way. She placed her shaking hands in her lap.

"I'll . . . be quiet," she finally managed.

"Good." George turned to Bryce. "What the hell are you smiling about?"

Bryce shrugged. "The weather. It's my favorite time of the year."

"Bullshit," George said. "What's happening with the break-in at Ailey's? Did he give you a list of what was missing?"

"He couldn't say exactly. The old goat's still a lousy bookkeeper, I guess. Mickey found a syringe by the window where the entry was made, so we're assuming the intruder took some of those. As for drugs, Ailey says he'll let us know."

"What do you think? Some punks from the city again?"

"Maybe," Bryce said. "But Ailey says his dog never made a sound."

"So? Was it in the store, or up in the apartment?"

"He's been keeping it in the store at night since last year's break-in."

Mickey stepped forward and bent his wiry frame to show George a tear in his sock. "Yapping little bastard nearly tore my leg off when I walked into the back room. Those wienie dogs are vicious."

"Dachshunds," Hannah said automatically.

George, Mickey, and Bryce looked at her.

"Sorry," she mumbled.

"The dog didn't know you," Bryce said to Mickey.

"And he knows you?"

"Sure." Bryce grinned and looked at Hannah's deliberately averted head. "I bought my first rubber from Mr. Ailey."

"So did I," Mickey said. Then he laughed. "But I'm not the one who cleared his shelves every week."

George grunted. "So what you're saying, Bryce, is the dog knew you were only breaking in to stock up on Trojans, and because he knew you, and because he's a big proponent of safe sex, he didn't bother barking."

Hannah adjusted her glasses and turned her head to see if the chief was serious. When she saw his smile she turned away again.

"Something like that," Bryce said with a grin. "It was a pretty clean job, unlike the last time. Nothing was out of place and Ailey didn't know he'd been burglarized until he felt a draft coming under the door this afternoon. He walks back, sees one square of the back room window broken, and hurries to call us. We'll know more when he's had a chance to go over his inventory."

"Right now, the syringe is all we have to go on," Mickey added.

George showed his dentures in a wide yawn. "Send it

over to the sheriff and see if they can pick up any prints from the wrapper."

"In the works," Bryce said. "And since I can't talk Mickey into doing the paperwork, I guess I'd better get it over with."

Mickey jangled the keys to his cruiser. "Hey, buddy, my own shift just started. And speaking of shifts, I need to trade with someone Saturday. You wanna work graveyard Saturday night, Bryce?"

"I'll think about it," Bryce told him. "See you later, Mick." He sat down at his desk and opened his drawer to take out a report form. He glanced out the window and saw something that made him leave his desk suddenly and hurry past Mickey out the door. He caught up with the white Oldsmobile at the corner. He gestured for the man to pull over. The driver looked at him with narrowed eyes.

"Pull over and talk to me," Bryce told him. "I made a few calls. I know who you are."

The man pulled over. He leaned back in his seat and watched Bryce approach with wary eyes. "Who did you talk to?"

"Your office." Bryce reached in the window and shook the other man's hand. "I'm Officer Bryce McKee. Who are you investigating?"

"That's confidential."

"It'll stay that way. I'm in law enforcement, Mr. Clegg. I'm used to keeping secrets."

The man called Clegg curled his mouth. "You check out every strange car in town?"

"No," Bryce admitted. "Just those who look suspicious. You looked suspicious."

"Guess I'll have to work on that."

"Tell me who it is," Bryce said. "We may be looking at the same person."

"Sorry," Clegg told him. "When the IRS investigates, it's confidential all the way. I will tell you that he's a prominent person in your town. Good day, officer."

Bryce stepped back as the white Olds pulled away from the curb. Portis Jackson, he said to himself. The IRS was investigating Portis Jackson. It couldn't be anyone else. He returned to the station and sat down at his desk once more. He felt Hannah looking at him, so he glanced up at her and smiled before returning his attention to the report of the burglary at Ailey's drugstore.

"Who was that in the white car?" Hannah asked.

"The IRS," Bryce said.

Hannah darted a glance at George and exhaled through her nose. "Can't you ever be serious? I asked you a civil question. The least—"

"I am serious," Bryce said, and he looked back to his typewriter. Hannah gazed out the window a moment, her mind working. The IRS was in Dumford? That could mean only one thing. They were investigating the Miller family. All that opulence in the home of a truck farmer and his voodoo wife. It was about time *someone* investigated.

Hannah turned back and watched Bryce as he rolled the report form into his typewriter and began to peck at the keys. His long, slim fingers might have been those of a pianist. Hannah eyed the slender digits and hated every bone, nerve, and cuticle. He was so arrogant. So confident of his masculinity and his roguish grin and sparkling blue eyes. When he was younger she had known he would look just like his father. She had been wrong. Bryce was twice as handsome and three times the blackguard.

An anonymous note to Portis P. Jackson would wipe that smile off his face, now wouldn't it?

When George got up and went into the bathroom she threw a pencil at the dark head bent over the typewriter. "That was your doing, wasn't it, Bryce?"

"Hey. Dammit, you made me mess up." Bryce glared at her as he reached for the correction fluid.

"It was, wasn't it?" Hannah insisted.

"What the hell are you talking about?"

"The chief chewing me out. You were behind that, weren't you?"

Bryce smiled. "I'd love to take credit, Hannah, but George did that all on his ownsome."

"Ownsome? That's not even a word. And I don't believe you. He's never treated me so badly before."

"No," Bryce agreed. He squinted at the report form and carefully applied the correction fluid.

"You'd rather have Lura Taylor working in here, wouldn't you?" Hannah seethed. "I saw the way you jumped when George mentioned her name."

Bryce ignored her and blew on the correction fluid to speed its drying.

"And as for buying prophylactics at the drugstore, well I guess you didn't have one handy last February, did you?"

Bryce looked at her. "I meant to thank you for the cigars, Hannah. I wondered how you knew my ex-wife was even pregnant. But then you're always finding out things about other people, aren't you?"

Hannah blinked. "Your . . . ex-wife?"

He shrugged. "It's no use pretending innocence now. I knew it was you who put the cigars in my desk. It's no big deal. I went to visit her once to see if we could work things out. We had a few drinks and did what consenting adults do, but the next morning it was no go. She says she's not even sure the baby is mine. But thanks for the cigars anyway. I was mad at first, but I deserved it for the gag I pulled on you."

"Yes, you did," Hannah said with cautious indignation. "Uh . . . when is she due?"

His shoulders lifted. "Another few weeks. She says she'll let me know if it looks like me."

Hannah stared at his slumped shoulders and downturned mouth. She couldn't believe she had been wrong about this, but his blue eyes were actually misting over. He turned his head away from her.

"That's sad, Bryce," she murmured. "Forgive the cruelty of my joke if you can. I'm sorry."

"Yeah." He wiped at his face and sighed. "Me too. Sometimes things don't work out the way you want them to."

Hannah clucked her tongue in sympathy. "Isn't that the truth?" She stood and moved to the coffee machine on the table beside her desk. "There's some coffee left. Can I get you a cup?"

"Yes, thank you," Bryce said sweetly.

Chapter Fourteen

Near the end of his shift, Ben drove to Julius Hinshaw's place and parked his car on the road outside Julius's pasture. The man had called earlier and reported that someone had been on his property overnight, and it was probably the cow killer. When asked how he knew someone had been on his property, Julius claimed he had found tire tracks in his pasture. That explained why there had been no trail of blood when the calf was taken, Julius stated. Whoever it was had simply loaded the animal fresh from its mother's belly into the back of his vehicle and driven away. Ben and Bryce hadn't seen the tracks the first time because they hadn't been paying attention.

Ben had been paying attention, and he had seen no tracks around Julius's dead cow. It was possible, however, that the perpetrator had returned for a second calf and been unsuccessful in finding a suitable cow. He got out of his car at the gate entrance to the pasture and walked inside on foot. Julius didn't come out to meet him. He was caring for his chickens.

The tracks Ben found were wide enough to be truck tires.

A few depressions and pattern marks in the soft earth and some matted-down grass were all he found to look at. None of it was enough to take a molding from. Ben measured the tracks anyway and wrote everything down on his police pad. When he walked back to his car he saw Julius Hinshaw watching him from the door of his barn. Ben nodded. Hinshaw spat into the dirt.

In his car he glanced at his watch and saw that it was near the end of his shift. He drove back to the station and without speaking to anyone he checked out. Hannah's spurious attempts at humility didn't go unnoticed, but Ben was too tired to ask who had castigated her and what for that day. He drove home and groaned when he saw the Datsun in his driveway. On impulse he made a U-turn in the street and drove in the other direction. Ordinarily he would drop by Bryce's place on the west side of town and drink a beer, but their friendship had taken a downward spiral since Lura's return. Ben thought of running out to his mother's tavern, but Stella's was the first place Michelle would look for him when he didn't show up at home.

He thumped the wheel in frustration, and after a moment of deliberation he decided to get something to eat. It would be a nice change from having to look across the table at Michelle's anxious features. She had been studying cooking and was attempting to win his favor by showing how domesticated she could be. As a result, Ben had gone on a diet of beer and sandwiches. A microwave sandwich in the afternoon made Michelle and her mackerel soufflé in the evening easier to take. One or two Budweisers after he arrived home and Ben didn't blink an eye when he saw Lura leave her house for a date with Bryce.

His eyes blinked more than once when he strode into Milly's and saw Lura behind the counter. He sat down on a stool and watched her retie her pink apron around her slender waist before picking up her order pad. She turned and saw him, and her eyes flickered briefly before lapsing into a neutral, waitresslike gaze.

"Hello, Ben. Would you like to see a menu?"

"When did you start working here?" he asked.

"Today is my first day. A menu?"

"Sure."

She delivered a menu from under the counter and turned away to refill a coffee cup three stools away from him. Ben didn't recognize the occupant of the stool. Lura smiled politely at a softly spoken comment from the man, and Ben grew suddenly angry at the people in his town. He knew Lura had been looking for a job, and, with her degree, Ben had foolishly believed she would have no trouble finding one.

"Ready to order?" Lura asked him a moment later.

"Is this it?" he said to her. "Is Milly the only one who would hire you?"

Her voice was calm. "I can come back if you haven't decided yet."

She wasn't going to talk to him. Ben sighed and gave the menu a cursory glance. "What's the special today?"

"It's on the front, under the paper clip. Spaghetti and meatballs."

"Do you serve it with garlic bread?"

"Two pieces. More is extra."

Ben smiled. "Your first day and you sound like an old pro."

"Do you want the special?"

Her voice was so cool it put a frost on his own.

"Yes."

"Extra garlic bread?"

"No."

"Coffee to drink?"

"Water's fine, thanks. Do you have a paper back there?" He didn't want to stare at her while he was waiting for his food.

"I'll see."

She disappeared into the kitchen and returned with the crossword and comics section.

"It's the best I could do."

"Thanks," he said. He took a pen from his shirt pocket and pretended to study the crossword. The man at the counter finished his coffee and paid for his meal in cash before going outside to slip behind the wheel of a dusty white Oldsmobile. Ben found himself looking at the tires on the car.

He filled in a few of the boxes on the crossword and kept a surreptitious eye on Lura as she collected empty ketchup bottles and cleaned ashtrays. The uniform Milly had given her was too large, but he could still see the outline of her hips beneath the fabric as she moved from table to table. Her hair was caught up in a loose bun that gave definition to her normally soft jaw and rounded chin—and she still had the habit of catching the corner of her lower lip between her teeth when she was nervous.

Ben looked back to the crossword. She was nervous because of him. He concentrated on the clues for a while and looked up only when she slid a steaming plate of spaghetti and meatballs in front of him. The spices tickled his nose and made his stomach give a noisy growl of anticipation. He pushed the crossword aside and picked up his fork. Lura placed a small basket full of garlic bread beside his plate.

"Milly says you can have all the bread you want. Looks like it's going to be a slow night."

Ben thanked her and turned his attention to the food. He twirled his fork in the spaghetti and paused with the stringy mass in midair as he caught her watching him with a crooked smile on her face.

"You weren't going to say anything, were you? I knew I'd forgotten something."

She disappeared into the kitchen and returned to hand him a shaker full of Parmesan cheese.

Truthfully, Ben hadn't even thought of it, but he sprinkled some out anyway and handed the shaker back to her. The smile was encouraging, but she had already made it clear he was just another customer. He was glad when a group of square dancers twirled their way into the restaurant. Lura suddenly had her hands full and he could watch her at his leisure as she hustled menus and water glasses.

After a while he regretted indulging himself. He saw everything that had snared him the first time. The line of her neck, the curve of her breasts, the soft voice and the shy smile. Everything he thought about when he was with Michelle. The impact was enough to quell his previously raging appetite. When he heard her unique combination of chuckle-laughter behind him, he pushed his plate away.

"What's wrong with it?" a defiant voice asked, and he looked up to see Milly poking her white head through the order window.

"Not a thing," he said. "I wasn't as hungry as I thought I was."

"Too spicy maybe?"

"It's fine, Milly. Just right."

"Something wrong, Ben?"

"No."

"You sure?" You look—"

"I'm positive."

"You wanna take it home?" Milly asked, and without waiting for an answer she retracted her head and came out of the kitchen to grab his plate. When Lura approached the counter Ben asked her for his check.

She frowned and wiped her hands on her apron. "What happened to your food?"

"Milly's boxing it for me. Nothing is wrong with it and everything is fine. Just give me the goddamned check."

His brusqueness took her by surprise. She found his ticket and carried it to the register with a confused expression on her face. Milly brought Ben the box and shook her head as she hurried back to the kitchen. "Let's just say I don't like waste."

"Thanks," he called after her. To Lura he said, "I didn't want to offend you by leaving a tip."

Her lips tightened as she rang up his ticket. Wordlessly

she took the ten he handed her and gave him his change. He pocketed the money, picked up his box of spaghetti, and left her staring after him as he shoved open the door and walked outside.

Michelle's Datsun was still in his drive at home. He made another U-turn and drove directly to his mother's tavern. Stella shook her head when she saw him.

"Your roommate was here looking for you."

Ben sat down on a stool. "She's not my roommate. I'll have a Bud."

"You look like hell," Stella said. "When was the last time you ate anything?"

"About fifteen minutes ago."

She gave him a beer and watched him empty the contents of the can in three long swallows.

"Look at me, Ben," she said solemnly.

He wiped his mouth. "Sounds serious."

"It is. I've never seen you drink a beer like that."

"Like what?"

"Like your father."

Ben looked away from her. "Don't compare me to that sorry sonofabitch."

His mother stared at him. "Up till now that was impossible. You couldn't have been any less like him if you tried. Lately it's a different story."

"I don't know what you're talking about," Ben told her. "Are you going to give me another beer, or do I go to the liquor store?"

"That's what I'm talking about," she replied. "Your father sat on that very stool and said those exact words to me. I don't know what your problem is, but I'd guess it has something to do with Lura and that black-haired she-devil with the red fingernails. I always thought it was polish, but now I know better. Michelle is holding on to you so tight she's drawing blood."

Ben glanced up in surprise. His mother sounded like Berniece Miller.

"That's right," Stella said. "I've never liked the little twit and I don't know what on earth possessed you to take her between your sheets. Why don't you stop being a pincushion and tell the needling bitch to take a hike?"

"Pincushion?" Ben had to smile.

His mother lifted her brows. "Don't make fun of me. You know exactly what I'm saying to you. You want to dump her, but you're afraid Lura will be held responsible."

Ben stood up suddenly. "To tell you the truth, I wish to hell I'd never met either one of them. I'll see you later."

"Where are you going?"

"Home."

He intended to, anyway, but a quarter of a mile from his house he heard a flustered Haden on the radio requesting assistance from an equally flustered Hannah. Ben broke in on the transmission and asked what was going on. Haden's voice was relieved.

"I'm out at the Parry place, Ben. You won't believe what's in that house."

"I'm on my way," Ben told him.

"You're off duty, Officer Portlock," Hannah reminded.

"I know that," he snapped into the mike. "Don't bother George, Hannah. Let me see what's going on."

"All right," she said reluctantly. "Just make sure you keep radio contact."

Ben growled a curse at her into the mike before replacing it. He didn't bother with his siren, but he broke the speed limit on the way to the north side of town. The houses on the north side were sparser, with more land in between than in other sections. Ben drove to the vacant ranch house and saw Haden waiting for him at the curb. His skin was pale beneath the freckles dotting his nose and cheeks. He ran a quick hand through his red hair and refitted his hat as Ben got out of his car.

"I was just checking the place for vandalism," Haden began. "You know how the kids use this place for drinking and stuff. When I got up to the door I noticed a funny smell.

I didn't think too much about it until I went out back and found a broken window. The smell—"

"Is the door unlocked?" Ben interrupted.

"I unlocked it on the way out." Haden caught Ben's arm as he moved past him. "I'd put a handkerchief over your nose before you go in. It's pretty bad in there."

Ben walked to the door of the house. He turned as he noticed that Haden wasn't with him. "Aren't you coming in?"

Haden shook his head. "No. Sorry, but I nearly puked the first time. Honest."

"Okay." Ben turned the knob and pushed open the door. The smell was bad. He had experienced a similar odor several times as a city cop, and it was something he had never forgotten. Putrefaction had an aroma all its own, and once it passed the nostrils and settled into the lungs, eating anything for the next twelve hours was impossible. He took out a handkerchief and glanced back to Haden. "Where is it?"

"They're in the kitchen."

They? Ben clamped the handkerchief over his mouth and nose and stepped inside the house. His footfalls on the stained blue carpet sounded unusually loud in the empty space. It was little wonder the realtor had finally given up on trying to sell the place; the walls had been spray painted with esoteric teenage symbols and the names of various rock groups. But Ben didn't think the kids had been in the house recently. They were into the school scene now and wouldn't cluster for a party at least until homecoming week. Besides that, it was too damned cold in the place to drink and play grab-ass comfortably.

The house was ranch style, so the kitchen had to be just beyond the living room somewhere. He looked down the hall and saw more symbols on the walls before turning into a long, narrow dining room. The smell was permeating the fabric of the handkerchief, so he knew he was getting close to the source. He forced his feet to move faster, partly out of curiosity, mostly out of the desire to get it over with and get the hell away from the stench.

When he entered the kitchen he instinctively took a step backward. A calf was on the table in the breakfast nook, its small black head hanging limply over the edge. Ben moved slowly toward it, his stomach rising in disgust as he realized he was looking at only the trunk of the animal. The legs were nowhere to be seen.

The puppies floating in the sink stopped him again. There were six, each of them a different color. Their tiny paws were outstretched, their eyes mere slits. The water had made bits of their hides tear loose. The water itself was a murky brownish-green color.

Ben closed his eyes, but not before he saw what hung above the counter beside the refrigerator. He had fed her last night, but now his cat's stomach was empty. Her stomach was gone. One end of the coat hanger was twisted around a knob on the cabinet, the other end was looped around the cat's neck.

He didn't look for the kittens. He found the back door and burst outside with a combination of rage and nausea battling for dominance in his throat. His feet tripped over a basket of dead animals on the back porch, and he landed on his knees in the grass. He stared at the contents of the basket, now spilled on the lawn around him, and his throat hitched and spasmed. "Who the fuck is *doing* this?" he roared at the empty yard.

Haden came running around the side of the house, his pistol drawn. When he saw Ben's scarlet face he halted. The fury in the other man was new to him. Ben was always calm, always in control. The man kicking the shit out of the back door of the house was someone to stay the hell away from.

Chapter Fifteen

Laura awakened early Saturday morning and instinctively lifted the shade to look out her window. The morning was clear, the rising sun bright. The grass, leaves, and most of the car windshields on the block were covered with a light frost . . . and Michelle's car was not in Ben's driveway.

She abruptly dropped the shade and chastened herself for her last observation. With a determined flip of the covers she forced herself out of bed and over to the dresser, where she counted the money she had earned at Milly's. Twenty dollars in tips on her first day was a surprising amount to her. She had expected the townspeople to be surly with her, if not downright obnoxious, but they were apparently happy to have her in a position befitting her low standing in the community. As a mere servant they could accept her and even show a little generosity. For the moment, she supposed she was Dumford's errant stray—no one wanted her inside the house near the children or the furniture, but a few scraps tossed over the back fence couldn't hurt anything.

The perspicacious Milly had been quick to notice that a sandwich and a cup of coffee were not all Lura needed when she appeared in the restaurant Friday. The spritely older woman had propped herself against the counter on both elbows and given Lura an understanding smile.

"Pretty bad, I know. If it wouldn't insult you, and if you're tough enough to deal with the occasional jeers and pinches, I'm looking for a waitress."

She couldn't afford to pay more than three and a quarter an hour, but the tips were usually pretty good if a gal knew what she was doing and could handle herself in a crunch.

Lura accepted on the spot. She had worked part-time at Barney's Steakhouse the summer she turned seventeen, so she knew the routine. And she was grateful beyond words for the offer.

Once in uniform, there were whispers from those who knew her, and hushed voices as she delivered meals and carried plates away. Only a brave and uncaring few of her former acquaintances had actually spoken to her. Most, like Ben, were surprised to see her working there. His remark about the tip disturbed Lura, and the manner of his departure, but she had made it a point to forget the incident for the rest of the evening. Bryce had come along to make it easier. He'd swept into the restaurant just before closing and delivered no less than a dozen waitress jokes before asking her to go riding with him the next morning.

When he knocked on the door at three minutes after eight, Lura was dressed and ready to go. She placed a finger to her lips to indicate that her mother and brother were still sleeping, then she let Bryce in and whispered for him to wait while she dashed off a quick note to them. Once outside, Bryce swatted her bottom before opening the dented passenger door of his white pickup truck.

"I knew you'd take my advice about wearing thicker jeans."

Lura hopped into the seat and smiled. "I still have bruises

on my thighs from the last time. Maybe we should try bareback this morning."

"If we do you'll have bruises on your thighs *and* your knees," Bryce told her. "Now you know why ladies of yore preferred a different form of saddle."

"And you've never bruised?" Lura charged as he climbed in and started the engine.

He grinned at her. "I'll have you know I am the living reincarnation of a Union cavalry soldier. Berniece Miller the psychic told me so."

"You're kidding," Lura said.

"It's true," Bryce swore. "Mickey went out to see her once and he came back spouting all kinds of bullshit. I decided it might be fun, and lo and behold, I find out I served three years in the 5th Illinois Cavalry."

"How did you die?"

"She wasn't certain. She thought I might have perished at Andersonville."

Lura eyed him. "One out of every twelve Union soldiers supposedly had venereal disease. Are you sure that wasn't the cause of your demise?"

"One out of twelve?" Bryce looked at her in surprise. "Poor bastards."

"Do you really believe in it?" Lura asked. "In reincarnation, I mean."

"I believe in Mrs. Miller. The woman is phenomenal, Lura. If you don't believe me, go and see for yourself. Right now I want to show you something and get some female advice before we go on to the lease, all right?"

"What is it?"

"You'll see," he said.

He drove to the former home of his grandparents, a white two-story Colonial located just four blocks from Lura's own house. The last time she had seen the place it was empty and literally falling apart. Now she sat in the cab of the truck and sucked in her breath at the gleaming front columns and newly painted frame. The roof and the chimney had both been replaced, and a new wrought-iron railing curled and peaked its way around the upper-level terrace.

"Bryce, did you do this?"

"Every fucking bit of it," he said with a wry grin. "A big improvement since the last time you saw it, huh?"

"It's beautiful," Lura said. "You didn't change a thing in the original architecture." She turned in her seat to face him. "I had no idea you knew how to restore old houses."

"I didn't either," he admitted. "It's been slow going and expensive as hell. Come and see the inside."

Lura followed him into the house, and his pride was evident as he walked her through each room and relived every frustration encountered during the house's resurrection. The scrolled woodwork of the original staircase turned out to be too costly to replace, he told her, but the oak floors were the original, as was most of the kitchen cabinetry.

"What I want your opinion on," he explained, "are the walls themselves. I eighty-sixed that crappy flowered wallpaper, but now I don't know what to do. Should I paint, or buy new wallpaper?"

Lura crossed her arms over her chest. "Why are you asking me, Bryce? You should save these questions for someone who counts."

"You're a woman, aren't you?" he replied. "Don't all women know how to decorate?"

"Not necessarily. And every woman's taste is different."

Bryce frowned at her. "A lot of help you are. Just tell me what you would do. I can't leave it like this."

"Paint it something neutral," Lura suggested. "Then you can do whatever you like later."

"Neutral," Bryce repeated. "Something any style or color of furniture would go with, right?"

"Right," Lura said.

"Okay. Good idea. Let's lock up and get started on those bruises."

Lura watched him turn keys in not one, or even two, but in three locks on the massive front door.

"You used one key when we came in," she observed. "Why the tight security?"

"I don't want to come in and find a dead animal farm in the kitchen next time."

"What?"

"You didn't hear? Haden found a bunch of dead animals in a vacant house out north yesterday."

"Animals? What kind of animals?"

"All kinds," Bryce said with a shrug. "I guess Ben went a little nuts after he went inside. You know what a sucker he is for animals. Scared Haden half to death when he started yelling about a cat. I didn't know Ben had a cat, but I guess the dead one in the house was his."

Lura remembered the cat. It was gray and unmistakably pregnant.

"I wouldn't want to be in the cat-killer's shoes when Ben catches him," Bryce went on. "You weren't here when he nearly got suspended for beating the shit out of an attorney who ran over some ducks on Old Salt Road. The jerk didn't even stop, just leaves these poor ducks flopping around with everything broken. Ben pulls him over and tells him to ante up the proper paper. The lawyer laughs and says he's got to be kidding. He's late for court and who gives a shit about two or three fucking ducks? This was the wrong thing to say. The mighty hand of Ben Portlock came down upon his face not once, but several times. Once for each duck, I believe."

"And George Legget didn't suspend him?" Lura asked.

"Nah. He was mad at Ben, but he was sorely pissed at the attorney. The ducks belonged to George's niece."

Lura smiled and shook her head. Bryce had a way of turning the most sordid story into a humorous anecdote.

His mood remained light and cheerful as they took turns riding his roan mare through the swiftly changing green, amber, and yellow of the ten-acre lot he had leased. When they rode double in the saddle Lura noticed that he kept the horse close to the fence bordering Edie and Portis Jackson's property. When she asked him why, he lifted both shoulders and said, "No reason."

Lura was beginning to suspect otherwise, but she remained silent. It was only when Bryce stiffened at the sight of Edie opening her back door that she decided to say something.

"You could get a better view if you brought along some binoculars."

"What are you talking about?" he asked.

"How long, Bryce?" she replied.

"How long what?"

Lura sighed. "Tell me it's none of my business, but don't pretend you don't know what I'm talking about."

"I *don't* know what you're talking about."

Lura pinched him. "I've been out here with you twice, and both times you've kept one eye glued to that house."

Bryce stopped the horse and twisted around to look at her. "Aren't we the perceptive one?"

"We are." Lura slid off the horse and stood looking up at him. "Are you going to make me guess?"

"No." He threw a leg over the saddle and joined her on the ground. "I don't want to talk about it. Period."

"All right. I'm sorry." Lura walked with him as he led the mare along the fence and back toward the small stable.

"There used to be a house here, you know," he said. "If you look, you can still see where the foundation was."

"I remember," Lura said. "It burned down when I was a little girl. Who owns the land now?"

"Dr. McMurphy. He wants to start building a retirement home here next year."

"What will you do with Maggie?"

"I don't know." Bryce gave the mare's neck a tender pat. "Maybe the doc will let me keep her here."

Lura reached out and caught his hand. "Bryce, I'm sorry for meddling. I should have kept my mouth shut."

He squeezed her fingers. "It's okay." He paused; then he looked at her. "You're right, you know."

"I know," she said.

"The thing I can't figure out is why." He dropped the reins and allowed Maggie to wander the last ten yards to the stable by herself.

"Why . . . ?" Lura prompted.

"Why I want her." He plopped to the ground and looked toward the distant house with narrowed eyes. "Do I want her because I can't have her? Because she belongs to another man and doesn't want anything to do with me?"

"Or because she's carrying your child," Lura said.

Bryce's dark head lifted. "Christ. You are perceptive, aren't you? Am I that obvious?"

"No," she assured him. "I've known you for a long time, Bryce. The last time we were here I saw you watching the house and I remembered how you danced with her at Stella's. I've never seen you look at a woman the way you looked at Edie that night. Just now, when you were staring at her house again, I suddenly thought of all the work you've done on your grandparents' place. It's for her, isn't it? It's for Edie."

His eyes shifted away. "I don't know. Maybe it was in the beginning. You know how Edie is about money. I thought the house would give me a better chance, prove that I have something to offer. But I'm not a rich man, and Edie knows it. I can't give her the life she has with Portis."

"Does he know about the baby?"

"No. Just me, you, Edie, and probably Berniece Miller know about the baby. Hannah thought she knew, but I lied my way out of it and had her licking my fingers before I was through."

"Ben doesn't know? Edie didn't tell him?"

Bryce's mouth twisted. "Lura, Edie is ashamed of having slept with me."

"You mean because of your reputation."

He nodded. "She thinks I'm some hotshot cocksman

with a telephone list the size of the Los Angeles Yellow Pages."

Lura heaved a sigh and sat down beside him. The ground was slightly damp, but the morning sun was warm on her face. She plucked a still-green blade from a patch of brown grass and twirled it in her fingers.

"What are you going to do, Bryce?"

He looked up, and for the first time there was no sparkle in his eyes. His face appeared drawn, and the corners of his mouth were lined with weariness.

"I don't know. She rejects me at every turn, and frankly, I'm goddamned tired of it."

"Have you asked her to leave Portis?"

"Yes. You can see the result."

"Do you think she loves him?"

Bryce shook his head. "She loves money. And she loves her mother and brother. Other than that, who knows."

"She doesn't care for you?"

"Me?" He forced a laugh. "Let me put it this way, our one night together obviously meant more to me than it did to her."

"There's one way to find out," Lura offered.

His voice was skeptical. "Really? How? Do we call her up in a survey about extramarital affairs?"

"No. You leave her alone, Bryce."

"That should be easy. I haven't exactly been seeing her on a daily basis."

"I mean completely," Lura explained. "Don't talk to her when you see her, don't drive by her house, and stop riding Maggie by the fence."

"What will that accomplish?"

"Trust me."

"I want to, but I don't understand what avoiding her is going to prove."

Lura leaned back and smiled. "Try it for a few weeks and watch what happens. As things stand now, you really have nothing to lose. And if she truly doesn't care for you, then you'll have some distance from the rejection and be able to deal with it."

Bryce grinned. "Are you sure you didn't get that degree in psychology?"

"Positive. My own life is proof."

"Speaking of which, have you been seeing anyone?"

"Just you."

He clucked his tongue. "Think of the damage it's doing to your reputation. Everyone knows what a wild, oversexed kind of guy I am. Word probably has it that I'm making up for all the years you did without."

Lura stood up and dusted the seat of her jeans. "Just how did you happen to receive such a notorious reputation?"

Bryce held out a hand and Lura leaned back to pull him to his feet. His head was already shaking. "Beats the shit out of me. I'm not the type to broadcast it every time I sleep with someone."

"Must be your pretty-boy looks," Lura teased. "People just naturally assume you're a stud."

Bryce groaned. "God, I hate that word."

"Stud?"

"Pretty boy. I may be handsome, but I am not pretty."

Lura laughed. "And you wonder where you got your reputation."

"Well, it's true," he insisted. "Why should I be modest when the facts are in the mirror every morning?"

"Thank God you're not vain or anything," Lura said in a dry voice.

"If I were vain I'd be glaring and pouting my way through life as a male model. Think about it."

Lura had to agree. "You're right. But I just thought of something. What if the baby looks like you?"

Bryce's smile was sweet. "I've considered that. But I imagine Edie has, too. She's probably been to the library and copied all sorts of medical literature to back up any story she tells. Portis the Tortoise probably won't know the difference or even care. Kayleen St. Clair and the IRS are his main concerns at the moment."

"The Reverend's sister?"

"The very same. I followed the fat bastard to her house one night."

"Do you think Edie knows?"

"I'm not sure. I've been tempted to tell her, but she wouldn't believe me. She'd think I was making it up."

Though they were out of sight, Lura directed her gaze toward the house. "What a mess, Bryce."

"That's not the worst part," he said. "I can't prove anything, but Edie's either the clumsiest woman on earth, or the sonofabitch hits her hard enough to leave bruises."

Her startled gaze was sufficient response, but Lura had to voice her shock. "He hits her?"

"I've seen bruises on her neck myself. And why else would she wear pants and long sleeves all goddamned summer?"

Lura said, "I can't believe Ben would allow that to happen."

"I can't either," Bryce said. "God only knows the lies she's told him. And you want me to leave her alone. Stop checking up on her."

"Bryce," Lura said firmly, "if Edie puts up with abuse simply for the sake of money, then she deserves everything she gets and you're better off without her. She can't have any respect for herself."

Bryce turned impatiently away from her and scanned the horizon. His jaw was tight as he said, "If you're so fucking smart, how did you end up in prison?"

Lura froze and stared at his back.

"Answer that one," he bit out. "And how much respect did you have for yourself when you laid your drunk old man across those railroad tracks? I never asked you, Lura, did you stick around to see the train slice him in half?"

Lura's hands flew to her mouth to stifle the cry that

158

emerged from her lips. She spun on her heel and moved away from him with jerky steps. The ground was hard and lumpy under her feet, and she stumbled as she tried to break into a run. Her palms hit the ground with a jolt, and the knees of her jeans made a zipperlike sound as they slid across the damp surface of the grass. In less than a second she was up and moving again, her breath coming in ragged gasps as she pushed herself across the field. Bryce was shouting at her, but she couldn't make out his words. When she reached Edie's fence she placed the toe of her shoe in the chain link fence and half-climbed, half-fell onto the other side.

Edie came out of the house at an awkward trot and stooped to help Lura to her feet. "My God, Lura," she cried. "Are you all right? What happened?"

"I'm fine," Lura breathed, and she held on to the other woman until she was certain her quivering legs would support her. Her stomach was still rolling.

"What did he do?" Edie demanded.

"Nothing," Lura whispered. "Can I use your phone?"

"Of course. Your face is white, Lura. Are you sure you're all right?"

"Yes, I'll be fine. Just a little winded."

The air left her lungs again when she walked inside the house and found Ben hanging up the phone in the kitchen. His own eyes registered surprise when he turned and saw her.

"Lura wants to use the phone," Edie explained. "She came barreling over the fence and nearly broke her neck."

"What did he do?" Ben demanded.

"Nothing," Lura repeated. "I just want to call Phil and go home."

Ben stayed her hand as she reached for the receiver. "I'll take you. I was ready to leave anyway."

"He was," Edie said quickly. She bussed Ben's cheek and nearly shoved him toward the door. "Portis is due home any minute now."

"Shall we go?" Ben asked, and Lura followed him through the house and out the front door. As they climbed into Ben's Jeep, Bryce's white pickup slid into the driveway beside them. Bryce jumped out of the cab and ran to the passenger side of the Jeep.

"Lura, we need to talk."

Ben said, "Move away from the Jeep, Bryce. She wants to go home."

Bryce remained where he was. The eyes he trained on Lura were earnest. "Please, Lura. Dammit, I never meant to hurt you. I was mad at you for telling me what I already knew. The things I said just came out."

Lura's eyes were two blue-black circles of pain as she looked at him. "I know you didn't mean it, Bryce. But I want to go home now."

"I'll take you."

She turned and looked straight ahead again. "Ben can take me. It's on his way."

"Jesus, Lura, don't look like that. Can't we just talk?"

When she didn't respond, Ben started the Jeep's engine. Bryce hung on, then he reluctantly let go as the vehicle began to move.

"I'll call you," he promised her.

Lura kept her eyes on the windshield. She couldn't look at him.

As the Jeep left the driveway, Edie came out of the house and stood beside Bryce. "What happened?" she asked.

Bryce turned to look at her, and there was no tenderness in his eyes as he raked his gaze over her frowning face. "I hurt her for no good reason that I can see. Not that it's any of your business, *Mrs.* Jackson."

The contempt in his voice stunned Edie. She was still slack-jawed when he turned his back on her and stalked to his truck. Only when he was inside the cab with the engine running did she think of what to say.

"What was *that* supposed to mean, Bryce?"

He didn't hear her.

160

Chapter Sixteen

Lura didn't look up until Ben turned down the wrong road. It was a dirt lane that led to only one farmhouse and was therefore classified as a dead end.

"Are we making a stop?" she asked.

"A short one. Boyer Burke found a dead doe on her place this morning. I want to look at it. It won't take long."

"Are you on duty?"

"No. I'll only be a minute, all right?"

Lura nodded and sat quietly as he parked the Jeep in Boyer's drive and tapped on the horn. Boyer came to the door and smiled when she saw Ben. One dark brow lifted when she saw Lura, but soon the smile expanded to include her as well. Boyer stepped onto her porch and walked down the steps to meet Ben as he left the Jeep. There was a towel around her shoulders, and Lura could see that her hair was wet. Boyer shook her wet, dark curls and nodded to Lura in the Jeep before she spoke to Ben. "I was out walking Bo this morning when I found her. She's up on the bluff, about fifty yards south of the big walnut tree with the orange band around the trunk. Give me a holler if you can't find her, and

161

I'll come out and show you. I'm thinkin' someone dropped her with a shot, and then I came home and scared 'em away. Poachin' bastards. Didn't have time to dress her, I guess." She turned to Lura then. "You're welcome to come in the house while he's a'lookin'."

Lura opened her mouth to accept the friendly offer, but Ben asked her to remain in the Jeep.

"I won't be gone long," he said.

Boyer smiled and shrugged before returning inside the house. Ben went off in search of the doe, and Lura sat and attempted to pull her thoughts together. What Bryce said to her had brought all her demons rushing back, with a force so terrible she had nearly blacked out from the assault. The memory that accompanied his words had been achingly vivid. She didn't want to think about it. Not now. Not ever again. If she was going to rebuild her life she couldn't afford to think about any part of the past. And that included Ben, she reminded herself. She blinked as she saw him suddenly reappear. He had been gone less than five minutes. He held up his index finger to her, then he went to knock on Boyer Burke's door. They spoke for a moment, then Ben returned to the Jeep.

"What was it?" Lura asked as he climbed inside.

"Boyer was right. Someone killed the doe and ran off before dressing her. A clean shot through the head."

"It wasn't what you were looking for," Lura said.

Ben looked at her. "How do you know what I'm looking for?"

"I don't. Bryce mentioned something this morning about dead animals in a vacant house. I thought they might be related."

"So did I," Ben said. He backed the Jeep out of the drive and drove down the dirt lane. A half mile from the highway, he pulled the Jeep to the side of the road and turned off the engine. He turned to Lura and said, "I can't do this. I can't just take you home and pretend that we have nothing to say to each other."

Lura glanced outside the Jeep and wondered what Boyer Burke had thought to see her with Ben. Boyer had lived in Dumford all her life. She lived by herself, but she knew everyone and heard most everything. What was she thinking? Lura wondered as she gazed at the trees bordering the road. The maples and oaks looked like a child's painting, with splotches of red, yellow, and orange dabbed in at random. From somewhere, Boyer's place probably, came the scent of woodsmoke. It was a comforting, homey smell. Lura filled her lungs and exhaled slowly. She might as well talk to him. He wasn't going anywhere until she did.

"Why did you go to the city, Ben?"

"To forget you," he said frankly. "When you didn't answer any of my letters, or allow me to see you, I decided I needed to get away."

"Did you meet anyone while you were there?"

"Yes," he said.

A squirrel on a nearby branch caught Lura's attention. She watched its fragile body weave in and out of the oak tree, every step calculated, no movement wasted.

"Why did you come back to Dumford?" she asked.

"Because I didn't meet anyone who mattered. And because the guilt drove me insane when Edie told me what a tough time Phil and your mother were having. I felt responsible."

"So you gave them money."

"I wanted to help. Was that wrong?"

"From my viewpoint, yes. What have you done for yourself in between helping my family and being an all-around good samaritan?"

The bitterness in her tone made Ben look at her. "You mean why aren't I wealthy and driving a new car, or why don't I have a wife and three or four kids by now?"

"Both," she said.

Ben looked away from her. "I don't know. Somewhere between Dumford and the city I lost my ambition to be a rich man. I had an opportunity to go to school in the city, and I found myself taking night classes in criminology. It's just my bad luck that police work doesn't make a man wealthy, because that's all I've ever wanted to do."

Lura nodded. "I remember. What about the wife and children?"

"I don't think I have to answer that. Deny it as I might, it's pretty self-explanatory. And believe me, I have denied it, to myself more than anyone. I never wanted to believe that I was waiting for you."

"Why?"

"It was pointless, wasn't it?"

Lura had no response. She focused her attention on the squirrel, who was now studying them just as intently. Ben followed her gaze, and for a moment they were silent.

Finally, Ben said, "I've never seen Bryce so apologetic. Tell me what he said to you."

She sighed. "It was nothing, really. He just brought up something I haven't thought about in years. I thought I could deal with it, but it was like being stabbed with an invisible blade. I couldn't breathe or think or do anything but run away."

"Do you want to talk about it?"

"Not now."

"Come here," Ben said.

Lura looked at him. "No, Ben."

"Either you come here, or I'll come and get you."

"Why?"

"Because I need you to."

When she hesitated he reached for her and pulled her onto his lap. Her forehead rested against his jaw; he supported her back with one hand and laid the other across her hip.

"You've filled out," he said.

The side of her mouth twisted. A churning sensation began in her middle. "I gained six pounds. All in the hips, I think."

His fingers squeezed. "I always thought you were too skinny. Your bones stuck out."

"They don't anymore."

Ben exhaled into her hair. "You know you're driving me crazy, don't you?"

Lura closed her eyes and said nothing.

"Someday you're going to have to tell me, Lura. You're going to have to tell me why we haven't been doing this every day for the last eight years. I still need to know."

Her fingers clenched in her lap. "Please don't," she said. "Don't talk."

"I have to." His arms tightened their hold on her. "Don't let me sit here and wonder if you hate me so much you can't bear to touch me."

The churning in her middle intensified. "I don't. I don't hate you, Ben."

His hands came up to lift her chin and force her to look at him. "Then why are you so cold to me? Because of Michelle?"

Lura was silent.

"I used her," Ben said, his eyes searching Lura's. "And now I'm paying for it. I'm ashamed of how I've treated her. I let her into my life because she looked like you. I even pretended it was you when I made love to her."

Lura turned her face away. "I don't want to hear this."

"It's the truth. You were gone, but I still wanted some part of you in my life. I haven't touched her since the day I found out you were home. I saw you and wanted the real thing again. Right now I want you so bad it hurts. Remembering what it felt like to be inside you makes it even worse."

"Ben, *don't.*" Lura lifted her hands to her ears, as if to block out what she was hearing. "It wouldn't be the same now. Nothing between us would be the same."

"It could be," he argued. "If you could only trust me, Lura. You have no idea what you did to me all those years ago. You have no idea what I went through when you wouldn't speak to me. When you wouldn't tell me why."

"I couldn't," Lura said. "I still can't. Please take me home now, Ben."

Ben's voice lowered as he forced her to look at him once more. "Don't try to tell me you don't feel anything right now. We can't go on the way we have been. I lie awake nights and burn at the thought of your being so close. I leave the front door unlocked on the chance that you'll come in some night. I count the steps to your bedroom window and go crazy every time I think of Bryce touching you."

A tear spilled out of Lura's eye and rolled down her cheek to hover near the corner of her trembling mouth.

"Ben, I wish you wouldn't do—"

His mouth caught the tear, and then her lips. His hands came up to imprison her head, and he kissed her until the fists she pushed into his chest forced him to stop. Lura covered her mouth with trembling fingers and moved back to her own seat. Ben cursed under his breath. He breathed in deeply before attempting to speak. "I'm—"

"Take me home now," Lura said. "Please."

Ben placed his hands on the steering wheel. "Nothing," he said. "Nothing has changed."

"That's not true," Lura told him. "You still can't forget what I did, and I can't make you try. Eight years ago you said it would always be between us if you kept quiet about what you saw. You didn't keep quiet, but it's still between us."

"I thought you could explain it, dammit," Ben flared. "I thought you could tell me you hadn't just committed a cold-blooded murder, that you had some justifiable reason for killing your father."

Lura's voice was controlled. "I told you before that I did what I had to do. That should have been reason enough."

"I need more than that, Lura. For God's sake, did he molest you? Did he beat you?"

She silenced him with a glance. "It's over, Ben. It's been over for years, but only one of us seems to realize it. Now, if you won't take me home I'll get out and walk."

He started the engine and jerked the Jeep onto the lane with angry movements. Lura saw the squirrel make a panicked dash for safety, and then the tires were leaving a billowy trail of dust behind them as they sped down the dirt road. Once in town, Ben secmed to calm himself enough to drive at a normal speed. Lura glanced at him several times and found his jaw clenched, his mouth a grim white line. She had to remind herself that this was the same man who had held her with such tenderness only minutes ago.

"What?" he said brusquely. "Why are you looking at me like that?"

She tore her gaze away. "I'm sorry. I was just wondering if I ever really knew you."

"I could say the same," he replied.

When he reached their street, Ben pulled into his own drive. Lura opened her door and got out as soon as the Jeep stopped. She paused before turning to go.

"Ben, I'm sorry things have to be this way. I really am. Please try not to be angry."

He slammed the Jeep's door and walked around to stand in front of her. "Too late. You're so hung up on your precious fucking secret that you'll willingly ruin both our lives to keep it. That makes me a little angry."

Lura met his hard gaze with a bristling anger of her own. "Me? You're the great lover of truth and justice. And even though justice has been served, you won't accept what I say and simply let it go."

"I can't," he said.

"I know. You're too good to be true, Ben. I knew that eight years ago, and I know it now. You try so hard not to be like your father that you put saints to shame with your heartfelt morals and your sense of obligation. I loved you for it once, and for that reason alone I couldn't trust you. There's a lot of room for interpretation in the area between right and wrong, but nothing can change what I did that night, no matter which end of the spectrum that act falls. I want to forget it, but I can't unless you and everybody else in this town will let me."

"Forget it?" Ben's voice cracked, his brows meeting in disbelieving anger. "Without knowing why you ripped the heart out of my chest and left me bleeding without a fucking word? Without knowing why you destroyed our future? I would have died for you, Lura. You were all that mattered to me. You were my goddamned *life*."

Lura stepped forward. "Ben, I . . ."

He jerked away from her outstretched hand and backed up to his front porch. "You knew, Lura. That's what hurt me the most. You knew what you meant to me, how crazy in love with you I was, and you didn't think twice about putting me through hell. I can't forget that."

The door slammed on his retreat. Lura took a step after him, her entire body quivering with a sense of loss. Then she stopped. There was nothing more to say. Nothing that would make a difference. After a moment she turned and walked away.

Further strife awaited her across the street. When she entered the house she found her mother in tears and her brother pacing the living room floor with a dark scowl on his face. She sat down on the sofa beside Annette and put her arms around the thin, quivering shoulders.

"Phil, what's happened now? What's going on?"

"Where have you been?" he snapped.

"Riding with Bryce. I left a note."

"Bryce has been calling every five minutes for the last half hour."

"Ben brought me home. What's wrong with Mama?"

"Let her tell you."

Annette gave a low moan and covered her face with her hands. "Mean, mean, mean."

"What?" Lura asked. "Mama, what's happened?"

"Mean." Her mother pointed a finger at Phil. "He is so mean to me."

Lura looked up. "Phil?"

"This isn't working," he replied, still pacing the carpet in front of the television. "I thought it would. I thought we'd be able to leave her alone in the house for the few hours both of us are gone."

He stopped before Lura. "I was supposed to work today you know."

"Yes," she said tentatively.

"Mrs. Pendleton called while I was getting ready to leave. She said she saw you wandering down the street early yesterday morning and she thought I should talk to you. I didn't think anything about it until I realized you worked the early shift yesterday and weren't even here. Yesterday afternoon Mama was asleep on the sofa when I came home from school. Five minutes after I walked in, Michelle called and says she saw Mama running across the neighbor's lawns to get to the house just a few minutes before I came home. She's been out running around when we're not here."

"Mama?" Lura pulled her mother's hands away from her face. "Is this true?"

"Saltines!" Annette shouted. "I hate saltines and I want Ritz or no crackers at all! Make him be nice and give me a quality cracker, Lura. I like Captain Wafers, but I can't stand Captain Crunch."

Lura tried to smile. "Definitely too much television. The air probably did her some good."

"Somehow I doubt that," Phil said.

"Well, what do you propose we do? I have to take what hours I can get. So do you."

Her brother's eyes lowered to the floor. "I've been mulling it over, and I think it's time we applied for state aid. We can take her to Larned."

"The state hospital?" Lura was incredulous. "Phil, how can you even suggest such a thing?"

169

"Easily. Who knows where she goes or what she's been doing on these little forays of hers. Mrs. Pendleton thought she was you, Lura. Remember that. Besides, it's for her own good and you know it."

"No." Lura shook her head. "We can't do that. Not after everything I've—for God's sake, Phil, she's our mother. We're all she has."

"I know," he said in a quiet voice. "But I can't worry about her and concentrate on school and my job at the garage all at the same time. If I knew she was safe and being taken care of by someone it would be different."

"But why can't we—"

"Lura, I'm going to apply for a scholarship at WSU. I want to go to college next year."

"A scholarship? At Wichita State?"

"That's right. I want to live and work in the city. I already have a job lined up at a garage there. Finis Ewing talked to the guy who owns it and he said for me to come and see him after graduation."

"I see," said Lura.

"Do you?" Phil started pacing again. "I wonder if you really do. I've done my part, Lura. I've held things together long enough. Now I have to start thinking about what I want."

"I think it's wonderful, Phil."

He stopped and blinked. "You do?"

Lura nodded. "All of it. I'm proud of you for wanting to go on to college. And I think it will do you good to move to the city and go to school there. But as for Mama, we need to talk about this hospital business a while longer."

"Fine. And in the meantime, are you going to babysit her? Are you going to quit the only job you've been able to find to stay home and make sure she doesn't wander off?"

"I don't think that's necessary, Philip. I'll think of something."

Phil snorted. "Philip. Oh, that's nice," he said sarcastically. "Phil when we're pals, but Philip when I say something you don't like. Think, Lura. What happens when you want to get married? Do you drag Mama along with you and hope your husband doesn't mind supporting a brain-damaged, television-tongued mother-in-law?"

Lura looked at her hands. "I'm not planning on getting married anytime soon."

"No, I guess not. You already look the part of the old maid, so why not play it out?"

Lura's eyes rounded in disbelief. "Why are you being so cruel?"

"Well don't you think it's about time? A few years ago I wouldn't have dreamed of sending Mama away, but dammit, Lura, I'm a man now. I need to make some kind of life for myself apart from my family. I know that's not the way we've done things in the past. I know the Taylors have always stayed together and made sacrifices, but I can't do that anymore. I need to be free."

"And the only way you think you can do that is if Mama is in some kind of sanitarium?"

"Jesus." Phil put his hands to his head and spun away from her. "How can I get through to you? You saw what she did with the fork. What if she takes it into her head to jump in front of a truck one of these days? She could have been pulling fast ones on me all along, beating me home from school and work each time. It makes me sick just to think about it."

Lura turned to her mother and gripped her firmly by the shoulders. "Mama, where did you go when you left the house yesterday? Where did you go on your walk?"

Annette wiped her nose with her hand. "I went for a walk yesterday?"

"Yes. Where did you go?"

Her mother frowned. "I usually visit Ordney, but sometimes he isn't there."

"The cemetery?" Phil scoffed. "There's no way. She couldn't make it that far north without being seen."

"He came back as an animal, you know," Annette said

171

soberly. "I think he's a squirrel now. A big one, with huge yellow teeth. Sometimes I have trouble finding him, but I always do. Ordney was dumb as a cow, really."

"How do you find him?" Lura asked.

"Dead, mostly. Don't you find him dead?"

Lura took a deep breath. "The squirrel, Mama. Where do you see the squirrel?"

"Usually in a tree."

Phil made a noise of exasperation. "For crying out loud, Mama, where's the goddamned tree?"

"Don't you dare speak to me like that!" Spittle flew from Annette's mouth as she shook her finger at him. "You watch your tongue, young man, or I'll call the network censors and yank my advertising."

"Mama," Lura said gently. "We're only trying to find out where you go on your walks."

Her mother waved a hand. "I'm really too tired for one right now. Maybe tomorrow, all right?"

Lura dropped her head in defeat. Phil sat down in the chair by the sofa and ran a hand through his dark hair before offering her a cigarette. She turned him down.

"What I really need right now is a drink."

"There's a beer in the refrigerator."

"You want one?"

"No, I think I'll go on to work. What about you? Are you working tonight?"

"At five."

Phil checked his watch. "It's after two now. Why don't you drop her off at Marie's on your way in and I'll pick her up when I get out of the garage. You'd like to visit with Marie today, wouldn't you Mama?"

"She's so fussy," Annette replied. "Truly, I don't know where she gets her airs. Our mother wasn't fussy at all. I didn't know her that well, of course, but she seemed very nice. Marie had to have picked it up from that English governess. The fourth one, mind you. My brother was a walking, talking terror when it came to governesses."

"Brother?" Lura echoed. "Mama, you didn't have any brothers."

"I most certainly did. But we were forbidden to speak of him after he died. He raped two girls and murdered another before they caught him. He was seven years older than Marie and eight years older than me. Brought huge shame on mater and pater, he did. I'm telling you it was one scandal after another in my family. Just as one quieted down we created another."

"How did he die?" Phil asked.

"Who?"

"Your brother."

Annette frowned. "What brother? I have no brothers."

Phil rolled his eyes. "Okay. What happened to this brother that you didn't have? How did he die?"

Annette turned to Lura and frowned curiously at her. "Do you know what he's talking about?"

Lura stood up and turned on the television. "I don't know anything, Mama. Why don't you find something to watch until I take you over to Marie's house."

The beer didn't help. Lura placed one hand against her throbbing head and wondered why she had so fervently longed for her freedom while in prison.

Her thoughts flitted from her mother's claim of a dead man returning as an animal, to the squirrel she and Ben had watched earlier. A squirrel with yellow teeth.

Dumb as a cow.

Ben's cat.

An image presented itself in Lura's brain, accompanied by a terrible, sickening suspicion, and before she could control it, the beer in her stomach was making its way up and out of her mouth.

"No, Mama," Lura croaked. "Oh, please, God. Not again."

Chapter Seventeen

A week passed before Edie saw Bryce McKee again. She had come to the post office to mail a letter to Miss Mary Florence in Oklahoma City. The letter thanked her for the news of Max Portlock's death and explained that the money held in his name would now be divided among his heirs. Edie thought of it as a bit like fishing—the bait was on the hook, and now all she had to do was sit back and wait for the lying, tough-mouthed carp to jump out of the water and land on her front porch. She hadn't told Portis that her father was actually alive. She thought it might come as more of a surprise to Portis if he thought he was being killed by a dead man. And as he always checked the mailbox to see what she was mailing, Edie decided it was best to take the letter to the post office herself.

As she was walking by Milly's she happened to look inside the window and see Bryce sitting on a stool at the counter. Lura was nowhere in sight, though Ben had said she was now working in the restaurant. After a moment's hesitation, Edie pushed open the door and walked inside. Bryce turned his head as the bell tinkled, and a frown creased his brow as he recognized her. The frown deepened as she approached the counter and took a seat three stools away from his.

"My goodness, don't you look pretty?" Milly said as she came from the kitchen. "Where on earth did you find that pretty blue frock, Edie? It's just darling."

Edie beamed. "Out of a catalog. Is Lura here?"

"Oh no, she had to cut back her hours to keep an eye on her mother. Most devoted daughter I ever saw. Are the two of you hungry?"

"Two?" Edie said. Then she laughed as Milly pointed to her swollen belly.

"I've got some scrumptious chocolate-pecan pie with your name on it," Milly enticed.

Edie's eyes lit up. "Chocolate-pecan?"

"You betcha. Ask Officer McKee if it doesn't melt in your mouth. He just ordered a piece."

Bryce smiled at the woman and held up a forkful of pie in salute. "It's delicious, Milly."

Edie placed her thumb and finger together. "I'll have just a little piece. And a glass of milk."

"Coming up." Milly was back with both in less than a minute. She waited until Edie's eyes had rolled in ecstasy over the first bite before excusing herself again.

"Got vegetarian lasagna as the special tonight and I need to get things cooking. Holler when you want your check."

The pie was delicious, but something inside her was wrong, Edie decided. She took a sip of milk and waited for the odd sensation to pass. Then she realized it was the baby. It was kicking at her insides with unusual gusto, almost as if it were trying to turn itself. As the motion shifted, she looked down to see the front of her blue dress flutter. On impulse she got off the stool and walked over to Bryce. When he swiveled to look at her, she took his hand and placed it on the movement.

"Feel that?" she whispered happily. "Feels like it's doing a flip-flop in there. Can you feel it?"

Bryce swallowed hard and nodded before pulling his hand out of her clasp. Edie looked at his stiff features and blinked in hurt surprise before moving slowly back to her stool.

Why wasn't he talking to her? she wondered. He wasn't even looking at her. He just sat there eating his pie, drinking his coffee, and reading his paper. She looked at her watch and realized it was his lunch hour. She'd always wondered what he did for lunch. She watched him out of the corner of her eye for a moment before realizing she'd never really seen him when he was quiet. He was always smiling and joking and teasing, even when he was upset with her.

He used his napkin correctly, she noticed.

What was different about him? The dark shadow on his cheeks? The fact that he needed a haircut? She looked closer at his dark, unruly hair and saw a touch of gray beginning just above his ear. It surprised her. She couldn't remember having seen it before.

"Bryce?"

He didn't look at her. "What?"

"Is, uh, Ben working today?"

"Yes."

"Oh. I haven't seen him lately. Is he still trying to find out who killed those animals?"

"Yes."

Edie took a bite of her pie and chewed for a moment. Not even the chocolate could make this new uneasy feeling go away. It had to do with Bryce, and the way he refused to look at her. Edie glanced at him again, and she finally realized what was different about his face. The impact made her eyes well up with sudden emotion.

"Bryce?"

The catch in her voice made him look at her. "What?"

"Why do you look so sad?" she whispered. "I've never seen you look sad before."

His eyes turned cold. "Milly, you'd better come out here," he said loudly. "Something's wrong with Edie."

"What?" Milly shrieked from inside the kitchen. She was at the counter in less than three seconds. In another ten she was practically spitting at Bryce.

"For heaven's sake. Haven't you ever seen a pregnant woman cry? You scared me to death, Bryce McKee. I thought we had an emergency here."

"Sorry," he said. "Don't bother with my check. I'll leave the money on the counter."

When he was gone, Milly folded Edie into her arms and soothed her. "Poor thing. I know my pies are good, but they're nothing to cry over. What's wrong, punkin? Got a case of the pregnant blues?"

Edie nodded and snuffled a little before lifting her head. "I'm better now. I don't know what set me off."

"Well, it doesn't take much. You want another piece of pie to take home with you?"

"Do you have another?"

"Sure do. You always did have a terrible sweet tooth."

"My teeth are all capped now," Edie said with a guilty smile. "The sweets caught up with me."

"Only person I know who likes sweets as much as you do just walked out of here. I don't know how that man keeps such a hard gut with all the sweets he eats in here. Guess he works it off at that big house of his."

"Big house?" Edie echoed. "Ben says there's not enough room to turn around in Bryce's place."

"His grandfolks' house, Edie. Bryce has got the place all restored. I drove by yesterday and thought I'd taken a step back in time. He did a good job."

Edie frowned. "But what is he going to do with it? Is he going to sell it?"

"Not to hear him talk," Milly said. She winked at Edie then. "Usually when a man takes such pains over a house, he's doing it for a woman. Hannah Winegarten told me he thought he was going to win his ex-wife back, but it fell through. Word has it that she's pregnant, due almost the same day as you, but she told him she wasn't even sure it was his baby. He's been looking pretty hangdog lately, so maybe he'll end up selling the place after all. It's a shame, since he put so much work into it. But that's the way it goes with those city women, I guess."

"I guess," Edie said. "Can I have that pie to take home now? I need to be going."

Minutes later she was walking out the door and heading for the phone booth in front of Ailey's drugstore. She fumbled a quarter out of her purse and plunked it into the slot, all the while cursing Bryce McKee. How dare he make two women pregnant at the same time!

Edie used directory assistance to find the woman's phone number, then she dropped in more quarters and she hastily punched in the number before she forgot it. The phone was answered on the ninth ring with a sleepy hello.

"Is this Twila McKee?" Edie asked.

"Yes," the woman said, "and I work third shift so this better be damned good."

"Sorry. I just wanted to know your exact due date."

"My what? Who is this?"

"Aren't you Bryce McKee's ex-wife?"

"Yes."

"And aren't you pregnant?"

Twila McKee laughed in her ear. "Not hardly. How is Bryce, anyway? I haven't seen him for two or three years now."

"He's fine," Edie said.

"Are you his girlfriend? How did you know my name?"

"Oh, he talked about his marriage once," Edie said uncomfortably.

"Uh-huh. And what made you think I was pregnant?"

"I don't know. Look, I'm sorry to have disturbed you. I'll let you go back to sleep now. Uh, wait, just one more thing. Why did you two get a divorce?"

"You must be a wife or a girlfriend," Twila said. "It wasn't any big thing. We just had a conflict of interests.

He's a family man, and I wasn't ready to settle down in stretch mark city yet."

"Sesame oil is great for that," Edie said. "I don't have any—" She caught herself. "Well, thank you for telling me."

"No problem. When you see him, tell him I said hello and that I'm still into studs. He'll know what you mean."

"Okay, I will," Edie said. "Good-bye."

When she hung up the phone she was thoroughly confused. Why would Hannah Winegarten tell Milly such a thing? And why would anyone tell Hannah such an outrageous lie?

"Oh Lord," she whispered suddenly. *"Bryce."*

He had cooked up the story to get Hannah off Edie's scent. That had to be it.

Wasn't that sweet of him? Edie thought.

But if he had gone to such trouble to cover up his paternity, then it must mean he was giving up on pestering her . . . mustn't it?

For some reason, that thought brought the uneasy feeling back.

And there was still the house to wonder about. Edie glanced at her watch and decided she might as well drive over and see it before Portis was due home. It wouldn't hurt just to look and see what Bryce had done to the place. Edie couldn't believe he hadn't mentioned it to her before, particularly when they had talked about his grandparents on the phone during the caramel incident.

When she saw the place Edie couldn't believe her eyes. She had intended to simply drive by and pretend to be toodling along through the neighborhood, but the tall, majestic columns and the pristine white exterior beckoned to her. She left the car idling in the drive and walked up to the front window. Inside, she could see the gleam of polished oak floors and the sunny reflection from the panes of

179

French doors just off to the right, leading to either a den or a library.

"A cattleman," Edie murmured to herself. "Old Man McKee had Hereford cattle, I remember."

But the house had never looked like this, not even when Edie was a child. What happened to all their money? she wondered. Maybe Bryce's father had squandered it all away when he took over. That was entirely possible, Edie decided. But where had Bryce come up with the money to restore the place? The work must have taken months to do on his puny civil servant's pay.

Still, she observed, if he had any money left, he really should buy some wallpaper. Painting the place in neutral colors would do in a pinch, but paper was certainly preferable. Personally, she thought she would buy a nice quiet print with a delicate, understated border. Maybe she could suggest it the next time she spoke to him. If he ended up selling the place, it might bring a better price to have some nice decorating touches.

Her thoughts paused there as she remembered the white-haired Milly's conspiratorial wink and the comment about men only doing such things as restoring houses when they were thinking about a woman.

That myth had already been debunked. He wasn't restoring the place in hopes of winning back a pregnant ex-wife, because the ex-wife wasn't pregnant and she hadn't even seen him in two or three years.

So why . . . ?

Edie's heart blocked her throat as she suddenly considered another possibility.

Could he have been serious all this time? Declaring where he was going and who he was taking out. Calling to check up on her and coming by to see if she was doing all right. Asking her to leave Portis.

"No," she breathed. She knew better, didn't she? To think what a fool she would make of herself if she actually believed he wanted her. Bad enough that she had allowed herself to become yet another of his conquests, but to let herself believe for a minute that he would give up his single life for her . . . No. He had simply been having fun with her those times he came by, making sure she didn't forget where the baby in her womb came from. Bryce had been teasing her for most of her life. He wasn't serious about her. He had never once said he loved her in all his attentions. He had never even mentioned love.

"It's too bad," she said to her stomach in a wistful voice. "We wouldn't mind living in this house, would we? We love to pick out wallpaper."

Chapter Eighteen

Hannah maintained her oath of silence in the station, though it was acutely uncomfortable and completely unnatural for her to do so. Sometimes she thought she might become violently ill if she didn't open her mouth and let the words out. When Bryce and Mickey argued on whether the harvest moon was in September or October she had been dying to tell them that a harvest moon was the full moon closest to the autumnal equinox. It wasn't always in one month or the other, she wanted to tell them. But no, George was constantly there with his big ears and warning glances, so she was forced to let the men remain ignorant on the subject of Harvest moons.

Silence was indeed difficult for an ex-schoolteacher, but the atmosphere in the station itself had been lighter since she and Bryce had patched up their little squabble. She was still wary of him, of course, considering his parentage. But he was so utterly melancholic over his ex-wife's coming child that it was difficult to show him anything but sweetness and sympathy. In her own tactful way, Hannah had made certain everyone else knew the reason for Bryce's morose behavior. She wanted to spare him the painful questions people always ask when someone appears blue for no apparent reason. Hannah thought he appreciated it, for he often smiled at no one else but her.

Ben Portlock didn't smile at anyone anymore. He had become so rude, ill-tempered, and uncommunicative that Hannah was tempted to wonder if the witchy Berniece Miller had cast a spell on him the day he drove out to see her. It was a terrible thing to witness the downfall of a good man. Hannah would swear Ben had lost five pounds, if not more, in the last week. His cheekbones couldn't stand it; his face looked positively gaunt. When George mentioned his appearance and asked his diet secret, Ben just looked at him.

The thing with the animals gnawed at him constantly, Hannah believed. She had heard him talking on the phone with someone, asking whether it was the same knife, and if any other information had been collected. She assumed it was the coroner. Though George had told him to leave the case alone and let the sheriff handle it, Ben was ignoring the chief. He had friends who told him what he wanted to know, but apparently no one had told him anything that helped. As far as Hannah knew, they had found no trace evidence of any use in the Parry house.

Slicing up animals was a revolting business. It made Hannah shiver in her bed at night to know such disquieting things—floating puppies and legless calves—had been going on so close to her own house. As a result she kept her eyes peeled more than usual for erratic and or aberrant behavior in her fellow Dumfordians. So it was that Hannah happened to stumble on some particularly erratic behavior in one of the town's most prominent citizens.

It was late when she left the station, almost ten in the evening. Cory Simmons was manning dispatch and already half asleep. His vacation had been extended when the relative he was visiting passed a severe case of intestinal flu on to his guest.

Cory was still weak, and still taking regular doses of Kaopectate, so Hannah had been loath to leave him at her post until it was absolutely necessary. Kurt would be having fits wondering where she was, and Hannah would have been a terrible liar if she didn't admit the thought of his panicking gave her a small thrill. In spite of money and manhood, he had to depend on her, didn't he?

She was savoring this thought when she drove by the old depot and noticed a tiny light glowing within the small wooden structure. Her foot tapped the brake in anger. Why did people always pick the northern edge of town for their nefarious activities? Drugs, oversexed teenagers, *puppies*. There was no telling what was going on in the deserted depot.

But it was best to take a peek before she called it in, she told herself. She didn't want George angry with her for causing a fuss over some transient. She turned off the headlights of her antiquated Rambler and steered onto the road leading over the tracks. On the other side of the depot, hidden from normal traffic, was a car she recognized.

What on earth would Portis Jackson be doing here at this time of night?

Hannah took her foot off the accelerator and let the Rambler coast until she was ten yards from the BMW. She sat a moment, deliberating, but curiosity overwhelmed her. Leaving the engine running, she emerged from the car. There was a second of hesitation as she debated whether to leave her door open or closed, but she quickly decided being safer was better than being sorry. She left it open. The dome light had been burned out for years, and there was none of the beeping, buzzing, or dingdonging found in newer cars with doors left ajar.

Practiced in the ways of stealth (a prerequisite for effective eavesdropping), Hannah avoided the railed porch entirely and moved to stand on the grass under the nearest window. Balancing on her tiptoes, she peered through the cracked glass and saw that the source of the light was a single weak-beamed flashlight sitting in the middle of the boarded floor. The pudgy Portis paced angrily through the beam, the hem of his overcoat flapping as he whirled to face someone Hannah couldn't see.

"Don't fuck with me, girlie. I'm warning you. I'll make your life miserable."

The invisible someone gave a high, feminine giggle.

"I wonder if your parents are into voyeurism, Portis? Do you think they'd enjoy watching a copy?"

Hannah saw Portis dart toward the female shadow. There was the sharp, cracking sound of flesh on flesh, and then his voice, hoarse and filled with rage.

"Don't even *think* about it, you ugly bitch. Don't even think about it."

The woman laughed again. "Wouldn't Big Daddy offer up some bucks to keep it out of circulation?"

"What the fuck do you want from me?" Portis whined in frustration.

"I haven't really decided yet," came the amused reply. "The pictures will do to begin with. And money, of course. After that, we'll see."

"What pictures? I don't know what you're talking about."

"Oh, please. Don't make the mistake of thinking every woman is as stupid as your wife. I know you still have the pictures and I want them. And the negatives."

"We'll trade," Portis said.

"No, we won't. I don't have that much to lose, my fat friend. Not like you. If any of this comes out I can always leave town. I'd rather not hurt the family, but if it comes to that, tough titty. Can you say the same, Portis?"

Portis began to whimper. "But we had such a good thing going. I took you places and indulged every whim. Why do you want to spoil it like this?"

"Like this?" The woman gave a low, menacing chuckle.

185

"This is what is known as getting thee before thee gets me. Don't pretend I haven't been at the top of your list of things to take care of since the night of the party."

Hannah's calves were cramping. And her ears were positively blazing. She was dying to know who the woman was, and just what this conversation was about, but she couldn't trust her joints to hold her. Before she could hear Portis Jackson's answer she had to lower herself and step quietly away to massage her legs. As she was rubbing, she suddenly decided she had heard enough. There was no sense in endangering herself by staying.

On the way back to her car she began ticking off a list of people she could tell. George Legget was out, definitely. She had half a mind to call up poor Edie and tell her just what a lout she was married to. But Edie was so close to term she might go into early labor over an emotional upset like this. Ben? Lord knew what he would do to his sister's unfaithful husband. In his present state he was likely to go off the deep end and—

Who was that *woman?*

Kurt shouted at her the moment Hannah entered the house. She rushed into his room, her face glowing.

"You'll never believe what I just heard down at the old depot!"

Her brother's curses lasted exactly fifteen minutes. In that time Hannah changed his sheets and fed him a melted cheese sandwich and some hot broth, all the while phrasing and rephrasing the tale she would tell when he stopped.

"Are you ready to hear it now, Kurt?" The first telling was always a rough draft. She would listen to herself and trim off the excess verbiage to intensify the more salient points in future performances.

Kurt's grunt was his assent. Hannah settled herself in a chair by his bed, and, deliberately not looking at what his hands were doing, she began. Three minutes into her story, Kurt interrupted her.

"Who was the woman?"

"I don't know. Just listen, would you?"

Another grunt. The sheet around his middle was quivering, but Hannah managed to ignore it and go on. When she finished, Kurt said, "Did they see you?"

"Of course not."

"Then you haven't lost your touch. You always were a sneaky little bitch."

"Don't speak to me that way. Tell me what you think they were talking about."

Kurt chuckled. *"She* was talking about money."

"This isn't funny, Kurt."

"Sure it is. Blackmail is always funny, because it usually happens to the smug sonofabitch who deserves it the most. You know what kind of pictures they were talking about, don't you?"

Hannah shook her head.

"Think, teach. What kind of pictures would you be worried about?"

"Dirty pictures?"

"And what would Portis be worried about his parents watching? You don't watch pictures, Hannah, you watch movies. In this case, I'd wager six Percodans it was a dirty movie."

"Portis Jackson starring in a dirty movie?"

Kurt groaned. "You are so abysmally dense, Hannah. Haven't you ever heard of VCR cameras?"

"Lord . . ." she whispered.

"And now that I've figured this out for you, get over here and give me a shot."

"You said you could give them to yourself."

"I have been, but by hand hurts."

"I wonder why," Hannah muttered. Then, "Wait, Kurt. What do you suppose she meant by being on his list of things to take care of since the night of the party?"

"I have no idea. Give me the shot."

187

Hannah tore the wrapper off the syringe. "There's been only one party lately. Do you suppose Portis and this woman had some argument the night of Edie's party?"

"The shot," Kurt growled.

"And that was the night Calvin Horn was . . ." Hannah's eyes rounded in alarm. "They found dirty movies in Calvin's house, Kurt!"

"So? Would you shut up and give me the goddamned shot?"

"All right," Hannah snapped. She prepared the syringe and inserted the needle with careless aim. "There must be something to this, Kurt. I can feel it. Maybe I shouldn't tell anyone just yet. Maybe I should try to find out what this is about myself. Wouldn't George be proud of me?"

Kurt farted and sighed at the same time. "Maybe you should do a little blackmailing of your own."

"That's the morphine talking, Kurt. Who would I blackmail?"

"Portis Jackson."

"Why?"

"For money."

Hannah stiffened. "I am an employee of the police department. I am a law-abiding—"

"Hold on to your panty shield, Hannah. It was just a suggestion." Kurt smiled then. "You know what would be fun, though? Write him a nice little note. Give him something to worry about. Who knows what you'll flush out of the woodpile?"

"A note?" Hannah's brows lifted. She had once thought of sending Portis an anonymous note for another reason. She looked at her brother. He wasn't yelling at her, and he had actually stopped playing with himself for the moment. He was enjoying the intrigue, she realized.

"What would the note say?" she asked.

"Try something like, 'I saw who you are, and I know what you did.' Just like those two girls in that old movie."

"What happened to the girls in the movie?"

Kurt waved one bony, yellow hand. "Their parents spanked them or something, I don't remember. Better yet, tell him his lover has been talking. That ought to stir things up."

Hannah frowned at him. "Where do you come up with these ideas?"

"Soap operas. You wouldn't believe the shit and shenanigans they go through."

"I don't know," Hannah said doubtfully.

"If you don't do it, I will," Kurt threatened with a malicious grin.

"Don't be ridiculous, Kurt. You can't even get out of bed without help."

"I wouldn't have to. I've got a phone right here. I can make anonymous calls."

"I could move it," Hannah said. "Take it out."

"You do and the minute you're gone I'll scream until our sweet, lovable neighbor comes running."

"Why? Why do you want to do this?"

He shrugged. "I'm bored. And if you think staying late at work and making me starve is going to speed my demise, think again. A bored man lives longer than he wants to, my sweet sap of a sister."

"I should never have told you," Hannah said in a rueful voice.

"I'm glad you did. I always knew Portis Pee was a walking dick for brains. He used to visit my practice in El Dorado for penicillin shots. I never saw him when he didn't have a dripping pecker."

Hannah snorted in disgust and stood up. "Call him if you like. I'm not sending notes to anyone."

"Then what *are* you going to do? Gossip about the vice-president of the bank until George cans you?"

Hannah's mouth twisted. "I don't know. I need to tell someone. What if the 'night of the party' business had something to do with Calvin Horn's murder?"

"We'll find out," Kurt said. "Bring me the phone book."

189

"What are you going to do?"

"Bring it, dammit!"

Hannah scurried into the kitchen and came back to fling the thin book at him. Kurt looked up the number he wanted, then he asked Hannah to dial it. She did so, her heart pounding, and then she handed him the receiver. "It's ringing. Maybe he's not home yet."

Kurt coughed and said, "Portis Jackson? Didn't wake you, did I? No, I didn't think so. Listen, I know all about what you did to Calvin Horn . . ." He stopped talking and handed the receiver to Hannah.

"What?" she whispered. "What did he say?"

Kurt's grin was a death mask. "He hung up. There's your answer, Miss Sherlock. Now what are you going to do?"

Hannah grabbed the nearest bottle of pills from Kurt's dresser and shook out two. After she had swallowed them dry she looked at her brother.

"I still don't know, Kurt. I just don't know. What do you think?"

"I think I'm getting sleepy."

"Kurt!"

His hand was moving back to his groin. Hannah resisted the urge to shake him. She didn't want to touch him.

"Kurt, please. How can I prove it? I can't go to George without proof."

Kurt showed his white, chalky tongue in a yawn. "Find the video movie. Maybe it has Calvin's prints on it."

"How? Won't it have other prints on it, too? Suppose it doesn't have any prints at all on it?"

"Suppose you get your sagging ass out of here and let me go to sleep," he snarled.

"All right. Good night." Wringing her hands in worry and frustration, Hannah left him. She was on to something big here, and he wanted to *sleep*. This was her chance to make George Legget choke on humble pie, her chance to prove how useful her keen eyes and ears could be. Going to sleep was unthinkable. Nay, inconceivable. There would be no dreams of Huntington Beach and the elusive spring on this night.

Chapter Nineteen

Portis walked the length of his den and back again, his eyes never leaving the phone on the mahogany desk. The skin of his face, neck, and hands itched intolerably from a sudden onset of flaming hives. Kayleen was back in the depot, her skull shattered. Portis knew he needed to go back and move her body before dawn, but running had been his first reaction. And then to come home to a phone call from a stranger, a man claiming to know about Calvin. Exactly what did he know? He had to mean what Portis thought he meant. He had to have been talking about Calvin's murder.

And now Kayleen.

Portis scratched absently at the tops of his hands as he paced. Her death had been an accident. He hadn't meant to slam her so hard against the wall. Not really. She had laughed and taunted until he couldn't take it anymore. And she had called him *fat*.

He squeezed his eyes shut and tried to think of what to do with her body. Was there very much blood? He couldn't remember.

Think! he begged himself. Don't just walk around and scratch yourself raw. There's a way out of this, Portis. There's a way out of everything. You're an intelligent man. You're a community leader. Remember when you got yourself into trouble at the bank with those securities? You were brilliant. You slid out of that like a greasy dog in a buttered bun. You were slick with those loans, pardner. They borrowed fifty, you wrote down sixty and double booked your ass out of a jam. This is the same. Just concentrate on the facts and forget the fucker on the phone.

Evidence. Okay. Hands, clothes, car. She hadn't scratched him, so the hands were no problem. The clothes he wore would have to be burned after he moved the body, which was too bad, considering it was his favorite overcoat. He thought he looked like Gene Hackman in *The French Connection* in that coat. Portis had more hair, of course.

He stopped himself and scratched angrily at his neck. The facts. His BMW would need to be cleaned and vacuumed as soon as possible. He could have Edie do that. He might as well take her car back to the depot to avoid recognition and have her do both cars tomorrow. It would seem less suspicious to everyone concerned if he made it seem like a routine clean and wax the cars idea.

Okay. So far, so good, he thought. Now, take the body where? He didn't want it found anytime soon, so there would have to be some digging involved. Soft ground, preferably. Thank God there hadn't been any hard freezes yet.

Who the fuck was that on the phone?

Portis clenched his jaw and pummeled himself on both sides of his head.

Forget that for now! Concentrate on the facts.

The facts.

God, this was so bizarre. Killing Calvin had been different; Portis hadn't actually seen it happen. But this, this was the real thing. Her shoulders had been in his hands and it was so easy to snap her forward and ram her back against the wood surface. The sound had alerted him to the seriousness of the situation, that wet-sounding crunch with just the hint of a crack. Her eyes had rolled back in her head only to freeze with half the whites showing. Her arms and legs had done a funny little dance, and then he had smelled something awful. That was when he knew she was really gone. Dead people shit their pants.

So had Portis, but he wasn't dead. He could feel it now in the stickiness of his shorts as he paced. There was no time and no sense in changing them. He had to decide what he was going to do with the body.

It would be nice if he had some kind of acid, he thought. Acid or lime, something to speed the decay along and leave him less to worry about. He pictured what she would look like when they found her—and they would eventually, Portis knew. She'd look just like the gutted pig he had stumbled across in Calvin's dump.

He hadn't told Kayleen about that pig. Tell someone about something dead and they want to have a look, no matter how ill they know it will make them. He himself had done everything in his power to forget the sight and go on hunting for—

The tape! Jesus Christ, where the hell was that thing?

Portis paced with fresh intensity. Someone, the good Reverend probably, would go through her things in a search for clues when she turned up missing. But no, he quickly thought, Kayleen was too smart to hide it in her own home, wasn't she? Of course she was. She would have put it somewhere safe. Somewhere private. Like her *safe fucking deposit box in his own goddamned bank.*

He smiled and stopped scratching for a moment. The silly bitch. Right under his nose. Why hadn't he thought of it before? He knew she kept her key in her purse, and getting the bank key wouldn't be a problem. He could—

"Portis?"

His buttock muscles clenched. Edie stood in the doorway and blinked sleepily as she looked at him. "It's after midnight. What are you doing?"

"Working," he spat at her. "I'm thinking and working. Go back to bed before you ruin my concentration."

"I'm hungry," Edie said. "Can I fix myself something to eat?"

Portis advanced on her before she could back away. His blow caught her on one eye and across the bridge of her nose.

"Why don't you try the caramels in the Bisquick box? Or maybe the Snickers bar inside the paper towel roll? And if you're really starving, why not add the Hershey's Almond bar wrapped up in the Ex-Lax package?"

Edie stopped cringing long enough to frown at him. "I'm not trying to change the subject or anything, Portis, but what's happened to your skin? You've got splotches."

His arm rose again and she twisted away and stumbled down the hall to the bedroom. When the door slammed behind her Portis shoved his hands into his pockets. He had caught himself thinking how easy it would be to go after his large-bellied wife and kill her. How easy it was to kill, period. To end a human life.

He shook his head and forced himself away from the bedroom door. He had to go down to that depot and get back before his shorts dried to his skin.

But where, dammit? Where could he take the body to let the greedy sow rot in undiscovered peace?

Sow. Pig.

The dump.

All right. The monstrous mounds of trash were the answer. Bury the bitch under one of those and you've got it made, Portis told himself. Nobody sifts dumps for missing persons. They might hang posters and form search parties, and they might comb countrysides looking for shallow graves, but nobody—with the dead exception of Calvin Horn—would sift through mounds of trash for a missing woman.

The new garbage hauler wouldn't be a problem. He wore some kind of plastic suit that made him look like a goddamned astronaut. He obviously wasn't going to get his hands dirty by doing any dump rummaging.

That's it, Portis thought with relief. Now to think of a way to tie in Kayleen's pictures. Maybe he could plant them in her house and give the Reverend a little surprise when he went searching for a clue to her disappearance. The saintly St. Clair might even take pause before calling in the authorities if he thought his sister was simply playing dress up with the devil somewhere.

Portis unlocked a drawer in his desk and removed the photos. He flipped through them, removed one of his favorites for old times' sake, then shoved the rest inside his jacket. It was time to make a move.

A brief glance into the bedroom found his wife stretched across the bed and snoring softly. He quietly closed the door again and slipped downstairs to find her purse. The keys to her Audi were sticky; a sniff told him it was butterscotch. Portis shook his head and wondered if babies could be born addicted to sweets. This one was going to come out crying for Reese's Pieces instead of mother's milk. Portis supposed it didn't matter. The kid was doomed any way you looked at it.

Once outside and in the car it angered him to find her gas tank nearly empty. He filled it up once a month, and by his calculations, he still had another week to go. Just where the hell did she go during the day while he was slaving his ass off at the bank? He made a mental note to ask her, and if she gave him some bullshit of the simmering potpourri variety, he decided to take her car keys away. See how she liked walking to the goddamned doctor every week. The gas was enough to get him where he needed to go, but the tank would have to be filled up tomorrow. Edie could do that before she washed, waxed, and vacuumed. The job of doing both cars ought to keep her wandering butt busy, Portis decided.

His sphincter gave way completely when he reached his destination and found the depot empty.

The flashlight in his hands jerked from one corner to the next in a panicked search, until he realized even the blood on the wall was gone. He sat down on the floor in a daze. *What the fuck was going on here?*

Kayleen hadn't walked out of the depot, that much he knew for certain. Someone, some lousy corpse-stealing sonofabitch, had come and taken her body and cleaned up the place.

The man on the phone, Portis thought. It had to be. The prankster had watched him do Kayleen as well as Calvin, and was now going to blackmail Portis for both of them. This was too much. This was just too much. Cover up one pile of shit and some cat walks in and digs another hole. Who could it be? The baby-snatcher? The nut in the ski mask Kayleen had seen at Calvin's place?"

Right, Portis thought. He was dealing with a crazy here. A sicko who carved up animals. Now, what was he going to do about it? He could wait and see what the asshole had in mind, of course, but you couldn't really trust an insane person. It was best to follow through with the plan. Portis would plant the pictures and burn his clothes tonight, then he would have Edie take care of the cars tomorrow. Whenever—and wherever—Kayleen turned up, there would be no evidence to link her death to Portis. And if the crazy decided to carve her up a little, so much the better. The location of the tape was Portis's only real concern. While he was in her house he might as well have a look around. He was certain it would be in her safe deposit box, but it wouldn't hurt to be sure. Who knows? Portis told himself. You might squeeze your ass out of this yet, you slick bastard.

The moment Edie heard the car leave she left her bed and crept to the kitchen. There was plenty of evidence to get rid of before Portis returned from wherever he was going. She snatched the Snickers bar from inside the paper towel roll and paused. Where *was* he going? To see his secretary? She was tempted to call Kayleen and warn her that a smelly case of hives was coming her way, and that the look on his face probably meant the telephone cord was going to be put into use. But she didn't. She had enough problems of her own without trying to save some slutty secretary from a night of Southwestern Bell bondage. She had to think up a clever lie about her puffy eye.

The swelling wasn't too bad, but she knew there would be discoloration tomorrow. How was she going to hide it this time? Edie had used every tale in the tome about bumping into cabinets and doors and telephone lines. After her last visit, a disgruntled Dr. McMurphy had threatened to put her in a rubber room until the baby was born. The idea didn't sound so bad, really, because this pregnancy business was becoming increasingly uncomfortable. Standing up or sitting down was a chore, and a full night's sleep was only a fond memory. Edie was ready for the ordeal to come to an end, whether Portis was alive or dead. At times like this she just wanted to pack her bags and forget the whole thing. She was tired of being punched by the fat pig. If Bryce called at this moment she would beg him to be serious and take her—

Her heart skipped a beat when the kitchen phone gave a shrill ring. She snatched up the receiver in disbelief and said a breathless hello. There was no answer.

"Bryce?" she whispered.

"Is this Edie Portlock?" a man's voice queried.

"Used to be," she said cautiously. "Who is this?"

"Hello, princess. Sorry to be calling so late. How are you?"

Edie's voice thickened as her eyes welled up. "Daddy, is it really you? Where are you?"

"Oklahoma. How are you, sweetheart?"

"Oh, Daddy, it's so good to hear your voice."

"It's good to hear your voice, too. Who died, Edie? In your letter you said something about—"

"I lied," she told him.

"I figured as much," he said with a sigh. "What's wrong, princess? You sound like you're crying."

Edie lifted a hand to wipe her nose and inadvertently poked herself in the eye with a candy bar. The smart made the tears flow faster, and in sudden anger she threw the Snickers bar against the kitchen wall.

"Daddy, why did you tell me you were dead?"

"That was stupid, wasn't it? I should've known it wouldn't work."

"Mom recognized your handwriting. Why did you do it?" she repeated.

"Never mind that now. What was so important that you had to find me?"

"I'm pregnant. You're going to be a grandfather."

Silence was his reply.

"Daddy, did you hear me?"

"Uh-huh. Just letting it sink in. The last time I saw you, you were still in A-cups and cotton undies."

Edie dropped her second bomb. "The baby doesn't belong to my husband."

Her father emitted a snort of surprise. "Jesus, girl. Are you sure I have the right Edie?"

"I'm sure."

"What does your mother think about this?"

"She doesn't know. Nobody knows."

"Not even Ben?"

"Not even him. Daddy, can you come home? I need your help with something, and I need it soon."

"How is Ben?"

"He's fine. He lives in our old house."

"Is he married yet? Have any kids?"

"No. He's going to be the next police chief."

Max Portlock laughed. "Now why doesn't that surprise me? What about your mother? She still running the tavern?"

"Yes. And she's not married either, in case you're interested. Can we talk about me now?"

"Sure we can. Would it be safe to say Bryce is the father of your baby?"

Edie gasped. "How did you know?"

"You said his name after you answered the phone, remember? Is this the same Bryce your brother moved in with when he left home?"

"Yes," Edie admitted in a low voice. "He came over one night while Portis was out of town and . . . well, it just sort of happened, you know?"

"Uh-huh. Sure. I know you've been crazy about that boy since you could walk."

"I have not," Edie muttered.

"Have too. You used to write his name in that little notebook you had, over and over." Max's voice became serious then. "But you married Portis Jackson, is that right? I'm surprised you landed him."

"I was too," Edie said frankly. "But I didn't know he was sick, Daddy."

"Sick? What do you mean, sick? Is he dying?"

"No. I mean he likes to hurt me."

"You mean he hits you?"

Edie nodded, then she said, "All the time. Worse since I got pregnant, because he knows the baby isn't his. I want you to come back here and get rid of him for me, Daddy. Can you do that?"

"Good God, girl," Max said in a harsh voice. "Are you entirely brainless? Just get the hell out of there."

Edie's eyes filled again. "Does that mean you won't come and help me?"

"Help you what? Kill a man? Why in God's name haven't you told your brother about this?"

"Because after beating Portis to pieces he would make me come and live with him. I don't want to do that to Ben."

"And you wouldn't have your money," her father said knowingly. "Right?"

"Right," Edie mumbled. "What's wrong with liking money?"

"Liking it is fine. Killing for it is what I have a problem with. I can't believe you'd ask me to do something like that."

"I'd do it myself if I knew how," Edie told him. "I can't think of any other way to get rid of him and still have money for my baby. I want my baby to have everything it could ever want. All the best. I don't want it to ever have to worry about being poor. Not like I did. The only problem is, I know Portis is going to treat my baby worse than he treats me, and I can't bear to think of him hurting it. I love it so much."

"What about Bryce?" Max asked. "Doesn't he have a stake in this?"

"It's all a game to him. Daddy, are you going to come and help me or not?"

"I can't," he said, and suddenly his voice sounded hard. "I wouldn't come back there if I could."

"Why not?" Edie cried in dismay. "I was counting on you."

"Then you're in a world of shit, because I'm not going anywhere. I have a new life now, Edie."

She frowned. "Are you remarried?"

"For the last ten years. She got me dry and kept me that way."

"Does she know about us?"

"No. Why do you think I'm calling so late?"

"I see," Edie said, though she didn't see. This was her father. This was the man who had held her, cuddled her, kissed her hurts better, and tucked her in at night. How could he divorce her presence in his past? How could he pretend she was from another life, when she was standing here very much alive and needing him so desperately?

The pain was worse than a slap from Portis. She felt betrayed by her own flesh.

"Does your new wife have money?" Edie asked in a level voice.

"She's loaded. You understand, Edie."

She did, and it sickened her. She forced herself to remain calm. "I suspected something like this when you wanted me to think you were dead. You have no reason to come back."

"I knew you would understand, Edie. You're your father's daughter, through and through. As for this other business, all I can tell you is to forget this killing crap and trust your brother. He's a better man than I ever was."

I know that now, Edie thought. Aloud, she said, "I can't talk anymore, Daddy. I'm glad you called, but I have to hang up now."

"Put an ad in my paper when the baby comes," he said. "Let me know whether it's a boy or a girl."

"I will," Edie lied. "Daddy, before I go, can I ask you something?"

"Sure, princess. What is it?"

"Did you ever love my mother?"

"Sure I did," Max told her. "As much as I can love anybody. You know what I mean, honey. Love can dress up a coat with fancy seamwork, but it doesn't fill up the pockets. You take care of yourself, Edie. I'll be thinking of you."

When the dial tone sounded in her ear, Edie slowly hung up the receiver and looked around herself with a new and painful awareness. Max hadn't left them because things had been tense with Stella, or because he had tried and failed to beat the sensitivity out of Ben. He had left them because of money. Or rather the lack of it. The tavern had to be maintained by a will to work and sheer determination, qualities Max couldn't find in himself or in the bottom of a beer bottle.

Ben knew. He had known all along what Edie refused to see. How it must have galled him to hear her idolizing the man, when he was nothing but a cheap, hard-hearted freeloader living off their mother's blood and sweat.

A wave of disgust and self-loathing washed over Edie as she thought of the pride in Max's voice when he pronounced her her father's daughter.

It wasn't true, was it? Not really. She wasn't like him. She truly loved her mother, and Ben, and she loved her baby. Money wasn't all she thought about.

"I hate you," she whispered suddenly to the microwave oven.

"And you," she said to the gleaming dinette with the outrageously expensive array of silk flowers in their white porcelain vase.

"And you, and you, and you," she said to the range, the refrigerator, and the six-hundred-dollar plant window.

"I don't like you much either," she said to the dented Snickers bar on the ceramic tile floor.

On impulse she got out the phone book and looked up Bryce's name. She picked up the receiver and punched in the number with stiff fingers. As she listened to it ring she wondered how to phrase her question to him. Did he really want her to—

"Hello?" a sleepy female voice answered.

Edie froze.

"Hello?" the voice repeated, and a second later Bryce came on the line. "Who is this?" he asked.

Hanging up didn't occur to Edie.

"It's me," she breathed. "I'm sorry to disturb you. I'll let you go back to . . . whatever."

Bryce started to speak, but Edie replaced the receiver and leaned back against the counter with a deep sigh that bordered somewhere near a sob.

"I knew it," she said to her reflection in the toaster. "And everyone thinks I'm so stupid." She glanced down to her belly then. "But I had to try, didn't I? Just in case he wasn't joking."

So what now? she wondered.

Her eyes found the Snickers bar on the floor.

"No," she said between her teeth. "Eating that isn't going to solve anything."

She left the kitchen and walked into the bathroom, the only room in the house where she could think clearly. When she saw her eye in the mirror, she seriously considered

203

taking Portis's wooden spoon and shoving it through his ear while he slept. The fat, hairy bastard deserved a lot worse.

Too bad she wasn't brave enough. She had known that from the start, hadn't she? No guts, no murder, no money.

Money, murder, misery, marriage—they all started with the letter *M*. How about an *L*? she asked herself. As in leave.

She looked around the kitchen once more, then she made up her mind. All right. She would. She would prove she wasn't like her father. Portis could tell any story and blacken her name all he liked. She didn't care anymore. Ben would keep her until the baby came, and he might even help her find a job after its arrival.

The mere thought of a job made Edie slightly nauseous, but she fought back the sickness with a vision of Portis hovering over her baby's crib with a spoon in his hairy hand. It would never happen, she vowed.

Her suitcases were open on the bed when Portis came home. He took one look at the hastily folded contents and puffed up his chest in rage.

"What the fuck is wrong with everyone tonight? What the hell do you think you're doing?"

Edie came out of the walk-in closet and bit her lip in an effort to still her sudden trembling. If he saw any fear it would be worse for her.

"I'm leaving you, Portis."

"You're what?"

"You heard me. And don't you dare try to stop me."

Portis sauntered over to the bed and casually tipped one suitcase onto the floor. "I told you what would happen, Edie. I warned you of what I would do."

She looked at the clothes that tumbled out of the suitcase. Her voice sounded braver than she felt. "Why? Why would you bother, Portis? You get what you want from Kayleen."

"What?" His red eyes narrowed. "What did you say?"

"You heard me. I'm talking about Kayleen, your secretary, lover, and vacation mate. Don't pretend you don't know what I mean." Edie struggled to get down to the floor and pick up the clothes and the suitcase. "But I don't care about her. I never did. I just want to leave. When I file for divorce I might use her as grounds to save time and—"

She wasn't able to finish. Portis grabbed her by the hair and jerked her head back to slap her hard across the face. "You're not going anywhere, you sorry bitch. Do you hear me?"

Edie tried to scream, but thick, hot blood blocked her mouth and throat. She beat at his bulky frame with her fists and felt stinging pain as he pulled her by the hair across the floor. Her knees burned on the carpet as he tugged her along, and she finally managed a sharp cry of pain as he shoved her inside the closet and viciously kicked her in the spine.

"Forgetting who I am, aren't you?" Portis wheezed as he slammed the double doors shut. "I'm the guy you don't want to fuck with, Edie. If you think I'm going to let you run off and cry to your brother and the rest of the town about what a bad man I am, you can think again. You're not going anywhere until I say so, you money-sucking slut."

"Keep your money!" Edie shrieked at him from behind the doors. "I don't want anything from you!"

"That's good," Portis said, "because you've just gone on a starvation diet. When you decide you like living here after all, maybe I'll let you out. You're not going to fuck things up for me, girlie. Not now."

"I have a doctor's appointment tomorrow," Edie warned.

"Not anymore, you don't. Now shut your ass up before I come in there and shut it for you."

Edie shut up. Her aching body couldn't take any more abuse. She curled up on her side and blinked in the darkness as she worried over the fierceness of his attack. He definitely hadn't been playing sex games this time. But he couldn't be serious about leaving her there until she changed her mind, she told herself. He wasn't that crazy.

Chapter Twenty

George Legget lifted his hands in the air and uttered a noise of exasperation that echoed in the quiet station.

"I realize I'm just a figurehead, but will someone please tell me what the hell is going on around here?"

Hannah looked up from her desk. "What do you mean?"

"What do I mean?" George pointed to Ben and Bryce, who had returned from shift duty and were silently filling out reports. "Nobody talks anymore. It's quiet as a goddamned church in here. Christ, McKee, I know it's bad when you tell your jokes, but it's worse when you don't. And Hannah, you've been looking like a cat choking on a rabbit for the last two or three days. I don't know what the hell your problem is, Portlock, but I wish somebody would clue me in. I've never seen so many sad-assed faces in my life."

Bryce and Hannah looked at each other. Ben's attention remained on his missing person report. When the phone rang, Hannah snatched it up. After answering, she looked at Ben. "It's for you, Officer Portlock. I'll transfer it over."

"Thanks." He waited, then picked up the receiver and identified himself.

"Hi, Ben, this is Boyer Burke. I never got around to thanking you for getting that doe out so quick. I appreciate your taking the time to take care of that for me and I wanted to—"

"The doe?" Ben said in confusion. "The man I sent out there said he couldn't find her. I thought you'd already taken care of it."

"Huh," Boyer said. "Well, if you didn't and I didn't, then who did?"

"Maybe it was our man after all," Ben murmured, half to himself.

"You just said he couldn't find her."

"Not that man. But the gun still doesn't make sense. He's never used a gun before."

"Who hasn't used a gun before?"

Ben blinked. "Sorry, I was thinking aloud. I want to thank you for calling, Boyer." He started to say good-bye, then he changed his mind. "Wait a minute. The morning you found the deer, who did you talk to?"

"Hannah Winegarten, there at the station."

"Anybody else? Any neighbors, or anyone close by?"

"No one."

"Okay. Thanks a lot."

Ben told her good-bye and hung up his phone. Hannah had called for Haden on the radio that morning, but Haden had been busy, so Ben had used the radio in his Jeep to tell Hannah that he would take the call and run out to Boyer's. That meant the only people who knew about the dead doe were Hannah, Haden, Boyer herself, and—

Ben had a sudden vision of Philip Taylor's police band radio sitting on the kitchen table in the Taylor home.

No, he told himself. Don't even consider it.

He shook his head, as if to clear the vision from his brain.

He didn't like what he was thinking. A poacher wouldn't have come back for the deer. The meat wouldn't be any

208

good. But what if a poacher had shot the deer, and someone else, someone Ben didn't want to think about, had come and taken the deer's corpse before Ben or Boyer could have it removed? Someone with access to a police band radio.

"Well?" George said sharply. "Come on. How about it? Is someone going to talk to me today? Bryce, what about Ailey? Has he told you what was taken in the burglary?"

"He thinks he's missing some sodium pentobarbital."

"What? Truth serum?"

"Close. He sold it to the vet occasionally."

George snorted. "What for? To get the truth out of animals? Fifi, did you take that pork chop off the table? Tell the truth now, you bad little dog."

Bryce had to smile. "Ailey said the old vet used it to put animals to sleep. The new one uses gas and doesn't buy it."

"How much was taken?"

"Ailey couldn't say exactly."

"Great. He'd last five minutes in a tax audit. Maybe that IRS guy you told me about is really here to look at him." The chief glanced at Ben then. "Anything of interest evolve for you today, Inspector Portlock?"

Ben jerked the report from his typewriter and moved to place it in the file basket on Hannah's desk. "Nothing that would interest you, Chief Legget."

"Well, fuck you too, bad boy. Jesus, I'm just trying to get a little response around here."

Bryce finished his own report and hurried to catch up with the departing Ben.

"Hey," he said once they were outside. Ben paused with his hand on the door of his patrol car.

"What?"

"What do you say two old buddies act like old buddies and drink a beer together?"

Ben hesitated before shaking his head. "Can't do it tonight. Some other time."

"Okay. Say, how's your sister getting along? Is she coming pretty close?"

"Yeah, I guess," Ben said. "I haven't talked to her for a couple days. Listen, I'll see you tomorrow."

"Sure." Bryce shoved his hands in his pockets and wandered down the sidewalk toward Milly's. Ben watched him a moment before getting in the patrol car and starting the engine. He didn't have any plans tonight. He just didn't feel like company. Not with his mind working the way it was.

When he found Michelle's Datsun in his driveway he felt his muscles tense. She climbed out of the car as he arrived, and he groaned to himself as he saw the hopeful smile on her face.

Her smile had always struck Ben as being somewhat incongruous with the rest of her. It had a way of making her appear sweet and guileless and almost childishly innocent. Almost.

"It's been a week," she said to him. "I couldn't stand it another day."

Ben left the patrol car and walked past her to his front door. "Come in, Michelle. I want to talk to you."

She followed him inside, where she immediately kicked off her black pumps and unbuttoned the jacket of her charcoal suit. She was still smiling.

"I've missed talking to you, too, Ben. You know I really should have let Lura have the school secretary job. All that boring paperwork is right up her alley. Do you have anything decent to drink?"

"Sit down," Ben told her. "You won't be staying long enough for a drink."

"Oh. Are we going somewhere?"

"You are."

The smile wilted. Her violet eyes lost all pretense of ignorance and became wary. "In that case, I think I'd prefer to stand."

"Suit yourself." Purposely avoiding the couch, Ben sat down in the chair nearest the door. When he looked at Michelle, she put her hands behind her back and spread her feet apart, facing him as if she were in front of a firing squad. Ben wondered if she imagined herself to have the psychological advantage in that pose. He said, "I don't want to come home and find you sitting in my driveway ever again. I thought I made that clear to you the last time we spoke. Obviously, I didn't."

Michelle's shrug was light. "You said to give you some room, and that's just what I did. If you want another week, just say so."

Ben stared at her. "Christ, you're hard-headed. I don't know how to make it any clearer, Michelle. I've tried to avoid hurting you, but you're being deliberately obtuse. The fact is, I don't want to see you this week, next week, or any week thereafter. Do you understand?"

Michelle abandoned her stance to drop down to the couch with a determined plop. "Why?"

"Do I need to give you the reasons? Isn't it enough that I say I don't?"

"Just give me one reason. You owe me that much."

Ben's fist dropped to his knee. "Dammit, why don't you show some pride and leave? I'm not going to turn this into a debate."

"One reason," Michelle repeated. "I want one."

"I don't love you," he said flatly.

"Is that it?" She gave a high, bitter laugh and collapsed against the cushions. "My God, you really had me worried for a minute. I thought it was something serious. I don't love you either, Ben."

"Then why are you here?"

"Do I need to give you the reasons?" she mimicked. "I will, if you like. You are what is known as a catch in this town. You have the most promising future of any eligible bachelor around. Everyone knows you'll be chief when George Legget retires."

Ben rubbed his face. "You amaze me, Michelle. You really do. Even when you're being blunt you manage to skirt the truth."

Her violet eyes glittered. "The truth being . . . ?"

211

"That this doesn't have anything to do with me. It's about you and Lura. As I recall, you didn't know I existed until the day I asked her out. Then you dropped everything and came after me. You couldn't stand the thought of someone actually preferring her over you. You still can't."

Michelle sat up. "That's absurd."

"Is it?" Ben charged. "Then why did you beat tracks to my door the day I came back to town? Why did you snatch that job at the school away from her? Why is every other word out of your mouth some slur against her?"

"My, my, aren't we being protective?" Michelle replied. "Do go on, though. I'm all ears."

"You don't want me," Ben asserted. "You want to prove some ancient, misdirected point to Lura and yourself."

Michelle yawned and checked her breath against her palm. After a moment she said, "Are you finished? Is it my turn yet? You've got eyes, Ben. Both of us know she's nowhere near my level. I'll admit to some rivalry when we were younger, but it was only because she had something I wanted. She had you. I still don't know how she managed it, but Lura knew I had my eye on you and suddenly you were going out with her. So you see, it's *she* who has always been envious of *me*. It's easy to see how you came up with a different interpretation.

"Now, I admit I don't love you," she went on, "but the sex was always wonderful, and I do like and admire you. I think we're both too mature to put ourselves through the angst-ridden discomforts of love, aren't we? We're not teenagers with throbbing hearts anymore, we're adults with adult needs and desires. Try to deny it if you will, but we were good together once, and we can be good together again. I can give you anything you need, Ben. Passion, strength, companionship, warmth . . ."

When he said nothing, she moved to a kneeling position before him and placed her hands on the tops of his thighs. "I realize Lura's return has been an ordeal for you. You've never spoken of it, but I've sensed the guilt you feel over what you did. Don't confuse those feelings with something more meaningful. If you truly cared for her, you would never have turned her in all those years ago. Eventually, you'll realize this on your own, but I'm not willing to sit by and watch you suffer until you do. Have you taken a good look at yourself lately?"

Ben sighed and extended a hand to stroke the silky black length of her hair. His voice was deceptively soft. "Michelle, you don't have a clue, do you?"

Her lips curved in satisfaction as she rubbed her cheek against his hand. "A clue to what?"

"To me. You once said you weren't stupid. You're going to have the chance to prove it."

Michelle lifted her head to study his face. His eyes were a brilliant, shimmering green with dark flecks of blue.

"How?" she asked.

"By having the brains to get out of here before I lose control and snap your fucking neck."

"I won't!" She slapped his hands away and slid back on the seat of her skirt. "You have no idea what you're saying, Ben. You think you're still in love with her, but you're not. And she doesn't love you. She never has. Lura wanted you for the same reason I do, because people in Dumford respect you. Lura wasn't a frog when she was with you, she was the pitching star's girl, the local hero's fiancée. She loved the attention, but she never loved you. I knew she didn't, and that's why I hated her so much. It was so unfair to you."

"Get out," Ben said.

"No," Michelle wailed. "You're mine now. I'm so much prettier than she is, Ben. She looks like a bag lady, for Christ's sake. I'll make you a better wife, and when you run for sheriff I'll be right there beside—"

"I'm warning you," Ben said calmly. "You can walk out or be dragged out."

On came the tears. He had expected them before now, but he knew he wouldn't be disappointed. Her mascara made rings under her eyes as she worked up a good sob.

"If you make me go, I'll kill myself," she swore. "I've invested too much time in this relationship to lose you now. I will. I'll kill myself, Ben."

He reached down to his hip and unsnapped his gun holster. "Then do it now and let me call the county morgue. I don't care how you get out of my life, I just want you out of it."

The rings around her eyes widened as she looked at the revolver he extended to her.

"Well?" Ben said.

Her expression said she expected him to jerk it back when she reached for it, but he surprised her by letting her take the revolver into her hands.

"What does she have that's so goddamned special?"

"You're stalling, Michelle. Do it or get out."

The tears stopped. Michelle's lips tightened in sudden anger and the ringed violet eyes narrowed to slits.

"You used me. All this time I was just someone to fuck until Lura came home. Right?"

"Right," Ben said. "Did you confuse that with something more meaningful?"

"You bastard."

He expected her to turn the revolver on him and pull the trigger. He didn't expect her to throw it at him. He tried to duck, but the flying metal caught him on the left brow and plowed into the flesh. A dark red spurt of blood was followed by a warm stream that coursed over his cheek and ran thick down the line of his jaw.

At sight of the blood Michelle emitted a frantic squeak and grabbed her purse from the couch with one hand while snatching her discarded heels from the floor with the other. Ben came out of his chair in a threatening motion, but she dodged him and ran for the door in a blind rush. In less than a second she was outside. In another five seconds Ben heard the Datsun's tires scream in tread death as the car left his drive.

He closed his door with a smile, and painful though it was, he found himself chuckling as he moved to retrieve his revolver. Anticipating her threat, he had unloaded the revolver before getting out of his car. The scene hadn't gone exactly as expected, but the look on her face at the sight of his blood was priceless. Ben had to hold his stomach as he made his way into the bathroom to survey the damage. He hadn't felt this good in days. She was gone. Finally.

The cut wasn't bad, he decided—three or four aspirin and one large bandage would take care of it. A small price to pay for his freedom. He poured peroxide on a clean washcloth and pressed it hard against the wound to stanch the still trickling blood. The tenderness of the swelling made him wince, but he endured the sting of the peroxide without a sound. His thoughts were already returning to Boyer's dead doe, and the theories his mind was presenting him. If he admitted what he was thinking to himself, he wouldn't be able to look at his reflection in the mirror.

She may have gone for starlit walks, but Lura couldn't have done those horrible, grisly things to those animals. At least Ben didn't think she could. Eight years ago he had guessed wrong about what she could and couldn't do, but he believed he knew her well enough to—

He turned away from the mirror and reached for the box of bandages on the shelf above the toilet.

No use kidding himself about that. He didn't know Lura. He didn't know her at all. She had made that abundantly clear to him.

After applying the bandage he left the bathroom and walked into his bedroom to pick up the bag of diaries. Hannah's journal had left him ambivalent, and he knew his ambivalence was evident to her. He could only guess what had happened after her last happy journal entry about plane tickets and packing and secrecy. California had been a blistering disappointment for Hannah, and the man who had lured her there was responsible for creating the brittle, embittered Hannah of the present.

Ben didn't know what to say to her now. He had to fight the urge to apologize each time he saw her. He felt as though he should apologize for reading her journal and intruding upon that most private period of her life. It had made him feel embarrassed and angry and ashamed to be reading her carefully penned words on those half-burnt pages.

But that didn't stop him from looking at the other diaries. There was still a chance, remote though it might be, that Calvin had seen something in one of them that had directly or indirectly figured in his death.

After carrying the bag out of his bedroom he decided to sort through the contents and see how many diaries there were to read. He dumped the contents of the bag and began arranging the books in two piles on the floor in front of the couch. When he came across a small blue notebook with steel ring binders, he paused. It was different from the other diaries in the bag, most of which had leather tongues and little metal locks on the covers. This looked more like something bought for school use. Curious, he flipped it open and found a poem scrawled on the inside cover:

> *No thought you have is yours,*
> *For it's all been thought before.*
> *The feelings you know are the same,*
> *So common they even have names.*

A product of the author, who evidently fancied herself a budding poet, Ben thought. His interest piqued, he dispensed with the start of the notebook and plunged right into the middle pages. Some of the diaries he had looked through were empty but for the first few pages, where the author had doubtlessly looked back upon what was written and decided to abandon the project. Others were completely filled, as was this one from the looks of it. Ben settled himself into a comfortable position on the couch and began to read.

Five minutes later he forced his eyes away from the page and took a long breath.

I can't read this, he thought. Not this one. Hannah's journal was different. This would be wrong. This is none of my—

"Fuck it," he said aloud. "I'm reading it."

Chapter Twenty-One

"I've been here almost an hour and you haven't said three words to me," Bryce complained.

Lura finished stacking the water glasses behind the counter before looking at him. "Then why are you still here?"

"Call me tenacious. Call me stubborn. You can even call me a butthead if you want to, but don't go on ignoring me. It's driving me crazy."

Lura's mouth curved. "You do look a little distraught."

Bryce lifted his brows. "That's over a dozen words now. I'm doing better." He paused to look around himself before continuing. "I've tried to call you every day. I want to apologize again for the things I said to you. I know I upset you, and if I thought you had plenty of Bounty back there I'd shed blood on your counter just to show you how sorry I am."

"That won't be necessary," Lura said. "I haven't returned your calls because I've had my hands full with work and Mama. She hasn't been feeling well lately, so I've been trying to keep an eye on her."

"Is it serious?" Bryce asked.

"No, it's just enough to worry over. How are things with you?"

His voice lowered. "If you mean Edie, I haven't seen her. She called me a few nights ago, but I had company. When I got on the phone, Edie mumbled something and hung up."

"Company?" Lura echoed.

Bryce's mouth twitched. "I decided I'd been celibate longer than was healthy."

"So you're giving up on Edie?"

He shrugged. "I don't have much choice. We both know what kind of person she is, and I'd be a complete fool to go on telling myself otherwise."

Lura saw something in his face that made her pause. "Bryce, this started a long time ago, didn't it? In school you hung around with Ben, but you were always teasing Edie. I remember that much."

His smile was grudging. "The seven years between our ages meant a lot more then than it does now. Not to mention the fact that Ben would have killed me if I had laid a finger on her. By the time she was old enough, she'd already decided that I was bad news for a girl's reputation. Then she married Portis."

"So you moved to the city and got married yourself," Lura said.

"It wasn't what you're thinking. I really thought I was going to make a life for myself away from Dumford. When the marriage failed, there didn't seem to be any reason to stay there. I quit my job at the ranch and came home."

Lura excused herself to deliver a check to a foursome at a table. When she returned, she said, "You worked on a ranch in the city?"

"It was southeast of the city," he explained. "The owner inherited the place and had no idea how to make money off cattle. I showed him how. She was his sister, incidentally."

"Who was?"

"The girl I married and divorced. There were some fine horses there on the ranch, too. I bought Maggie from him before I left. Twila's got a stud farm now, I heard."

"What happened between you?" Lura asked. "You and Twila."

"She wanted to party, I wanted to stay home. She called me a hick, I called her a bimbo. And so it went."

"Funny," Lura murmured, "but I can't imagine you as being settled down."

"Neither can anyone else, apparently," Bryce said in a dry voice.

Lura nodded in sympathy and looked past him. The foursome in the booth had finished their coffee and were ready to leave, so she excused herself to ring up their check. When she returned this time, she hesitated before asking her question.

"Bryce, tell me if this is too personal, but how did you and Edie come to—"

"Don't ask," he interrupted. "Let's just say it was something I thought both of us wanted."

"I'm sorry," Lura said.

Bryce grinned. "Not half as sorry as I am. I think I've aged ten years in the last nine months. See the gray in my hair? In another few years I'll look like you. And while we're on the subject, I think I've solved the mystery of your pubic hair."

Lura's cheeks heated. "Oh really?"

"Uh-huh." He pointed to her face. "Your eyebrows are still dark. That's a dead giveaway."

She considered flipping him with his coffee spoon, but he was already coming around the counter toward her. When he put his arms around her, she looked at him in surprise.

"If we were smart, we would've fallen for each other instead of those knucklehead Portlocks," he said. "I won't ever hurt you again, Lura. I promise."

Lura hugged him, then leaned back. "If you do, I'll ask for that blood you offered earlier."

220

"It's a deal." Bryce stepped away from her and poked his head through the kitchen window. "Milly? Where are you?"

There was some rustling in the back, and then Milly's white head appeared. "You made me lose count. Napkin inventory is serious business, Bryce. What do you want?"

"A chocolate-pecan pie of my very own. How about making me one?"

"Sweet Jesus," Milly spat. "You interrupt me for that? Pick it up tomorrow, and be prepared to pay extra."

"Thanks," Bryce called. To Lura he said, "Thought I'd check to see if she was hiding under the window. Next to Hannah, Milly's a saint, but they're both afflicted with elephant ears. I'm not sure how it happens, but I think it has something to do with lack of sex. The juices dry up and go to their heads or something, I don't know. Here, let me see your ears, Lura. I just want to check my theory."

Lura laughed and batted him away. "My ears are fine, thank you. It's your theory that needs work."

"Speaking of work, would it be out of line to ask for a little service?" a cold voice asked.

Bryce and Lura turned to see a grim-faced Michelle approach the counter.

"I've been sitting in a booth for five minutes. What does it take to get waited on?"

"Bullshit." Bryce moved around the counter to stand beside her. "You just walked in the door. I heard the bell tinkle."

Michelle ignored him and sat down on a stool. "This place is dead tonight. Had much business since you started working here, Lura?"

Bryce looked closely at Michelle and whistled through his teeth. "I've seen carrion on the road look better. Who does your makeup, coon eyes?"

Lura bit her lip. "Would you like to look at a menu, Michelle?"

"No. I'd like a cup of coffee if it's not too much trouble."

Bryce propped an elbow on the counter. "So what's the problem, Michelle? Did you chip a nail, or what?"

She glared at him. "Don't you have anything better to do with your time?"

"Not since 'Little House on the Prairie' was canceled. Come on, Mishy. Who made our widdle friend cry?"

Michelle's ruby fingernails clicked against the cup of coffee Lura placed before her.

"No one made me cry. If you must know, I've just ended my relationship with Ben."

Lura kept her face expressionless when Michelle glanced up to see her reaction. Bryce clucked his tongue.

"I'm sure it was painful."

"It was," Michelle admitted. "But one of us had to have the strength to do it."

"How noble of you," Bryce said. "How's Ben taking it?"

"Not very well. He flew into a rage, and I think he may have hurt himself."

"You didn't stay to find out?"

"I was too frightened."

Bryce nodded. "Yes. Ben Portlock in a rage is a frightening thing to behold."

"You're not taking this very seriously," Michelle snapped.

"About as serious as Ben is taking it, I'm sure."

The coffee shook itself out of her cup as Michelle threw herself off the stool. Bryce and Lura watched her stalk out of the restaurant and heard the bell on the door jangle loudly with her departure. When she was gone they turned to look at each other.

"He dumped her," said Bryce.

Lura arched one brow. "What do you think she meant when she said he may have hurt himself?"

"I dunno. She probably drew blood before she left and rationalized that it was all his fault. Maybe I'll drive by and see if he needs a rabies shot." He stood up on the rungs of his stool and leaned across the counter to kiss her on the cheek. "I'll see you later. Don't take any napkins home with you tonight."

Lura smiled and waved him on. As she watched him go she touched the cheek he had kissed and found herself wondering over his earlier statement. She almost wished she and Bryce had fallen for each other. Unlike Ben, Bryce had no moral compact with the everloving truth.

She was still thinking about it an hour later as she switched off the ignition of the Toyota and sat gazing absently across the street. She pinched her arm when she caught herself smiling over Michelle's story. It wasn't funny. She knew why Ben had ended his relationship with her cousin, but the fact that he had wouldn't bring Lura and him any closer together. Until he could accept her silence, there would be nothing but bitterness between them.

She wanted it to be different. Didn't he believe she did? She hated the silence more than he could ever know. But the truth would only widen the schism. Once again, he would be compelled to do the right thing, and in this case, Lura knew it would have devastating results. Her own actions may have been wrong in the eyes of society, but at the time she had believed she was preventing a much greater wrong. Now, however, she wasn't so sure.

Lura wished she could go to him. Tonight, when all the houses were dark and the gibbous moon was the only light, she wished she could steal across the road on bare, silent feet and open the door to his house. He would be sleeping in the bed by the window, with pale stripes of moonlight illuminating his face and hair. The room would be quiet, the only sound and movement the slow rise and fall of his chest. His body would be warm beneath the carelessly crumpled—"

"Lura, are you coming in?"

Lura's heart nearly stopped when her mother approached the car. She exhaled, then sucked in her breath again as she saw what her mother was wearing. Annette was dressed in jeans, a bulky sweater, and an overcoat. Perfect gear for a walk on a brisk October night.

"Where have you *been?*" Lura asked as she threw open the car door.

"Ben? Ben's at home," Annette said with a frown. "His car is right there, see?"

The slam of the car door seemed to echo up the block. Lura took her mother's arm and guided her up to the porch.

"Mama, where's Phil? Is he asleep?"

"Did you know your sixth sense is more sensitive in the fall?" Annette replied. "Something about the coolness of the weather and the changing atmosphere. I feel it, don't you?"

"Let's get inside." Lura inserted the key and felt the knob twist in her hand. Phil opened the door and breathed an audible sigh of relief.

"Thank God. I thought I'd lost her. I fell asleep on the couch and when I woke up she was gone."

"Out for another walk, apparently," Lura informed him as she led Annette to a chair at the kitchen table. "What time did you fall asleep, Phil?"

"I didn't exactly check my watch."

"Phil . . ."

"Must've been after nine. Why?"

"She's been wandering around for more than an hour, that's why. Are you cold, Mama? You haven't taken your hands out of your pockets. Do you want some tea, or some hot chocolate?"

"Do we have any Nescafé?"

"Christ," Phil muttered. "I'm ready to get cable anytime you are, Lura. HBO doesn't have commercials."

She ignored him. "Tea or hot chocolate, Mama. Those are your choices."

Annette sniffed. "I don't want anything. I want to go to bed now. I have a dream to continue."

"Not so fast," Phil said. "First I want you to sit down

and tell us where you've been. You didn't dress up like this to go out and find your squirrel friend, did you?"

"I don't know what you're talking about. I don't associate with squirrels. Although I wouldn't mind a nice rabbit. We used to eat them quite regularly at home, you know."

"I know. You've told us all about baked Bugs Bunny before. Right now I want to hear why you sneaked out of the house the minute I was asleep."

Annette drew herself up. "Lura Josephine, would you please tell Philip Napoleon to stop treating me like some Romper Room refugee? If I want to have jam on my graham crackers, what business is it of his?"

Phil looked at his sister. "Are you ready for a vote on the nuthouse yet?"

Lura's jaw dropped, and before she fully realized what she was doing, her hand shot out and slapped her brother hard across the face.

Annette began to applaud. "Keep going. I saw this on 'Remington Steele.' Philip looks like him, doesn't he?"

Her children ignored her. Phil's gaze was cold as the surprise on his reddened face gave way to contempt.

"I stopped kidding myself the day you came home, Lura. The first time I saw the pity in your eyes, I stopped telling myself we could be a normal family. When are you going to stop kidding yourself?"

Lura rubbed her stinging hand against the skirt of her waitress uniform. "I'm sorry I did that, Phil. Please forgive me. I hear what you're saying."

"I don't think you do," he said, and as she opened her mouth to reply, he turned on his heel and left the kitchen. A moment later Lura heard the door to his bedroom close with a controlled click. She looked helplessly at her mother.

"What am I going to do, Mama?"

"I don't know," Annette said in a low voice. "Maybe you should see an attorney." She brought her hands out of her pockets to wipe at her runny nose. "I really don't know what I've done to . . . Lura?"

Lura was having trouble breathing. Her mouth was open and her lungs were heaving, but she couldn't seem to find any air as she stared at her mother's bloody hands. The blood was so thick it had dried black and crusted around the fingernails.

"Mama, what have you done?" she asked in a choked whisper.

Annette followed Lura's horrified stare to look at her hands. "My sixth sense was in prime condition. It still is. That's why I'd like to finish my dream. I need to see what happens. I don't like two-parters, but what can you do?"

Lura's throat was blocked. Her eyes were stinging. She pulled her mother from the chair and drew her over to the sink. Annette stood patiently while Lura poured dish soap on her hands and turned on the water.

"I don't know what you're so upset about," Annette said. "You really are a foolish girl, Lura. Ever since you were a child you've cried at the drop of a cat."

"Cat?" Lura said in a trembling voice. "Was it another cat?"

"No, you can't have another cat. You kids didn't take care of the first one."

Lura watched a tear from her cheek fall and join the rust-colored water in the sink. "You really are sick, aren't you Mama?" she said dully. "The first time I thought you had a good reason. I thought I knew why you did it, and I wanted to protect you. I didn't know anything, did I?"

"You still don't," Annette said sharply. "For instance, do you know why Renée had so many problems? His blood was tainted. That's right. His blood was tainted black with lust and greed and misery. They told them it would happen. They warned them not to have children. And this town is no different. Dumford blood is tainted. It runs black as pitch with the same lust, greed, and misery that killed Christ himself. You don't see it because it's got thick skin that doesn't bleed when it's cut. It's dead skin. Dead skin with golden hair and wide blue eyes that look—"

"Shut up," Lura sobbed. "I don't understand a word of what you're saying, so please just be quiet and don't talk. I don't want to hear any more."

"Fine," Annette said. "But I told you so. You don't know anything. He wouldn't inherit a dime until he was married, and even then he'd have to split everything with his half sister, so he solved the problem by marrying her. He had it all, he did. Papa was so smart. Smarter than his own father, who was another murderer, by the way."

Lura stopped scrubbing her mother's hands. "You're talking about . . . your father married his half sister?"

"Did Marie tell you that? Shame on her. We were forbidden to speak of it. All the way back. Murder in the blood for generations. Did you ever hear of Gilles de Rais?"

"Mama . . ." Lura put her hands to her face and shook her head. "I can't take much more of this. I'm sorry, but I can't."

Annette's expression turned quizzical. "Didn't I ask you for a cup of cocoa a moment ago?"

"I'll get it for you now. Dry your hands and go to your room. You can drink it in bed."

Lura prepared the cocoa and sat with quivering limbs while she watched her mother drink it. When the cup was empty she took it and carried it around the room with her as she checked the windows. In the hall she stopped outside her brother's room and knocked lightly on the door.

"Phil, are you asleep?"

"No," came the muffled response.

She opened the door and saw him lying on the bed. She made her way through the dimness and sat down on the edge of the mattress. Phil put his arms behind his head and waited.

"I've done some thinking," she said.

"Did I hear you crying?"

"Yes. I've decided you're right. We need to get her out of here as soon as possible."

"Why the sudden turnaround?"

Lura tried to shrug. "I was wrong. Phil, can I ask you something?"

"What?"

"How well do you remember the night Dad died?"

Phil's voice became cool. "Not very well at all. I guess I've blocked it out or something. Why?"

"No reason," Lura said. "I'll call the doctor first thing tomorrow."

"He'll tell you it's for the best. You'll see."

"Yes," she murmured. "Well, good night."

"Good night. And don't worry, Lura. We're doing the right thing."

The irony of those words didn't escape her as Lura left her brother's room. The right thing. She wanted to scream. Instead, she thought about Phil. He knew. He knew what their mother had done that night long ago, and he doubtlessly knew what the woman was doing now. So why did he continue to hide it from Lura? Did he think she wasn't aware of what was going on? Again, the irony was inescapable. Here they were, both devoted to protecting their certifiably insane mother, yet they continued to lie to each other about the facts of the situation.

Lura wanted to kick herself for not realizing those same facts sooner. But how was she to have known? Her mother's mind was a mysterious knit of confusion that unraveled itself one squirming stitch at a time. Rape, incest, murder ... She wanted to believe those stories were the product of a chemically damaged brain, but something, some taint in the blood perhaps, told her they were true.

Eight years of my life, she thought. Eight years wasted because I refused to look beyond love and acknowledge the fact that my mother is dangerously ill.

Lura's first impulse was to run away. Go back to her quiet jail cell and hide from the rest of the world. Or go to Ben and beg him to help her trudge through the mire of truth and come out with a clear conscience. There were limits to family loyalty weren't there? The protection of a loved one had to end somewhere, didn't it?

The questions were moot, she realized with a sigh. Tomorrow she would begin proceedings to have her mother committed. The courts would do the same if she went forward with the truth. One way or another, justice was still being served.

With that thought Lura retired to her bedroom and made ready for bed. She slid between the sheets and took several calming breaths, but guilt prevented her eyes from closing. The blood on her mother's hands stained her eyelids and fused the image with another: Ordney Taylor collapsed on top of the kitchen table, blood oozing from a jagged trench carved into his abdomen. Lura's mother stood over him, his bone-handled hunting knife in her hand. Phil, his eyes dilated with shock, hunched in the corner and stared fearfully at his salivating mother.

Lura battled the image, but the scene was already in motion. Her nostrils strained against the remembered stench of bourbon, blood, and the smell of her own vomit as her senses revolted at the sight of her dead father. Her mother had turned at the sound of Lura's heaves and dropped the knife. "Help me get him out of here," she begged Lura. "Please, help me. We've got to get him out of here."

Lura's shock had blocked her comprehension. She heard herself repeating the same question over and over: "What happened?"

Annette, her gray hair wild, hands dipped in blood, ignored the question. Spit glistened on her lips as she spoke. "I'll help you get him into his truck. Take him somewhere. Take him someplace where . . ." Her eyes rolled in panic as she inadvertently stepped on the knife. "Hide it. We have to hide what's happened here. Don't you see? He was drunk. He stumbled and fell . . . the tracks! Take him to the tracks, Lura. Push him out onto the tracks and make sure his stomach is where the train will . . . we have to hide this. You see that, don't you?"

"But, Mama, we can't—"

"For me, Lura! Oh, God, please, you have to do this for me! They'll take me away from you. Don't you know that? They'll separate us. They'll tear us apart!"

Numb with fear and panic, Lura had denied the urgent sense of wrongness and retched three more times before helping her ranting mother move the body into her father's truck.

"We have to do this," Annette swore as she handed Lura the keys. "You understand, don't you? Leave the truck there and come back as fast as you can. My car is still in the shop and I don't know how to drive his cycle, but you don't mind walking, do you? Run, if you can. Yes, I think you should run. I'll clean up the . . . mess. I'll do that and you do this and we'll all be fine. He was drunk, remember. So drunk he couldn't walk. He got out of the truck to pee and passed out on the tracks. The train comes along and . . . do you love me, Lura? Do you love me enough to do this for me? Do you?"

Lura did, though she didn't understand why. By the time she returned, her mother had sobered up enough to take a bottle of pills and lay down on the floor of the garage next to the fuming exhaust pipe of Ordney's motorcycle. In the house, Phil was still in the kitchen corner, his young face frozen in a white mask of horror.

The ambulance lights and siren were etched into Lura's memory with traumatic clarity. Her mother was taken away, and the police arrived an hour later. Ben had seen Lura on the way home from Stella's. Curious as to why she was driving Ordney's truck so fast at such a late hour, he had followed her. At the trial he testified that he saw her drag the limp form of a man across the tracks only minutes before the train came. Ordney Taylor was cut in half.

Lura squeezed her eyes shut and felt her stomach churn under the merciless pain brought by the memories.

I'm not going through it again, she promised herself. I love her, God knows I love her, but I can't go through that again.

In sending her mother away, Lura would stop the madness and still keep the secret. With any luck, she wasn't too late. By tomorrow she thought she would know if Annette's speech about dead skin with golden hair and wide blue eyes had any meaning. Lura could only pray it didn't.

Chapter Twenty-Two

When looked at through the eyelashes, coffee grounds reminded Hannah of ants. Brewed black ants. She hastily tossed out the used filter and filled a new one with fresh grounds. George drank too much coffee, she thought to herself. In another few years the caffeine would leave his bones as brittle as toothpicks. And the cigars he had taken up would ruin his olfactory equipment. She supposed he thought the halo of blue smoke around his head made him look the part of a distinguished soon-to-be-retired police chief. Hannah thought it made him look like a squinty-eyed crime boss from someplace like New Jersey.

If she tried, she could find at least a dozen other things to dislike about the man, but the silent derogation left a bad taste in her mouth and a sick feeling in her stomach. She had yet to redeem herself through the solution of Calvin Horn's murder, for there seemed to be no hope of following up on the conversation she had overheard at the depot. Kurt was no longer any help to her. He'd had his fun with the telephone, and he didn't care what she did to prove their theory. The urge to confide in someone else was battled daily, sometimes hourly.

She returned to her desk and glanced across the room at Bryce McKee. When looked at through the eyelashes, it was easy to pretend he was his father. Not the cruel, laughing stranger who had left her in a Huntington Beach motel room, but the gentle, humorous man she had fallen in love with. On a whim, she figured the difference in ages between Bryce and herself. He was only fifteen years younger than she.

Under the desk, her knees twitched. Hannah clamped her legs together and forced herself to concentrate on the papers on her desk. The filing was always light, so she had time to go through each report and see who had done what. Three speeding citations; a complaint about a neighbor's vicious dog; a drunken argument between a husband and wife (Hannah mentally filed this one away for future use); and a report of a missing person.

Now *that* was news, Hannah decided, as she read over the details. When she finished the report, her tongue was pattering against her palate. "I always knew that girl was trouble," she murmured to herself.

"What?" George lifted his head like a dog shaken out of sleep. "Did somebody actually say something?"

Hannah chose her words carefully. "I was merely making a comment to myself in reference to Ben's missing person report."

The chief looked around himself. "Where the hell is he, anyway?"

"He won't be in today," Bryce said. "Mickey's covering for him."

"What's wrong? Is he sick?"

Bryce shrugged. "He had a wicked-looking cut on his head, but other than that he seemed okay. I saw him last night and he said he had some personal business to take care of today."

"How'd he get cut?"

"I didn't ask," Bryce lied.

"Well, I hope to God he takes care of his problem. He's about to piss me off, you know," George warned.

Bryce smiled. "We don't want that, do we?"

The chief glared at him before turning to Hannah. "Now who did you say was missing?"

"I didn't," she replied.

George bared his teeth. "I'm *asking* you, dammit. Does everyone have to get in on the smartass act?"

"I don't know what you're talking about," Hannah told him in a cool voice. "You asked me who I said was missing, and I told you I didn't say."

The chief closed his eyes and shook his head. "Let me rephrase the question, counselor. Will you please tell me the name on the report?"

"Which name?"

"The name of the missing person," George ground out.

"Oh," said Hannah innocently. "It's Kayleen St. Clair, the Reverend St. Clair's sister."

Bryce sat up. "Who instigated the report?"

"The Reverend. Kayleen lives in that little house on the corner from the church, you know."

"How long has she been missing?" Bryce asked.

"Over three days now. Ben has some notes on the bottom here. Her car is parked at her house. No sign of forced entry. No tickets purchased or reservations made for bus or air travel. A girlfriend at the bank claims Kayleen traveled quite a bit with some rich boyfriend, but Ben notes that her luggage is at home in her closet."

"Any name on the boyfriend?"

"No. Ben has a question mark here, but no name."

"What's the big deal?" George said. "I'd say Inspector Portlock of Dumford Yard has everything under control. The rest of you guys could take lessons from him in turning routine reports into crime novels. I've never seen such a stickler for detail. He doesn't miss a—what the hell are you waving at, Hannah?"

234

She gestured to the door, and George looked around to see a grim-faced Alexander St. Clair enter the station. Under his arm was a manila envelope.

"Hello, Reverend," George said. "We were just working on your sister's case."

Bryce and Hannah traded a glance.

"I'd like to see Officer Portlock," the soft-voiced visitor requested. His salt-and-pepper hair, normally straight and neatly combed, looked to Hannah like a tuft of cotton candy fresh from a coal factory.

George's voice dropped to an understanding rumble. "Why don't you take a seat, Reverend? Ben is off duty today, but I'm sure we can help you. Like I said, we were just discussing the case when you arrived. Bryce was going to do some follow-up before he went out on patrol."

The Reverend looked at Hannah. "I don't think I should speak openly, Chief Legget. Is there somewhere we can talk in private?"

George snapped his fingers. "Hannah, run down to Milly's and pick up a dozen doughnuts, would you? And don't hurry yourself to get back."

She made a tiny noise of protest, but the chief's warning glance lifted her out of her seat. She looked longingly at Bryce as she reached the door; Bryce gave a light shrug and turned his attention to the Reverend.

Hannah squirmed on her stool while she drank a cup of tea and made small talk with Milly. When fifteen minutes had passed, she paid for the doughnuts and carried them out of the restaurant. As she stepped onto the sidewalk she saw Bryce leaving the station.

"Pssst! Bryce!"

He frowned when he saw her beckoning to him. After a slight hesitation he walked toward her.

"What is it, Hannah?"

"I didn't want George to see me asking you," she explained. "What evidence did the Reverend have in that envelope?"

"Why?"

Hannah brushed a stray auburn curl away from her forehead and tried to sound disinterested. "No reason. I just assumed it was something like pictures."

Bryce's eyes narrowed. "How did you know?"

"It was a good guess," she said. "Were they dirty pictures?"

"He didn't want to offend you. What did you do, peek in the window?"

"Don't be silly, Bryce. He wouldn't have asked me to leave if they were anything but dirty pictures. Are you going out on patrol now?"

"Yes." He paused then. "Hannah, why do I have the feeling you know something about this?"

She smiled brightly at him. "I couldn't say. I'd better get these doughnuts to George now. I'll see you when you come back."

He watched her as she moved past him and continued watching until she reached the station. Hannah was tempted to turn and blow him a kiss, but there was no time for such foolishness now that she believed she knew the identity of Portis Jackson's blackmailer. The fact that Kayleen St. Clair was missing added a horror story taint to her suspicions about the bank vice-president. First Portis had the pictures and Kayleen had the tape. Now the Reverend held the pictures and Kayleen had disappeared.

So where was the tape?

In Portis Jackson's possession, of course, Hannah told herself. He paid off Kayleen and sent the pictures to the Reverend out of spite after she left. That, or he had killed Kayleen and—

Hannah shivered. She could be on the trail of a desperate murderer here. But she still had no proof. She needed something, anything, to take to George.

By lunchtime she knew what she had to do. It was a long shot, but if anything had been overlooked in Kayleen's house, it would take a seasoned snoop like herself to find it.

Being female, Kayleen was sure to have all sorts of secret hiding places that would pass unnoticed by a man's inexperienced eyes. Hannah had several secret caches herself, one of them full of missives from a beloved swine named McKee. She took them out and read them whenever she felt herself softening toward men. They served as both memento and cruel reminder of a love betrayed. Kayleen St. Clair would be no different. Somewhere she would have a lock of hair, a photograph, or cherished love letters of her own hidden away. Hannah hoped for all three.

At twelve o'clock she told George she would be going out for lunch. He answered her with a smirk and a cloud of cigar smoke. Hannah gathered up her purse and walked past him with her shoulders straight and her head held high. Once outside she rushed to the Rambler. She had no idea how she was going to get inside Kayleen St. Clair's house, but with only an hour for lunch she needed to hurry.

Hannah was dismayed to find a half-dozen cars parked in front of the house next door to Kayleen's place. She turned the Rambler around in the church parking lot, then realized the abundance of cars in the area would be the perfect camouflage for her own car. Who was to know she wasn't attending whatever function the neighbors were having? It was brilliant of her, she decided, as she parked the Rambler behind a shiny silver import.

Her brows knitted as she left the car and approached Kayleen's house. It was such a cute little place, with its flagstone walk and lemon-yellow shutters. The leaves of the oak trees lining the walk were blood red against the blue sky. The place was too pretty, too picturesque to be the home of a blackmailing home-wrecker, Hannah thought. Was there no justice in the world? Kurt's house was a dugout in the prairie compared to this sweet abode.

With a half-hearted sigh she walked to the picture window and peered through the opening in a pair of yellow drapes. When a pair of eyes peered back out at her, she stumbled back and clutched her chest in alarm. A moment later Bryce was out the door and taking her by the arm to pull her inside the house.

"What the hell are you doing here, Hannah?"

"You frightened me," she breathed.

"You deserved it. Now tell me why you're here."

"Why are you here?" she countered.

He dropped her arm. "To see if Ben might have missed something."

"That's why I'm here."

"Really?" Bryce said with a snort. "Did George give you a gun and a badge for the day?"

Hannah stepped past him and seated herself on a brown plaid sofa. The interior of the house was a disappointment. The gold shag carpet was desperately in need of cleaning, and the furniture was tacky beyond belief. It was a shame, really, Hannah thought, when the outside had showed so much promise.

"I thought I might be of some help," she offered to the waiting Bryce.

His expression said he didn't believe her. "Don't give me any of your happy horseshit, Hannah. Tell me what you think you know."

She rubbed the arm he had grabbed. "For your information, I happen to know the identity of the rich boyfriend."

"Big deal," Bryce said. "So do I. I've known it for some time."

The corners of Hannah's mouth drooped. "You have?"

"Uh-huh. Who do you think it is?"

"You first," she said.

Bryce scowled. "I asked you first."

"At the count of three we'll both say who we think it is," Hannah suggested. "All right?"

"All right," he agreed. "You count."

"Okay. One, two, three . . ."

Neither said a word.

"You don't trust me," Bryce said, "and I know I don't

trust you. Does the name of your boyfriend start with the letter *P*?"

Hannah nodded. "Does yours end with the letter *N*?"

"Which name? First or last?"

"Last."

"Okay. First name starts with the letter *P*, last name ends with the letter *N*. Is that right?"

"Yes."

"Is there an *R* in the first name of your guy?"

She nodded again. "Is there a *K* in the last name of yours?"

"Yeah. I think we have the same guy. How long have you known?"

"Not long. What about you?"

"Long enough," he said. "Tell me everything you know and we'll see what we have."

"You first," she said.

"Goddammit, will you stop that? I'm the one with the badge here, Hannah. Do you want me to haul you in for obstruction of justice?"

Her fingers tightened on her purse. "I don't want to tell you anything. I'll tell George, but I wanted to come and look for proof before I said a word. Did you find anything?"

"Not a thing."

"How did you get in?"

"Her bathroom window was unlocked."

"Oh," said Hannah. She would have hated to crawl in someone's bathroom window. "Where is your car?"

"Around the corner," he said. "Now, if you're finished questioning me, maybe you'd like to get the hell out of here and go back to work."

"I'm on lunch," she informed him. "And as long as I'm here, you may as well let me have a look around."

Bryce's hands went to his hips. "I told you I've already

239

looked. What do you expect to find that two experienced police officers missed?"

"If you're so sure I won't find anything, then where's the harm?" Hannah responded. "Who knows what a woman might find in another woman's house?"

Bryce arched one brow. "You could have a point there. Especially if *you* were the woman doing the looking."

Hannah smiled at the remark. "Where is the bedroom? I think I should start there. I don't know how much longer I can take this plaid living room furniture."

"Second door to the left." Bryce pointed down the hall. "You won't like the decor in there much better. I'm going out back to have a look in the garage."

"There's a garage?" Hannah asked.

"Detached. I don't think she used it. If you find anything you damn well better show it to me, Hannah. I'm going to frisk you before you leave."

Hannah blushed to herself as she realized the prospect of being frisked by him wasn't entirely unpleasant. To hide the color in her cheeks she hurried down the hall to the bedroom. She was going to have to do something about these sudden flights of fantasy. For twenty-five years she had fought every sexual impulse that happened her way—why was menopause taking so long to catch up with her chaste body?

Her heart skipped a beat when she stepped into the room and found a hundred pairs of eyes on her. James Dean looked sullenly down from every wall, his lips pouty, his gaze slightly contemptuous.

"The woman was obsessed," Hannah whispered to herself as she walked around. The pictures on the wall confused her. Portis Jackson was the physical opposite of the svelte young Dean. What had possibly attracted Kayleen to the hirsute banker? Money, of course. But what else? Did Portis like James Dean, too?

Hannah walked to the closet and eyed its contents. A

quick check of clothing pockets turned up two credit card receipts and three tissues. A probing in the toes of the shoes in the bottom of the closet turned up twenty dollars in randomly placed five-dollar bills. The empty purses gave forth eight bobby pins, six pennies, and seven tampons. A shoebox stuffed under a folded cardigan held nothing but unmatched earrings and broken watches. Kayleen was a jewelry packrat, it seemed.

The dresser was next. Made of wicker, it squeaked as Hannah pulled out each drawer and felt underneath for something taped to the bottom. In the drawers themselves were flimsy, filmy scraps of material that bore no resemblance to normal undergarments but were obviously meant to be worn as such. Hannah soon realized the missing Kayleen was doubtlessly what Kurt would call a "kink queen." Her suspicions were confirmed when Hannah came across an object similar to what Bryce had planted in her desk drawer at the station. Disgusted, Hannah left the bedroom and went to the bathroom to wash her hands before continuing the search.

Upon her return, she went to the bed and sat down to think. The mattress rolled beneath her and she sprang up again. Waterbeds were not on Hannah's list of life experiences. She patted the surface with a tentative hand and watched the resulting ripple with satisfaction.

"They're not as fun as they look," Bryce said from the doorway. He smiled at her start of surprise and made a waving motion with his hand. "They upset my rhythm, if you know what I mean."

Hannah cleared her throat and opened her mouth to make a suitable retort. She pointed to his hand instead and said, "You're bleeding."

Bryce looked at the cut on his palm. "I tripped over the septic lid and fell down on a piece of glass. Lucky I did, otherwise I wouldn't have seen the door of that storm cellar out there. Someone has shoveled a pile of dirt and leaves over the top of it. I moved the dirt, but the door has a spring hinge. I need you to come out and hold it open while I go down and have a look."

Hannah's swallow was audible. "What do you think is in there?"

"If the smell is any indication, something dead."

"Oh." Hannah's mind said no, but her feet followed him out of the house and into the leaf-strewn backyard. Her eyes darted nervously from Bryce to the rotting wood door of the storm cellar he showed her.

"It's heavy, but I think you can handle it. Just don't let go, all right? Hannah?"

"I . . . don't smell anything."

"You will once I open it. Turn your head to the breeze and keep hold of the door."

He took his flashlight in one hand and heaved up the door with the other. Hannah grasped the damp wood surface and turned her head, but the smell found her. She blinked and tried to hold her breath as Bryce disappeared down the stone steps. Within seconds he was back up again and Hannah watched in sympathetic horror as he turned his back on her and began to retch. When he finally straightened, his face was white. "She's down there," he croaked. "Cut up."

Hannah released the door and listened to it crash back to earth. "Cut up?"

"Mutilated," Bryce mumbled. He wiped at his mouth and took a deep breath. "I want you to go back to the station and have George call the sheriff. I'll wait here."

"First I have to tell . . ." Hannah paused and hesitated, then she started over again. "There was a tape. Kayleen was blackmailing Portis Jackson over a tape. A movie. I heard them arguing at the old depot three nights ago. I saw him, but I never saw her, and I didn't know it was her until the Reverend brought in those pictures today. Portis wanted to trade the pictures for the tape, but the woman said no. I think he did it, Bryce. I think Portis Jackson killed Kayleen. And Calvin Horn, too. Kurt called Portis and said he knew about Calvin, and Portis hung up on him."

Bryce was staring at her. "You overheard them at the depot and you didn't tell anyone?"

"I had no proof," Hannah said in defense. "Kurt said if I found the tape, maybe it would have Calvin's fingerprints on it. We still don't have any proof, Bryce. Portis probably found the tape when he killed Kayleen, and he sent the pictures to the Reverend, so he can't be linked to those. All we have is my word against his about the depot."

"He didn't send the pictures," Bryce told her. "They were found inside the house. Portis probably planted them here when he came to hide the body. If there was someone else who saw him, like that IRS guy, or maybe Edie—" His mouth snapped shut and he spun on his heel. Hannah followed him into the house and watched him snatch up the phone in the kitchen. He punched in a number and drummed impatient fingers on the wall as he listened to it ring.

"Who are you calling?" Hannah asked.

"We've got enough to bring him in for questioning. I want to warn Edie and make sure she's all right."

Hannah smirked and stood back. "I see you know her number by heart."

Bryce whirled and glared at her. "Get back to the station and do what I told you."

She ignored him. "It *is* your baby, isn't it? I knew I couldn't have been wrong."

Bryce hung up the phone. There had been no answer. "We've got more important things to worry about right now, not to mention the fact that it's none of your fucking business whose baby it is. Now will you please go back and tell George we have a body over here?"

Hannah adjusted her glasses and gave him her coldest

243

look. "Your father would be proud of you, Bryce. You make him look like an amateur."

Bryce was still frowning in confusion over the remark when the front door slammed behind her.

Chapter Twenty-Three

Edie cried when the phone stopped ringing. She had no idea how long she'd been in the closet, but if her husband's movements were anything to judge by, she guessed today was her fourth day. Before Portis went to bed the first night he had placed a chain around the knobs on the outside of the double doors to prevent her escaping. He removed the chain only to dump her waste pan, give her some water, and to feed her the candy she had stashed around the house. Each time he came, he asked if she had changed her mind about leaving him. That morning Edie had said yes, but Portis called her a liar and locked her up again.

She was tired. Tired of peeing in her good roasting pan, tired of trying to break the stupid damn chain when Portis was gone, and tired of eating nothing but chocolate. Besides that, the batteries in her book light had died the second day and left her with no way to read the last crucial chapter of the murder mystery she had stashed away in the closet. Not being able to confirm her suspicions about the killer's identity was aggravating beyond belief.

And she was worried about the baby. Despite the caffeine in the chocolate, or perhaps because of it, she had felt no movement for some time.

She wiped her eyes and nose on the hem of a dress hanging above her. She wondered who had been calling. Ben seldom called during the day. Her mother called only on Sundays. She knew it wasn't Max Portlock, now didn't she?

Edie's lip curled in the darkness. She got to her feet and stretched, then she did a few knee bends. When her joints stopped popping, she lifted her leg and kicked with all her strength at the center of the door. The chain rattled noisily, but it didn't break. Edie didn't know where Portis had come up with the chain, or what he normally used it for, but the sucker was certainly strong.

Frustrated, she put her sticky, chocolate-covered fingers in her mouth and placed a punishing kick at random. Her hand fell from her mouth and her jaw dropped in surprise when she heard a splintering sound from the wood near the hinges. She kicked again and stood back to look. Soon she began to laugh and cry at once. "Oh, Edie, you are so *stupid,*" she said aloud. "You've been kicking the wrong part of the door!"

With a flurry of kicks she attacked the area near the bottom hinge with caffeine-fed fury, until she heard the wood begin to separate from the metal. When she saw daylight she pushed out on the bottom of the door as hard as she could and heard the wood around the top hinge groan in protest. Humming with excitement, she backed up, counted to three, then threw both feet in a baseball slide into the lower half of the door. The pain of landing on her backside made her cry out, but there was now enough give in the door to force up the lower half and squeeze out.

Edie's eyes watered as her pupils adjusted to the light. She rubbed the tears away and realized she'd left her book in the closet. She thought of removing the chain and retrieving it, but when her vision cleared she decided to forget the book. She could always buy another one in the free world.

She didn't recognize herself in the mirror. Her blond hair was matted and oily, her face pale and thin. Her first impulse was to take a shower and apply makeup, but she abandoned her reflection and began to search for her suitcases. She found them under the bed, her clothes still crumpled inside.

"You bastard," she seethed. "I'm going to have to iron everything."

And she would have to forget about the clothes in the closet—unless she wanted to take a screwdriver to that top hinge and get the book as well. What was the big hurry, after all? she asked herself. The clock on the nightstand showed ten minutes after one. Portis wouldn't be home from the bank for hours yet. Edie could take that shower, put on that makeup, eat something hot, nutritious, and filling, and still be out of the house by the time he came home.

The tension in her muscles began to relax as she peeled off her clothes and stepped under the warm, steamy spray in the shower. The bruises on her body made her want to cry, but while toweling off, she was happy to feel a sharp and painful kick from the baby. It kicked twice more while she was preparing soup and a cheese sandwich, and the discomfort was so great that Edie had to walk around as she ate. She wandered through the house, wrinkling her nose at the messes Portis had made during her imprisonment and congratulating herself on not being the one who would have to clean them up.

His den was the worst. Empty potato chip bags, crushed beer cans, and a dried, half-eaten pizza littered the top of the table beside his black leather recliner.

The selfish pig could have shared that pizza with her, Edie thought angrily.

Her eyes grew round when she found one of his desk drawers left open. Portis always kept his desk locked. Edie had long suspected that this was where he kept his library of dirty videos, books, and magazines, and she was proved correct when she found a neat row of videocassettes beneath a pad of legal paper. She looked over the tapes and noted with a sneer that most had stupid, nonsensical titles, like *Goldilocks and the Three Bared.* This didn't surprise Edie.

What did surprise her was the tape marked *Birth the Lamaze Way.* He had to be kidding, Edie thought. Portis had refused to attend Lamaze classes, and he had forbidden her to use his money to pay for them. He didn't believe in them, he claimed. Portis thought women should go through birth the normal way, with plenty of pain.

Curious, Edie took the tape out of his desk and put it in the VCR. After adjusting the volume on the monitor, she sat down in the leather recliner to watch. It was a little late to learn Lamaze now, she realized, but she might pick up something useful. She decided Portis had taped it off television so he could watch the anguished faces of women in labor over and over again. The miracle of birth was probably a sexual thrill for the scum-sucking sicko.

As the picture replaced the snow on the monitor she began to frown. This wasn't a hospital. It was a bedroom. Worse, it looked like a motel room. An emergency birth, perhaps? she wondered. No, the woman on the bed wasn't pregnant. She wasn't even fat. She was breathing heavily enough, but—

Edie gasped as her husband strutted into view on the screen. He wore a military costume of some kind, and in his hand he carried a riding whip.

He looked ridiculous.

Edie laughed so hard her eyes teared up again. When she could breathe, she looked closer at the woman. It was Kayleen, all right, the slutty secretary from the bank. She and Portis were playing some kind of bondage game for the camera. And Kayleen actually seemed to *enjoy* being brutalized.

Disgusted, Edie stopped the tape and took it out of the

VCR. Holding the loathesome object with the tips of her fingers, she carried it back to the desk.

Then she paused. Her brows lifted.

A smile tickled the corners of her mouth as a dozen devious possibilities eagerly presented themselves to her. This was it. This was her ticket to the free world. Her husband's reputation, not to mention his career, could be ruined with the tape she held. She could get a healthy divorce settlement and live in comfort the rest of her natural life. She could bleed the fat worm dry. . . .

From the murky depths of her conscience she heard Max Portlock chuckling. Smiling like a benign Robert Young, he dog-paddled to the surface of Edie's thoughts and said, "Hello, kitten. Father knew best after all, eh?"

"All right," Edie muttered aloud. "Forget the money part. I can still use the tape to get a divorce."

Portis wouldn't dare to touch her once he knew she had the tape. He wouldn't even breathe in her direction without immediate and profuse apology. Not that he would have a chance to breathe on her. If Edie had known he was twisted before, the tape proved his illness beyond all doubt. It had to come from his mother, the closet dominatrix, Edie decided. Portis's father was power hungry and prone to white-faced rages, but his mother was constant in her demand for total submission. Portis was the crazed biological creation of two social deviants.

A riding whip, for crissakes.

Edie shook her head and left the den just as she had found it. After placing the tape in her purse, she returned to the bedroom to retrieve her suitcases. It was time to leave. Forget the book and the dresses in the closet; she could make Portis send them to Ben's house by special delivery if she wanted to. And how about that loan for her mother's tavern? No problem, Mom. How much do you need?

Laughter bubbled in her throat as Edie lugged the suitcases out to her car. The weakness imposed by her time in the closet seemed to dissipate under her newfound source of power. Everything was going to be okay. Her serendipitous discovery of the tape, the number one all-time bargaining chip, proved there was a God after all. When the cases were in the trunk, she turned her head and stuck her tongue out at the house before getting in the car.

Fifty yards from her drive, the engine spluttered and stalled. Edie ground the starter again and again, until she finally thought to look at the gas gauge. The needle hugged the wrong side of the E.

"Shit!" she hissed. "How could you do this to me?"

She left the car and ran back to the house to call Ben. The number at the police station rang on and on with no answer. Edie stopped counting after ten rings and hung up to call her mother. A barmaid answered and informed her that Stella had gone to the city for the day.

"I don't believe this." Edie slammed down the receiver and wrung her hands. Time was running out. She had primped and dawdled her way into zero hour and there was no one else to call.

"Okay," she said grimly. "That's it, then."

If she had to walk, then she had better hurry. She didn't want Portis to drive by and catch her on the road. Maybe she'd get lucky and catch a ride with someone. Her suitcases would have to be abandoned, of course, but she could negotiate for those later. All she needed was her purse and that tape. She could never leave home without it.

Chapter Twenty-Four

Ben came to three realizations through reading Lura Taylor's diary: Ordney Taylor had been a wife-beating, womanizing drunk; Annette Taylor was slightly screwy even before the death of numerous brain cells; and Lura had fallen in love with him long before the day Ben asked her out for the first time.

The feeling that he was intruding on sacred ground had stayed with him, but Ben's curiosity was greater. He had read each page with unwavering attention—until he found that nearly half of the entries had been written in French. Suspecting the worst, he had paged ahead to find the date of Ordney's murder. One paragraph, in French, was scribbled on the page. The following pages were empty.

That morning Ben had gone to the library to find a book on French, but the process of deciphering each word was beyond his patience. He had driven by the school then, toying with the idea of showing the passages to the French teacher, but he had found himself unable to place the book in the hands of a stranger. After long deliberation he left the house once more and drove to the home of the one person in Dumford he felt he could trust.

Her gold tooth gleamed when she opened the door and saw him. "Why hello there, Officer Portlock."

"Hello, Mrs. Miller," Ben said to the psychic. "How are you?"

"Fine, just fine. Have you come to warn me about more muckraking, or is this a social call?"

"I need your help," Ben told her. "Can I come in?"

"Sure can." Still smiling, she stepped aside to let him enter. The dress and the bandanna were yellow today.

"I'll come back if you're busy, Mrs. Miller."

"Call me Berniece," she said. "And don't be silly. Just sit yourself down and tell me what I can do for you on this fine fall day. That's a beautiful sweater, by the way. The dark green matches your eyes. I almost didn't recognize you out of your uniform. Can I get you some coffee to drink?"

"No thanks." Ben sat down on the long sofa and looked around himself. Nothing had changed. The place was just as immaculate, the decor just as pleasant. Part of it came from her, he realized. She added something special to the ambience.

"Thank you," she said, her black eyes twinkling.

"Jesus," Ben muttered. "I forgot you could do that."

"Show me the notebook under your arm," she suggested. "That's what you're here about, isn't it?"

Ben handed it over to her. "I don't know how to explain this, Mrs. Miller—"

"Berniece," she said. "And you can start by telling me how you came to have this." Her finger tapped the first page of the notebook. "Is this someone's write-down book?"

"Excuse me?"

"Diary. Journal. Private thoughts." Her black gaze was penetrating. Ben cleared his throat.

"Yes it is. I have a dozen others as well, all of them found in Calvin Horn's house the night of his death. No one knows I have them—except you, of course."

Berniece went on looking at him. "You took them because you thought they might have some meaning?"

"Yes," Ben said. "I don't believe Calvin killed himself."

"I see. And you've been reading these diaries and searching for clues. Why bring this one to me?"

"Some of it is written in French. I was hoping you knew the language . . . in Haiti."

Berniece nodded. "It's been years, but I'm sure I can give you a rough translation." She held up the notebook. "You think there's a clue in here?"

Ben nodded, not trusting himself to speak.

His hostess's smile was sad. "You're no good at deception, Ben Portlock. No damn good at all. Why not say it aloud and spare yourself the guilt of a lie? This diary has nothing to do with Calvin Horn."

"All right." Ben's gaze left her face and concentrated on her feet. "It belonged to someone I was once engaged to marry."

Berniece frowned. "What gives you the right to violate these pages?"

Ben stood up in agitation and paced the carpet in front of the sofa before sitting down again. "What would you have done in my place?" he asked her. "I'd be lying if I said I didn't enjoy reading it, but I thought I might find the truth about what happened the night she killed her father. Can you blame me for wanting to know why she did it?"

Berniece's eyes narrowed. "This is the Taylor girl, then. You were engaged to her and she didn't tell *you* why?"

"No." Ben turned his head away. "Maybe it's because I was the one who turned her in. Or because she wanted to hide something, I don't know. But I want to know. I need to know. Do you understand?"

"Unfortunately," Berniece admitted. "Reasons are important to you. A damn sight more important than they should be. You're asking me to put my fingers into ancient ground and dig up the ashes of this woman's past for your own gratification. Am I right?"

Ben looked at her. "If you're not going to help me just say so. I don't need another lecture on goddamn coupon perforations."

"I didn't say I wasn't going to help you," Berniece replied. "But I do want you to know what I see behind this request. You're just about on fire with wanting this girl, yet you allow this old and painful business to keep you from her. I find that tragic, Ben."

"Berniece, please."

"All right," she said on a sigh. She opened the notebook again and began flipping through the pages. Ben attempted to point out the last entry, but she waved him away. "Settle down, boy. Might be something earlier on."

Ben crossed one leg and fidgeted with the hem of his blue jeans when she stopped at a page and began to read. After a moment, her fine brows met in a deep frown. "I'm not familiar with some of the words," she told him. "French Haiti has a language all its own, Ben."

He sat forward. "You don't understand her French?"

A broad grin spread across the black woman's face. "I understand enough. Did you know you were her first lover? She says you were very gentle with her . . . at first."

Ben sat back again, his neck hot. "Do you have to read those parts?"

"No," said Berniece, "but I bet you wish you could. She goes into some detail here about your anatomy. Still that have scar from barbed wire on your left hip?"

"No, it moved to my right—will you please skip that stuff and go on?"

She ignored him. "Good Lord. Did you realize how much this girl adored you? You wouldn't get me down on the floor in some drafty old boathouse. Which lake was that?"

Ben moved to snatch the book from her and she jerked it up and away. "Okay, okay. Just having some fun with you. She really did love you, you know."

"I thought she did," he said bitterly.

"Bullsnot, boy. Now get back to the corner of that sofa there and make yourself comfortable."

His mouth tight, Ben sat and watched Berniece's face. As she read, her lips would curve, and each time she smiled he felt his flesh prickle with indignation. When she burst out laughing, he couldn't take it anymore.

"What? What's so goddamned funny?"

She blinded him with her gold tooth. "Lura gave a naked man a ride home one night. His initials are B. M. He was chased out of someone's house without his clothes, and he had a handful of leaves over his privates."

Ben frowned; then his brow suddenly cleared. "Bryce McKee. He told me a neighbor picked him up that night."

"Bryce McKee?"

"You know him?"

"I do."

"Is he a client of yours?"

"I can't say. Either way, I'd be half moron not to have noticed him. He's a handsome one, Bryce is."

"Right," Ben said.

Berniece looked at him. "Well, I'll swear. Is that envy I hear? You know in your heart there's nothing between Bryce and your gal."

"Maybe *I* do," Ben said quickly. "But how do *you* know there's nothing between them?"

The psychic grinned. "Okay, I guess you caught me. Are the two of you good friends?"

Ben shrugged. "We used to be."

"Until she came home," Berniece guessed. "Well let me tell you, he's half crazy over someone, but it ain't her. He wouldn't talk about it, but I did happen to pick up a few impressions. I think her name is Eve or something similar, so you can trust me that you don't have a thing to worry about. Now, can I trust that you won't say anything to him?"

255

Ben stared at her. "Eve?"

Berniece shrugged. "Something like that. Why? Do you know her?"

"That sonofabitch," Ben said softly. "I should have known from the way she acted at the tavern that night."

"Pardon me?" Berniece said.

"And the way he's always asking me how she's getting along." He looked at Berniece then. "Her name isn't Eve, it's Edie. My sister."

"Uh-oh," Berniece said with a sheepish smile. "So much for client confidentiality."

Ben waved a hand. "Don't worry about it. If she wanted me to know, she would've told me."

"You won't confront them?"

"No."

"Thanks, Ben."

"It'll wait until after the baby's born."

Berniece blinked and opened her mouth, but Ben cut her off. "How about translating that last page now? If we dig up any more scandals we'll have to call in Hannah to officiate."

His hostess laughed and began paging through the notebook. When she found the last paragraph she read it completely through before giving him a quizzical look.

"She talks about how anxious she is to marry you and break away from her family. She says she sometimes feels strangled by the same bonds that are meant to make her feel secure. She mentions several things about the wedding itself, her bridesmaids and so on, and then she hears someone shouting in another room. She goes on writing for another moment, then she says she'd better go and see what's going on. That's it. That's all she says. Does that tell you anything?"

"Maybe. I don't know." Ben held out his hand for the notebook. He didn't know what he had expected to hear, but that wasn't it. "I won't take up any more of your time, Berniece. Thank you for helping me."

256

She stood up with him and walked him to the door. "I'm going to help you some more, Ben. That knife is closer."

He stopped. "Closer?"

"The image is clearer. It's going to happen very soon now. Very soon. Give me your hand."

Ben extended his hand and she clasped it with both of hers. Her eyes closed in concentration.

"Berniece . . ." He shifted uncomfortably.

"It's no use," she said after a moment. "I still can't see the initials on the handle. The first one could be a *C*, or a *G*, or an *O*. Maybe even a *Q*. Take care of yourself, Ben."

"I will," he said. "Thanks again, Berniece."

He was in the Jeep and closing the door before he remembered his first visit to the psychic. She had told him to look between the black and white. Well, he guessed he had. The notebook pages were white and the writing was in black ink. But he still didn't know the truth. He knew Lura heard shouting that night and had gone to investigate.

It disturbed him that she had never said a word about her unhappy home life during their time together. She had always been cheerful and bright with him, never showing any of the pain he had found in the pages of the notebook. He supposed he'd been fooling himself about her ever having trusted him. She had never trusted anyone beyond her own family. Her drinking, squabbling, shouting family.

What kind of shouting had she heard that night? he wondered suddenly. Another knockdown fight between her parents? Other passages indicated that both she and Philip had avoided all possible involvement in the daily altercations between their drunken parents. Lura had used the time spent in her room during these battles to write in her diary. So why investigate this particular battle? What had made this one different from the others?

After a moment, Ben left the Jeep and knocked on Berniece's door again.

She greeted him with a grin. "Long time no see."

"What is the word for scream in French?" he asked.

"Same as the word for shout. Why? What difference does it make?"

Ben kissed her on her startled mouth. "The difference between committing a murder and covering up one. Thank you, Berniece."

"You're welcome, I'm sure." Berniece was blushing. "What are you going to—"

Ben was already walking to his Jeep. Berniece looked at his back and knew the answer to her question. He was going to the dump to burn some diaries. All but one. The one in his hand was going back to its author.

Chapter Twenty-Five

Hannah took malicious delight in the expression on Bryce's face when Haden charged into Kayleen St. Clair's backyard to report that Portis Jackson could not be found, and that his wife's car sat abandoned in the road a short distance from their house.

"Put out an APB on him," George ordered. "That fat sonofabitch better not have left town." The cigar hanging from the chief's lips had gone unlighted from the moment Hannah relayed the news about Kayleen. The end in his mouth was dark, damp with spit. George was not having a good day.

"He drives a silver BMW," Hannah offered. Then, watching Bryce out of the corner of her eye, she asked, "Where do you suppose his wife is?"

The chief turned on her. "What the hell are you still doing here? I've told you twice to leave. You don't have any business at a crime scene."

"It's my case," Hannah argued. "I know the facts."

"You know jack shit. And you might not even know him

if I turn around and see you standing here one more time. Now get your butt back to the station."

Hannah didn't move. "I called Cory and asked him to come in early. He's manning the station."

"Then go home," George barked. "Goddammit, what the hell is taking the sheriff so long?"

"Calm down, George," Bryce said. "You'll work yourself into another heart attack."

"Well, Jesus, it's almost dark. You'd think they'd put a priority on—there the sonofabitches are. It's about damn time. Haden, point 'em back here on your way out. And tell 'em to bring more than one bag. That ought to light a fire under their asses. Bryce, where are you going?"

"To call Ben again. He might be home by now."

"Just leave him out of this. I've got the situation under control."

"His sister might be at his place," Bryce said.

"So?"

Hannah smirked. "Ben's sister is Portis Jackson's wife, George."

"Oh yeah. Well, go ahead and call then. And Hannah, I'm not going to tell you one more time. If you're not out of here in the next thirty seconds, then don't bother to show up at the station tomorrow."

"It's not fair," Hannah protested. "I'm as involved in this as he is." She pointed at Bryce.

"One," George said.

When he reached ten, Hannah whirled and stalked away from them. She glanced over her shoulder and saw Bryce flutter his fingers in a facetious good-bye as he walked to the back door of the house.

Hannah hated him. And she hated herself for having entertained such ridiculous notions about him. Betrayed twice by the same man. Almost. It felt like that anyway. How could she have been so gullible, so naive? He would pay, she decided. He would feel the wrath of Hannah. More than anything, she wanted to punish him for those sexual flights of fantasy his charade had forced her to endure. And if he tried to steal this case away from her, she vowed she would become his worst nightmare. She was the key here. Everything hinged on her testimony.

She plopped herself behind the wheel of her Rambler and envisioned the headlines in the Dumford weekly. There would be a picture of her, of course, and a long story about how she had discovered the blackmail scheme through her own investigation. Bryce had found the body, but that was no big thing. The credit for solving the case belonged to Hannah. And not just one case, but two. Hannah was certain Portis Jackson would break down in custody and confess to the murder of Calvin Horn as well.

Things were going to happen around this town, Hannah told herself as she pulled away from the curb. The silver import was gone, the party next door apparently cut short by the nearby police invasion. The unknown owner of that import would know her name this time next week, Hannah predicted. And afterward there wouldn't be a party in town, be it Tupperware or Mary Kay, that she didn't have an invitation to attend. Naturally, she would be forced to decline a few—a certain amount of discretion was crucial in dealing with sudden fame—but most of the invitations would be accepted with grace and aplomb . . . as usual.

Oh, yes, things were certainly going to be different for Hannah in Dumford. George was excited and tempermental now, but he would soon calm down and realize how valuable she was to this investigation. The chief would treat her a little differently then. He would be forced to show her the respect she deserved. And he would definitely apologize to her for his rudeness. She might accept his apology. And she might not. It would depend upon how humble he appeared in the delivery.

Rehearsing her story for the reporters, Hannah drove on until blinks from other cars told her she had forgotten to turn on her headlights. She was surprised to see that dusk was accompanied by a light fog. Layered strands of whispery mist filtered through the Rambler's beams and seemed to become thicker as she drove north. The fog was so dense by the time she reached her turnoff that she thought her eyes might be playing tricks on her when she saw a tiny glow of light coming from the direction of the depot. She couldn't see the depot itself, but there was nothing else in the area.

Had Portis Jackson returned? she wondered uneasily.

Then she smiled.

Chalk up another one for Hannah. Not only does she solve the case, but she apprehends the—

No, she quickly told herself. The man was a murderer. Did she think he was just going to throw up his hands and surrender when she told him the jig was up? It was too dangerous to go in by herself. She would go home and call George at the St. Clair house. He would send someone over to check it out.

Who else would be in the depot? No one she knew. It had to be Portis Jackson, returning to the scene of the crime. All murderers did that, didn't they?

The credit for his capture would still be hers, even if someone else did the actual capturing. Let a man with a gun and a badge go in and do the physical work. That's what they were paid for.

Once in the house Hannah dropped her purse and went directly to the phone. There were noises coming from Kurt's room, but she ignored them and flipped open the phone book. She dialed Kayleen's number as quickly as her trembling fingers would allow, then she frowned as she heard a moan from her brother.

Oh, please, she thought. We're not back to the imaginary orgasms, are we?

"St. Clair residence," said a voice in her ear.

"Who is this?" Hannah asked.

"Who is this?" came the reply.

"Hannah Winegarten. I need to speak to George Legget."

"This is Bryce, Hannah. What do you want?"

"I want to talk to George. It's important."

"You can't. He's lying down."

"What happened? Is it his heart?"

"He had to take a pill. What was it you wanted to talk to him about?"

Hannah hesitated. If she called back later, Portis might be gone.

"What about Haden?" she tried. "Is he there?"

"No," Bryce said in a flat voice. "He's out looking for Portis Jackson."

"I know where he is," Hannah said reluctantly.

"You do?"

"Yes. There's a light in the depot. I think he's gone back there."

"Alone?"

"I don't know. I considered it too dangerous to investigate on my own."

"Smart move. I'll check it out as soon as I can."

His compliment maddened her. "Did you ever locate your sweetheart? Expectant mothers shouldn't be out after dark, you know. It makes expectant fathers worry."

Bryce hung up on her.

"Liars deserve every little sting," Hannah muttered as she replaced the receiver. "And you'd better get used to the feel, Mr. McKee, because I'm not through yet."

Her chin high, Hannah walked down the hall and stopped at Kurt's door.

"I wasn't late on purpose this time," she said to him. "I was involved with a case. Our case."

Kurt didn't answer. His eyes were focused on the television.

"Don't you want to know what happened?" Hannah asked. "It's worse than we imagined, Kurt. The woman is dead. We found her carved up in her own storm cellar."

When he made no reply, didn't even blink, she stepped into the room. "Kurt, are you listening to me? I'm telling you about a murder and you're watching a shampoo com-

263

mercial like it's the televised broadcast of the second coming."

She wrinkled her nose then. "Your sheets are soiled, aren't they? Is that what you're upset about? Well, I'm sorry, but as I've told you, I was involved with this case and it couldn't be helped. I'm the key witness here, you understand. No one knows as much about Portis Jackson as I do."

Kurt's eyes didn't move. And he still hadn't blinked. Suddenly wary, Hannah approached the bed. "Kurt, are you playing games? You can't be dead. I heard you moan just a minute ago."

She put tentative fingers on the nearest wrist and attempted to feel for a pulse. When she felt nothing she tried the other wrist.

"Damn you," she said suddenly. "How could you, Kurt? Do you realize how this fouls things up for me? How can I bask in the limelight when I'm supposed to be in mourning?"

With a jerk of her head she began to pace the floor around his bed. "This is typical of you. Don't give me any warning, no, just moan and die while I'm on the telephone. Now I have to call the mortuary. And tomorrow your lawyer. I'll be so busy with arrangements I won't have time to do the Kayleen St. Clair story with the newspaper."

Her pacing stopped as an idea came to her. "You know what I might do? I might take your money and buy that cute little house of hers from the Reverend. It was good of you to let me live here rent free all these years, but face it, this place just isn't me." Her mouth twisted as she looked at the body on the bed. "I am sorry you're dead. Don't think I'm not. You are my brother, after all. Sometimes I wondered how you could be, since we're so different, but that was all in the way Papa raised us, I guess. You got to do everything, while I had to stay home and be a good girl. We just didn't know each other that well, did we Kurt? We had different views of—"

"I *could* let you stand here and talk to a corpse all night," a voice said, "but you're boring the shit out of me."

Hannah's neck cricked as she spun. Her eyes bugged out in their sockets as Portis Jackson stepped from behind the bedroom door. In his hand was a long knife.

"If you want to know the truth, Miss Winegarten, your brother was a stupid asshole. And after listening to that windy little speech, I can see you're no rocket scientist, either. Jesus, the things people think about when someone dies. You're sad, but then there's the money, right? Money has a way of making everything better, doesn't it? Better than a kiss and a Band-Aid any old day. Most people, however, don't make investment plans while the poor sonofabitch's shit is still on the sheet."

"How . . . ?" was all Hannah could manage.

Portis sneered. "He called me at the bank today to play his little game. But you know what? I recognized his voice this time. I used to visit him at the clinic in El Dorado—did he tell you that?"

Hannah's mouth opened, but her voice box had gone dry. She settled for a stiff nod. The man standing before her looked desperate. His eyes were red, his face was splotchy. The corners of his mouth glistened with saliva.

"He screwed up at the end. Most folks say good-bye, or bye-bye. Your brother said 'buh-bye, now.' He said it to me for years at the clinic. He was surprised to see me again, I could tell. Liked to jack off, didn't he?"

Hannah found her voice. "You killed him. While I was talking on the phone."

Portis smiled and nodded. "Pillow over the face. But not before he told me what I wanted to know. And you just told me the rest. No one knows as much about me as you do."

"I lied," Hannah blurted. "Someone else knows, too. A police officer. I told him after we found Kayleen's body in the storm cellar."

"You're lying now," Portis said. He advanced on her and

265

grabbed a fistful of her hair. "Did the good Reverend find the pictures?"

"Yes," Hannah squeaked. His breath was hot on her face. The foul odor of his desperation assaulted her nostrils. "Please don't hurt me," she pleaded.

"Why do people always say that?" Portis asked. "You know damn good and well I'm going to hurt you. I have to."

"No, you don't. I wasn't lying about someone else knowing. They're looking for you and your wife right now. George put out an APB and everything."

Portis's laugh was harsh. "They won't find my wife. She's tucked away safe and sound. Did you say Kayleen's body was carved up a little?"

"Don't you know?" Hannah asked, and her frantic inquiry was rewarded by a tightened grip. She winced as he released her hair to grab her cheeks and squeeze her face.

"I asked you, didn't I? Now you're beginning to see why they won't be able to pin anything on me. I didn't carve up anyone . . . yet. I left her in the depot and our friendly neighborhood psychopath picked her up for me. If I do this right, he'll get the blame for you two, as well."

Hannah swallowed. "You mean you didn't kill Kayleen?"

"Of course I did, you idiot. You were there."

"No, I wasn't. I left before . . . anything happened."

Portis jerked her over to the bed. "Sit down right there and don't make a move. That's right, move his legs while they're still pliable. I have to tell you this pisses me off. Your brother said you saw everything at the depot."

"I heard an argument about a tape and some pictures. That's all," Hannah swore.

"And what about Calvin Horn?" Portis demanded. "How did you know about him?"

Hannah crossed her legs and then uncrossed them again. Portis was right in front of her, the hand with the knife hanging loosely at his side.

"We didn't know," she admitted. "We guessed. When I heard you and Kayleen arguing about the tape, I remembered that some dirty movies had been found in Calvin's house."

"Well, Jesus Christ," Portis spat. "You mean to tell me you pathetic pissants couldn't prove a thing? I come over here, risk my ass trying to cover it, and you're telling me I killed your jerk-off brother for nothing?"

"We could split his estate," Hannah offered. She clasped her hands together and tried to sit up straight. "I'm willing to offer you half of everything in writing if you leave here without harming me. You'll have money, and you'll have my sworn silence."

"How much money?" Portis asked.

"Your share would be at least fifty thousand."

Portis wiped a pudgy hand across his damp forehead. "I could use the bucks, but you fucking bitches are all alike. Turn your back once and it's blackmail city. Nice try, but it's no go."

Hannah threw up a hand as he stepped forward. "Wait! I have something else to bargain with. I know something."

"It won't save your life," Portis told her. "What you don't seem to realize is that I'm not walking out of here while you're still breathing. I can't afford to."

Heart racing with fear, Hannah said, "What if I told you I know you're not the father of your wife's baby?"

Portis's gaze narrowed. His knife hand twitched. "What makes you think I'm not?"

"Because I know who the father is. What's more, I know where he is at this very moment."

"Really?" Portis found this interesting. "Just how do you know all this, Miss Winegarten?"

"I keep my eyes and ears open, that's how. Did you or did you not leave her home alone one weekend last February?"

"I know when it happened," Portis said. "Just tell me the fucker's name."

"Is it worth my life?" Hannah asked in a trembling voice.

Portis pretended to consider the question. "It may be. But only if you leave Dumford. I can't have you living here knowing what you know."

"I'll leave right after the funeral," Hannah told him. "I'll go to California and live. You'll never see me again. I promise."

Portis was sarcastic. "You won't talk to the police before you go? As the *key* witness against me, they'll be relying on your testimony."

"I won't say a word," Hannah promised. "I'll just go. I'll slip out of town without telling anyone. I've done it befo—" She stopped herself, but Portis was already smiling.

"You and Baker McKee, right?"

Hannah blinked.

"Oh, don't look so surprised, Miss Winegarten. The whole town knew about your single slip with The Bakerman. California, wasn't it? Yes, I'm sure that's how the gossip went. Our saintly Miss Winegarten went and got herself some and had to leave town to do it. But that was then and this, my dear sixth-grade teacher, is now. Tell me the bastard's name, and maybe you'll walk away from this."

Hannah's eyes were round and somewhat glazed. "The whole town . . . knew?"

Portis looked at the ceiling. "You're pissing me off, you batty old bitch, and it's not a good idea to do that right now."

Her mouth opened and closed like a fish out of water, but nothing came out. Portis brought the point of his knife down and drove the tip into the flesh of Hannah's thigh. When her scream died away, Portis said, "I'm tired of fucking around with you. Torture doesn't bother me. I could do this all night." He grabbed one of her hands and pressed it against his crotch. "See what it does for me?"

Hannah tried to yank her hand away, but Portis held it

firm against his swelling privates. She squeezed her eyes shut and tried not to think about the blood seeping out around the thin metal blade in her leg.

"Tell me the name," Portis said.

His breath made Hannah want to gag. Her voice box had gone dry again.

"Okay, you asked for it. Another inch and we'll hit the femoral artery. You'll spout blood like a geyser and I'll probably come in my pants."

Hannah believed him.

"It's . . . Bryce," she whispered.

"Louder. I didn't hear you."

"Bryce. Bryce McKee."

"The cop? You're lying."

Hannah shook her head. "No. It's Bryce. He's just like his father was. He's even worse."

Portis snorted. "And I suppose he's the one who knows everything you know? He's the police officer you mentioned earlier?"

"Yes," whispered Hannah. "He knew about you and Kayleen before. He said he did."

"Bastard probably followed me," Portis mused. "I've had that feeling for a couple of weeks now. Where is the sneaky cocksucking sonofabitch? You said you knew where he was?"

Hannah's gorge rose and fell in an effort to fight a sudden wave of nausea. The blood, the pain, and the penis beneath her hand were too much. Something was coming loose inside of her, something was tearing away. It was an effort for her to push the words out. They came in a garbled rush: "He's on his way to the depot. I saw a light there and thought it was you. I hope you find him. I hope you kill him. I hate . . . *God,* how I hate that man. He's just like his . . . cut that smile right off his . . . He thinks it's funny. He thinks it's . . ." She jerked her head up and looked wildly around the room. "Do something before he leaves! He's meeting her in Los Angeles and he thinks it's *funny*. Oh, my God, he won't stop laughing. Make him stop laughing at me, please. Stop him before he . . . stop him . . ."

As she babbled on, Portis frowned and withdrew the point of the knife from her thigh. He waited until she took a breath, then he drove the blade into her side. Hannah's throat hitched, but otherwise she appeared not to notice. She went right on babbling, spraying spit on Portis as she prated about notes, promises, and sacred red blood on white linen sheets. When she began to rant about the unholiness of abortion, Portis drew the blade from her side and inserted it in the area just below her sternum.

That worked. Her eyes grew round with surprise as she leaned slowly back against her dead brother's legs. She took out the knife and handed it to Portis as casually as if she were handing him a can of soda. Then she looked at him and smiled. "It's warm, isn't it? Feel how nice and warm the sand is?"

"Crazy bitch," Portis muttered.

Chapter Twenty-Six

At the same moment Hannah phoned the St. Clair house, Edie awoke to the sensation of gentle hands touching her belly. Rubbing. Someone was rubbing something greasy on her stomach. She tried to open her eyes and found it impossible; something was tied around her head so tightly she couldn't lift her eyelids. Her head hurt, she noticed. A spot behind her left ear was pulsing with pain. A mental reconnaissance of the rest of her body found her extremities tightly bound. She shivered when she realized she was exposed from the belly down. She couldn't feel her underwear. Her warm woolly socks were there, but she felt no underwear.

"Cold?" a voice asked in an inscrutable whisper.

Edie decided not to answer. She tried to remember what had happened. She had been walking. Walking down the road and hoping for a ride before Portis came by. She had made it to the main road—

"I asked if you were cold," said the whisperer.

"Of course I'm cold," Edie snapped. "I'm lying here without any underwear on. What did you expect?"

There was no reply. When numerous seconds had passed, Edie decided on the imperial approach. In her best stern and haughty voice, she said, "Who are you and just *what* do you think you're doing?"

"I'm a friend," the whisperer replied.

"I don't have any friends," Edie said. "At least none that go in for this kind of thing. Where are we? And what are you putting on my stomach? I never use anything but sesame oil. I don't—"

"Hush now. Don't get excited."

"Ex*cuse* me," Edie said. "But I think I have a right to know these things. Why am I tied up?"

"Please be quiet. You're ruining my concentration."

Edie snorted, indignant. "You're not doing much for me, either. Are you a man or a woman? I can't tell by your whispering."

"It's not important. Hush now, and let me watch for movement."

"Movement? I'll move for the death penalty if you don't untie me. Do you know who my brother is? He's going to be the next police chief, that's who." Edie paused then as she caught a whiff of something. "It smells like damp wood in here. It smells dirty, too. I hope I'm lying on something sterile. If I—"

"You are spoiled, aren't you? Spoiled rotten. And too stupid even to be afraid."

"I am *not* stupid," Edie protested.

"Then be quiet. Do you want me to gag you?"

"No. Did you hit me over the head with something?"

"I've been waiting for this opportunity. I've been waiting for you."

"Ben won't take this lightly. When I tell—" Edie stopped suddenly and sucked in her breath. "Wait, are you going to hurt me?"

"It's up to you."

"Great. You and Portis should meet each other. I'm afraid now, okay? Now I'm afraid."

272

There was a ripping sound, like that of fabric being torn.

Edie tried to sit up. "Was that my dress?"

Gentle hands forced her back down. "Just lie back and try to relax. I'll be ready to start in a minute."

"Start what?"

"My work."

Edie bit her lip. "Can I ask you something?"

"What?"

"Is that Vaseline or KY Jelly?"

Her question went unanswered. The whisperer went on making noises around her, occasionally touching her belly and feeling for movement within. Suddenly the voice said, "How are your chromosomes, Edie?"

"My what?"

"They carry hereditary characters. I've been looking into chromosomes lately."

Edie was irritated. "What does that have to do with anything?"

"It has to do with everything. Do you watch much TV?"

"I thought you wanted me to be quiet?"

Her captor ignored her. "There was a program on not too long ago. Fascinating stuff about inbreeding among the animal kingdom. It weakens the species, you see. Nature usually takes care of the inferiors, since the defects of the inbreds often make them easy prey for predators. But those who survive go on to breed, creating an even weaker strain. I resent the fact that nature has no way of dealing with inbred humans."

Edie tried to sit up again. "Are you suggesting that *my* baby is inbred? What kind of person are you?"

"I like to see things for myself."

"What are you going to do, watch my stomach all night?"

"No, I'm going to remove it."

"My stomach?"

"The baby."

"What?" Edie's voice filled the small room. Her outrage

quickly gave way to panic and fear. "You can't be serious. It's not due till next week."

"I have some ether. It might make you sick to your stomach, but—"

"No!" Edie cried. "You can't do this. Why don't you go to school and learn about chromosomes the normal way? You don't need to take my baby!"

Her captor gave a raspy chuckle. "School? I'm afraid they don't cover this area. Are you sure you don't want the ether? It's going to hurt, you know."

"You're going to cut me open?" Edie's eyes were wet beneath the blindfold. "What did I ever do to you? Why are you doing this?"

"I want to see the umbilical while it's still attached to the placenta. The last one had already been severed."

"The last . . . " Edie gasped. "My God, it was *you*. You took Joni Wilkson's baby."

"It died too soon. Are you ready now?"

"For what?"

"The incision. It . . . excites me . . . so I might not make it perfect. There's something very seductive about metal slicing through flesh. After the first time I was hooked. I've always dreamed of doing caesareans. I've been through one myself, you know, but performing one is—"

"Are you a woman?" Edie asked in horror. "My God, you must be crazy."

"No. I'm not crazy. No crazier than anyone else in this godforsaken town. Go on and scream if you have to, Edie. Without the ether it's going to hurt. The fog should muffle most of the noise. Here we go now. I'll start at the top."

The moment the cold metal touched her belly Edie opened her mouth wide and screamed as loud as she could.

The slicing of her flesh paused, and the whispering voice was closer. "I take it back. I didn't realize a scream would echo so much in here. It's distracting. Please take some ether or be quiet."

Edie was incredulous. "You're going to kill my baby and you want me to be quiet? Please don't do this. It hurts. Oh, Lord, is that blood I feel? Am I bleeding?"

"Not much. I only cut about three inches . . ." The whispering voice paused. In the next seconds Edie felt a cold whoosh of air from movement on the floor beside her. Instinctively, she knew her captor was no longer near. She opened her mouth and began to scream again, straining her lungs for volume. She screamed over and over, unconsciously counting her cries. A freezing hand over her mouth cut her off in the middle of the sixth scream.

"Oh, Jesus, Edie," said a broken voice. "What the hell is going on here?"

"Bryce?" she whimpered. "Bryce, is that you?"

"Edie, did Portis do this?"

"No," she sobbed. "I don't know who it was. Bryce, I'm *bleeding.*"

"I see that. I'm going to put a handkerchief on it, and then I'll untie you. Just calm down and try to stop crying."

"I can't stop crying. This person was going to take my baby. She was going to cut me open and take my baby out. I couldn't tell if it was a man or a woman because of the whispering, but then she said she'd had a caesarean, so it must have been a woman. There was all this crazy talk about inbreeding and chromosomes and—Bryce, would you please get this blindfold off me?"

He finished untying her hands and placed one of them on her belly. "Hold this firm now and we'll slow the bleeding down. It doesn't look too bad."

"Oh, thank God." Edie caught her breath then. "Are you looking at me? Bryce, don't you dare look at me."

"It's a little late, Edie. And it's nothing I haven't seen before."

"But I'm so *fat* now," she cried. "And I don't have any underwear on."

Bryce ignored her to work on the blindfold. When the

fabric came away she rubbed her wet eyes before looking at him. His face was taut, his blue eyes worried. She looked down at the handkerchief.

"You carry a red handkerchief?"

"That's your blood, Edie. Let me get your feet untied and we'll see if you can walk. Can you sit up?"

"Can I have your jacket? I *told* this person not to use my dress. I can't pull it down. Too much has been ripped away. Is that what I'm tied up with?"

Bryce took off his police jacket and draped it over her middle. "Happy now?"

"Thank you," she told him. Then her eyes began watering again. "Bryce, she was so crazy. She wanted the baby so she could look at the umbilical cord. The Wilkson baby didn't have one, and it died too soon, she said."

"Stop thinking about it." Bryce freed her ankles and pulled her into a sitting position. "And please stop crying, Edie. I don't have any more handkerchiefs."

"I'm sorry, but you'd cry too if it almost happened to you. I was so scared, Bryce. At first I was mad and I said some really stupid things, but then I realized she was serious and she was going to take our baby and I got so scared . . ." She paused and hiccoughed at the look on his face. He opened his mouth to say something, then he seemed to reconsider. "Think you can walk?" he asked her.

"What were you going to say?"

"Nothing. Come on, I'll help you stand up."

"You were going to say something else," Edie declared as he gripped her hands and pulled.

"No, I wasn't. Now help me."

"You were too. I could tell you were going to—"

They both stared as the floor beneath her feet suddenly puddled with water.

"Oh, shit," said Bryce. "Is that what I think it is?"

Edie looked at him. "I don't know. I haven't had any pains . . . I think."

"You think?"

She lifted a shoulder in a shrug. "I guess that means they're going to start, though."

"You guess?"

"This *is* my first baby," she reminded him. "I've been feeling crampy since I left the house today, but—"

"Okay, let's go," Bryce interjected.

"Where?"

"To the hospital."

"Oh no." Edie backed away from him. "I'm not going to any hospital looking like this."

"For crissakes, Edie. We need to get your stomach taken care of. Just tie the sleeves of the jacket around you and we'll go."

"We can stop at my car," Edie told him. "My suitcases are there. I can get some clothes and . . . where's my purse?"

"What?"

"My purse. Bryce, I need that purse. It's got the tape in it. Do you see it anywhere?"

Bryce looked around himself in disbelief. "I will never understand the way you think, Edie. Never in a hundred goddamn years. There it is in the corner. Just stay put. I'll get it."

"See if my undies are over there," Edie said. She saw him shake his head and heard him mutter something under his breath as he moved away from her. She checked the handkerchief under the jacket and decided to turn it to the other side. Holding the jacket between her knees, she shook out the handkerchief, folded it, then pressed it against her wound once more. The wound itself looked awful. Half sick from the sight, Edie glanced up in time to see her husband glide through the door of the depot and lunge at Bryce with a knife. Edie screamed in shock and saw Bryce whirl. The knife in Portis's hand disappeared in the blue shirt of Bryce's police uniform. Bryce sagged to the floor. Edie cried out his name and stumbled forward.

"Fancy meeting you here," Portis said to her as he jerked the knife out. "Did I hear you mention something about a tape? It wouldn't be a Lamaze tape, would it, you sly little bitch?" He tore the purse from Bryce's hand and unzipped the top to rummage through the contents.

"You picked a hell of a place to meet your boyfriend, wifey. That lantern's a nice touch, but it's a little chilly in here, isn't it? And who the fuck was that in the blue Camaro? Sonofabitch nearly ran me down in the road. You know, I bet you thought you had it made with this tape. I won't even ask how the hell you got out of the closet."

Edie was staring at Bryce. He wasn't moving. And there was something dark on the floor around him.

"Here it is." Portis held up the tape. "I admit it was stupid to keep it, but as long as you were holed up I thought I'd get my money's worth out of it."

He dropped the purse and approached her. "Were you thinking of running to your big brother with it?"

"Bryce . . ." Edie whispered. She couldn't tear her gaze away from him. He was too big and strong to be lying there so still. Wait—had his hand moved?

Portis jerked the police jacket away from her.

"What's this?" he asked when he saw the blood-soaked handkerchief. He peeled her hand away and looked at the wound. "A little on-the-spot caesarean?"

Edie felt her throat thicken as a sudden sharp pain ripped through her abdomen. "Bryce!" she cried out. "Bryce, are you all right?"

Her husband shook his head. "No, dear, I'd say he's definitely not all right. In fact, I'd say he's going to die pretty soon. Just look at the blood he's losing. Go on, I want you to see it." Portis shoved her, and she walked on stiff legs over to where Bryce lay.

"Take a good long look," Portis told her. "And while you're looking, remind yourself that you made this happen. This is your own fault. I just want you to realize that."

"Bryce?" Edie whispered. He was on his side, almost in a fetal position. She stopped in front of him and clasped her hands together when she saw the thick pool of blood around him. The tears rolled freely down her face. "You aren't going to die, are you?"

His lips moved. Holding her stomach, Edie leaned over him to hear what he was trying to say.

"That's my girl," Portis said. "Get down there and get a really close view. You might have to die with him. I haven't decided yet. I don't know if the murder spree thing would go over. I could get used to this, though. No piss in the britches tonight. A little rash is all. A few more times and I think I could get over that."

"Bryce, I can't hear you," Edie whispered to him. "What are you saying?"

"Move."

Edie didn't understand. She looked at him in confusion; then she saw his fingers unsnapping his holster. She was standing between him and Portis. Bryce was asking her to move out of the way. Instead, Edie quickly bent down and took the gun into her own hands.

"No!" Portis bellowed.

Without hesitation, Edie turned and fired as her husband rushed her. The first shot blasted into the wooden wall behind him. It was the loudest thing Edie had ever heard. Portis kept coming, his eyes bright and feverish with his rage. Edie fired again, this time actually hitting him in the arm, but the hand with the raised knife was still coming. In desperation she aimed for his heart and squeezed the trigger again and again, until her ears were ringing. Finally she saw him stop. The knife clattered to the floor as Portis clutched at the neat hole in his hand. He looked down at the blood spurting from one thigh as the leg buckled underneath him. Portis went to his knees and began to sway. Blood poured from his wounds.

Less than a yard away, Edie was tempted to try for his forehead. Portis didn't give her the chance. Sobbing like a child, he crawled away from her. He threw himself into the corner and collapsed into unconsciousness.

Edie refrained from the urge to spit at him. She dropped

the empty gun and turned her attention to Bryce, whose pale face frightened her as she kneeled beside him. She grabbed the tattered hem of her dress and ripped off yet another long strip to wad up and press hard against the seeping wound in Bryce's chest.

"My bleeding's stopping," she told him above the buzz in her ears. "I'll try to stop yours, too. I got Portis. I got him for you. Are you still conscious? Do you hear me?"

Bryce made a noise in his throat, and Edie felt a shuddering sigh pass through her body along with a sharp labor pain. "Please . . . don't . . . curl . . . up like that," she told him around the pain. "It scares me. I'm scared enough as it is right now. Our baby's coming. I'm having pains. I think it's coming fast."

Bryce opened his eyes. His lips were white. His voice was a whisper. "Tonight's the first time I've ever heard you call it ours."

Edie started crying again. "Well of course it's *ours*. Bryce, please don't die. Even if we aren't together, I want my baby to have its father. I was leaving Portis. I had my suitcases packed, but he put me in the closet. I got out today and I was going to make a life for myself away from him. I—"

"Edie," Bryce painfully interrupted, "if you don't go to my car right now and call for an ambulance, I will die."

"An ambulance! Oh, my God!" Edie pushed herself to her feet and trotted out of the depot. When she returned, she was struggling for breath. "They're coming. They're on their way. They'll be here in a few minutes." She stopped talking and clenched her teeth as another labor pain seized her. Bryce opened his eyes to see her sag down beside him. He watched her pant for a moment before extending a shaking arm to touch her pale, dirty face.

"Edie, I love you."

She turned her head to stare at him. Her eyes filled when she saw the seriousness in his eyes. "Are you saying that just because you're dying?"

Bryce moved his head slightly to tell her no. Then he

closed his eyes again. It was getting harder to talk. Harder to breathe. Edie reached for his hand and gripped it tightly as another pain assaulted her. Bryce felt the fuzziness in his head begin to grow. His thoughts began to wander, then he suddenly focused in on one thing. He opened his eyes and looked at the panting Edie. "Camaro," he whispered. "Edie . . . the radio."

Chapter Twenty-Seven

Lura arrived home from the restaurant to find her mother sitting on the front porch in the dark. With a muffled cry of exasperation Lura slammed her way out of the car and approached Annette's shivering figure.

"What are you trying to do to me, Mama? Is Phil asleep again? He was supposed to be watching you."

"He is watching me," Annette said through chattering teeth. "It's foggy, isn't it? Maybe God had some leftover cloud that he didn't know what to do with."

Lura pushed her mother inside the house and turned on the lamp beside the sofa. "Let me see your hands, Mama."

"Why?"

"Because if there's blood on them I'm either going to scream or go insane."

"Blood?" Annette chuckled and showed Lura two clean white hands. "People have a thing about blood, don't they? Its significance. Blood brothers, blood sisters, bloody hands, a bloody good cup of tea—what does blood have to do with tea, anyway? Blood, blood, blood. How can you tell by looking if it's good blood or bad blood? You can't. But bad blood can kill you. And it can kill others."

"Who . . . has it killed?" Lura asked hesitantly.

"Me," Annette said. "And probably you. Sin spawns evil."

"Are you saying—" A noise from the kitchen caused Lura to pause and cock her head. She heard it again, a woman's high, frantic voice. "Sit down and turn on the TV, Mama. I'll be back in a minute."

Lura walked into the kitchen and looked at the police band radio on the table.

"Make them hurry," the woman was saying. "He's still bleeding and I think he's going into shock. If anyone tries to take Portis first, they're going to die. I just want you to know that."

There was static, then a man's voice said, "They're on their way. Just try to relax."

Portis? Lura thought. The voice sounded like Edie. Lura sat down at the table, wondering what had happened and just who it was that Edie wanted to be taken before her husband. From the hallway she heard her brother's door open. Lura rose from the table and took a Pepsi out of the refrigerator before sitting down again. Phil came into the kitchen and smiled at her. "I was on the phone talking to this girl from school. I think she likes me."

"And I suppose you were so engrossed that you didn't hear Mama open the front door and leave?"

Phil's lips tightened. "I guess maybe I was. Did she wander off again?"

"How long were you on the phone?"

"An hour. Maybe longer."

Lura shook her head. "Teenagers. So, you think she likes you, huh?"

Phil shrugged. "I like her, anyway. Listen, I didn't fix any dinner. Mama said she wasn't hungry."

"She may be now," Lura said. "I'll fix something in a minute. I just heard something pretty strange come over the radio."

"Really? What was it?" Phil opened the refrigerator and scanned the contents with a bored expression.

"I think it was—"

The radio on the table crackled loudly. "Hello? It's Edie again. Are you there?"

There was static, then, "This is Simmons. Go ahead."

"The person who tried to cut me open tonight drives a blue Camaro. Bryce says Phil Taylor owns—"

The voice was cut off as Phil flicked a switch on the police band. He leaned against the counter and looked at his sister.

Lura swallowed. "Phil . . . ?"

"I don't believe this," he muttered. "She couldn't possibly have taken my car without my hearing her. I didn't even know she could still drive." He spread his hands then. "But Edie could be wrong about the color, you know. Shit, it's dark out there."

"She said blue, so she must have seen it," Lura said, and suddenly she was afraid. Afraid to ask her mother any questions. Afraid to know what Edie was talking about.

"Do we have any Dr. Pepper?" Annette walked into the kitchen with a hopeful expression. "I want the unusual. I'm tired of that same old cola taste."

Phil looked at the key hook hanging on the wall beside the refrigerator, then he approached his mother and felt the pockets of her natty cardigan.

"My goodness," said Annette as he pulled his car keys out of her left pocket. "I wonder how those got in there?"

"That's it," Phil said. "I'm not waiting for them to sign the papers, Lura. We're taking her in first thing tomorrow morning."

"In?" Annette echoed. "Where is in? What are you talking about, Philip?"

"In, as in looney bin," Phil said. "In, as in funny farm,

happy acres, nuthouse, and hospice for the criminally insane."

"Oh," said Annette.

"You smart-mouthed little bastard." Lura put an arm around her dumbstruck mother. "That was totally uncalled for, Philip."

"Really? Ask her what she's been doing tonight. Ask her what Edie Jackson meant about someone trying to cut her open. Ask her about the dozens of animal corpses buried in our backyard, most of them mutilated beyond recognition." Phil laughed at Lura's expression of surprise. "Yeah, I think we can stop dancing around each other now. We both know what she's been doing, and it's time we stopped covering up. Unless you'd like to go to prison for her again."

Annette put a hand to her forehead. "I guess this means we don't have any Dr. Pepper. Lura, could you come and help me pack? If I'm going to the farm tomorrow, I'll need to find my riding boots. I hope my father hasn't sold my mare. He threatened to, you know."

"I'm sure he hasn't," Lura said, and keeping her arm around her mother's shoulders, she led her slowly down the hall. Once inside Annette's room, Lura closed the door behind them and lifted a hand to touch her mother's face.

"I'm sorry, Mama, but he's right. You have to go tomorrow."

Annette swatted her hand away and turned to spit at the door. "Liar! *Ne vous fiez pas a lui.*"

Lura stepped back in surprise. "Why shouldn't I trust him?"

Her mother sat down on the bed and beckoned for Lura to join her. *"Menagez vos paroles: it nous ecoute."*

"We don't have to be careful," Lura told her. "He doesn't understand French."

Annette looked at her daughter a long moment before

sighing and putting her face in her hands. She sobbed once, then said, *"Il est coupable."*

Lura stared. "What? What did you say?"

Her mother repeated herself, then she went on. Lura listened to the rapid French and felt the blood drain from her face at what her completely coherent mother was saying.

"I didn't kill your father, Lura. It wasn't me. At first I thought the two of them had been fooling around and had had some kind of accident. Ordney was always letting him play with that knife. But then I realized what had happened was no accident. Philip was actually smiling as your father tried to put his insides back where they belonged. I was afraid to go in, afraid to touch Philip, but he let me take the knife away from him. He stopped smiling and sat down in the corner, just the way you saw him when you came into the room. I was holding the knife, and I knew you would think I had done it, so I allowed you to believe that. What else could I do? I couldn't let them take my son away. He was just a baby."

Lura was still staring. She had to clear her throat before she could speak. "I don't . . . is this . . . Mama, are you telling me the truth?"

"God help me, yes. I couldn't let them take him, Lura. Not my son."

"So you let them take me instead," Lura said. Her chest suddenly felt as if it would burst with anger. "And you allowed me to think you had killed Daddy in self-defense, so you could cover up his murder."

"I knew it was wrong the moment you left," Annette said. "Why do you think I tried to kill myself? I was in such a panic. I've lived with nothing but pain since. He's never stopped killing, Lura. Philip killed all those animals he told you about—horrible, horrible deaths—and he's gotten worse since you came home. That baby. And a blond woman. I had to hide her in her storm cellar. All for him, and he wants to send me away. He doesn't care. He's just like Renée was—the coldest, most convincing liar you ever saw."

"Eight years, Mama," Lura said dully.

"Forgive me," Annette whispered.

"I don't know if I can. This craziness . . . it's all been an act?"

Her mother ignored her. "He told me everything about his crimes. Everything. His gloating made me sick. He knew no one would believe me."

"That's why he doesn't like us to speak in French," Lura guessed. "But why wait so long to tell me, Mama? Why didn't you tell me the night you hid that woman's body?"

Annette's eyes misted over. "I was still hoping . . . she was already dead, you know. Philip told me she was dead when he found her. And then he told me he'd left her on her own front porch after he finished with her. He was so arrogant, Lura, so certain he would never be caught. He could always blame it on me, you see. Like tonight. He put those keys in my pocket when he was feeling around my sweater. When I'm gone, he'll probably try to blame things on you. You're the one who's been to prison for murder."

Lura wiped a line of perspiration from her forehead. Her skin felt cold, clammy with fear.

"When did it start, Mama?"

"What? His illness?"

"Yes." If that's what you could call it, Lura silently added.

"Before birth, perhaps. He is so much like Renée was. The first time I realized it was the day Ordney took him hunting for the first time. Your father forced him to gut and clean every kill. A week or so later Philip suddenly started asking me questions about reproductive organs. He was fascinated with the fact that he had come into the world by caesarean. He really made a mess of that poor dead woman's midsection. He took out her uterus, fallopian tubes . . . everything."

A sudden swelling in her throat prevented Lura from

speaking for a moment. When the nausea abated, she said, "Those things you told me about your family—were they all true?"

"Like what?"

"The incestuous marriage between your mother and father. And your brother being a rapist and a murderer."

Annette smiled. "What brother? Did Marie tell you that? Shame on her. I'll have to speak to her about her mouth."

Lura went still. She stared. The suddenly vacant expression in her mother's eyes made her flesh prickle. She opened her mouth, then she turned her head as the bedroom door swung open. Phil looked at them in disgust.

"I hope you've had a nice bilingual chat, ladies. Perhaps you'd care to uncurl your tongue long enough to come out and talk to Ben, Lura. He says he has something that belongs to you."

A mixture of anxiety and relief pulled Lura off the bed. Unconsciously, she avoided making contact as she moved past her brother. She stared at his hands and wondered if the black under his nails was grease or blood. He grunted and she looked at his face. He was a black-haired stranger with steely blue eyes and audibly grinding teeth. He was nervous, Lura realized, and he was watching her so closely that it made her nervous.

"We were talking about Mama's childhood," she offered. "In France."

Phil turned his head and looked at his mother. "Mama, you haven't packed a thing. I think we should start with a nightgown."

"All right," Annette said affably. She rose from the bed and walked to her dresser.

Once in the hallway, Lura turned. Phil gave her a frosty smile as he closed Annette's door. Lura started away, then halted in her steps when she heard the lock click. She rushed back, twisted the knob, and felt the hairs on her neck raise as she heard a muffled cry from inside the room.

"Phil, open the door!" Lura pummeled against the wood

then turned to shout down the hall. "Ben, come back here and help me! He's going to kill her! Phil, don't!"

Ben came down the hall at a run, his brow furrowed. He pulled Lura away from the door and splintered the wood around the lock with one solid kick. He entered the room with Lura right behind him. Both of them stopped just inside the door. Phil lay on the bed, his head in his mother's lap. His eyes were round and disbelieving. His hands were wrapped around a syringe sticking out of his chest.

Annette looked up and smiled. "Hello, Ben. It's nice to see you again."

"Annette—" Ben began, but she cut him off with a wave of her hand, as if she knew what he wanted to say.

"Don't bother. This is how my father killed my brother, Renée. Sodium pentobarbital right in the heart. It just stops, you see. Notice the surprise on his face? When Philip brought home that baby I knew I'd better see about getting some. I shouldn't have waited this long, really. No telling how many people he's hurt. But it works very fast if you use the right amount. Poor, sweet boy."

She looked at Lura. "Philip had the baby in his room for three days. I'll bet you didn't even notice. But I did. And the deer he brought home. Silly boy tried to put its intestines through the garbage disposal."

Sickened, Lura turned her face. "Mama, why didn't you tell me?"

"I thought I did. Didn't I just tell you?"

"I mean before. When he was *doing* these things."

Annette shrugged. "Maybe I didn't want to. When he told me what he was going to do to Edie Jackson, I thought about saying something, but then the 'Beverly Hillbillies' came on and—"

"What about Edie?" Ben asked sharply.

Lura looked at him and suddenly realized he didn't know. In a choked voice she told him what she had heard on the radio. Mouth tight, hands clenched into fists, Ben left the room. A moment later Lura heard his voice on the phone in the kitchen. She looked at her brother's unmoving form, his startled blue eyes, and she began to cry.

"Mama, why did you do it?"

"Do what?"

"Kill him. Why did you kill Philip?"

Her mother stroked the dark head in her lap, then she withdrew a knife from under her pillow.

"His blood was bad, Lura. He couldn't escape it. Not when it runs in your family for centuries. Here, I'll show you what it looks like . . . "

Before Lura could move, her mother had lifted the knife and plunged it deep into her own soft middle.

"No!" Lura rushed to her and reached for the blade. Her mother held on to the handle and shoved it even deeper. Blood poured forth and covered both of them.

"Bad," Annette whispered. "You can't escape it either, Lura. You should join us. It's not hard. And it's not that painful, really. You want to come with us, don't you? You don't want to be here all alone."

Lura put her head down and began to sob. "Mama, I'm—"

"I know you're afraid. But it won't hurt, Lura. I promise. There's nothing for you here. You'll always be different. You'll never be one of them. You're my girl, and you have my blood in your veins. Come with me. Me and Philip. You honored me once, honor me again."

"No!" Ben rushed forward and caught Annette's arm as she was about to plunge the knife into Lura's exposed back. He wrestled the blade away from her, and his face burned black with fury as he battled the urge to bury the blade in the woman's grinning visage. Finally, with only a glimpse at the shaky *O* and the crooked *T* carved into the bone handle, he tossed the knife into the hallway and turned back to pull Lura from her mother's bloody embrace. Annette held on, her fingers entwined in her daughter's long gray hair. Spittle mixed with blood ran down her chin as she spoke.

"You can't have her, Ben. She's my daughter, my blood, and no one in this filthy little town shall have her. She's one of us and she knows it. She loves me more than she'll ever love you. She proved it."

Ben looked away from her wild eyes to focus on Lura. "Don't listen," he said hoarsely. "Please don't listen to her, not this time. You're not like them. You never were."

"You're wrong," Annette said with a gurgling sound. "It's inside her. Tell him, Lura. Tell him how you're going to come and help me and Philip along. She wants to come with us. If not now, then later. She knows what to do once she has the chance. Dumford has nothing to offer her without us. Nothing. She's no one here."

Ben tightened his hold on Lura and put his mouth close to her ear. "Lura, I can't lose you again. Help me. Don't choose her this time, choose *us*. Pull away from her. Please."

Slowly, Lura's sobbing paused. Her hands came up to close around her mother's wrists, and her knuckles whitened as Lura began to pull. Ben felt her shudder as the hair tore away from her head in thick strands.

"I'm sorry, Mama," Lura whispered. "You'll have to go without me. I can't help you this time."

Ben grabbed Lura and held onto her. Annette looked at the hair in her blood-covered hands and smiled knowingly at her daughter. "Don't keep us waiting, Lura," she said, and died.

Epilogue

By the last week of November the leaves of every tree in Dumford filled the streets and yards. As Ben pulled into Berniece Miller's drive he noted that her yard was one of the few that had been raked and cleared of all fall debris. It was typical of Berniece, Ben decided. So much of what she dealt with was messy and unkempt that she probably made it a point to keep an immaculate house and leaf-free yard.

Berniece herself met him at the door, and her smile for him was huge. "Well, if it isn't the new chief of police, come to pay me a visit. What shall I call you now?"

"Ben," he said, returning her smile. "Are you busy?"

"Not a bit. I'm just on my way out to fill up the bird feeder."

"I'll come with you," Ben offered. "Where do you keep your birdseed?"

"In the garage on the second shelf. I'll get a jacket and meet you out back."

Ben went to the garage and found the birdseed. He carried it around the side of the house and smiled as Berniece came out and took his arm. They walked through the yard together and Berniece suddenly turned to him. "You're definitely a different man these days. Calmer. Less strained. That girl makes you happy, doesn't she?"

Ben nodded. "She does."

"But you're worried?"

"Yes."

"She's still having the nightmares," Berniece guessed. "Still battling the ghosts across the street."

"Yes," Ben admitted.

"Tell me about it," Berniece suggested.

"There's not much to tell. She shivers and mumbles, and once I woke up to find her in the kitchen holding a fork and staring at it. A dinner fork."

Berniece's nod was sympathetic. "Her family's hold over her was strong. So strong as to be unhealthy. I touched her when I met her in the grocery store last week, just to see how she was getting along. Her confusion is still great. Things are dark and jumbled for her yet. Right now she toys with the idea that her loved ones are somewhere she can reach them, if she can only make the journey. But of course she can't. She can't leave you. Her love for you is what keeps her in place."

"Will it always?" Ben asked.

Berniece stopped and reached for the birdseed. "Time is what she needs. Are you wedded yet?"

"Soon," he said. "As soon as she's ready."

The gold tooth appeared. "How nice. What about that Bryce McKee? He hasn't been to see me for some time now. Did he marry your sister yet?"

"The day after her emergency divorce was signed. They stood before a judge and Edie held the baby instead of a bouquet."

"A little girl."

Ben nodded. "They named her Analise."

"Are they happy?"

"Edie's delirious. Bryce is still a little upset with her for moving into the house while he was in the hospital. I guess the wallpaper she ordered was pretty expensive."

Berniece chuckled. Then she became serious. "And what of the hearing I read about in the weekly? How did that go?"

Ben exhaled. "Portis Jackson was arraigned on four counts of first-degree murder. Not only that, but he owes the IRS nearly a quarter of a million dollars in back taxes. They came down on him the same day of the hearing. Yesterday he fired his second lawyer."

"The trial hasn't even started yet."

"I know." Ben shifted his feet and looked at the sky.

Berniece looked at him before lifting the bag of birdseed. "All right, Chief. I guess we're through with the small talk. Tell me why you've come to me today."

Ben took the bag from her and dumped the contents into the bird feeder. "You know why. I need your help. I told myself I wouldn't take advantage of you, especially for police work, but I have to ask. I wouldn't be using every resource available if I didn't. I'll try to pay you for your services—"

A firm brown hand gripped him by the arm. Her black eyes were steady. "You realize what you're asking? If people find out you came to see me, you'll face scorn and ridicule and probably be laughed out of a job."

Ben covered her hand with his own and squeezed her fingers. "No, I won't."

"All right," Berniece said, satisfied. Then she gave his hand back to him. "You're seeking a man. A retarded man?"

"Alzheimer's," Ben said. "He's been missing two days." He took a white T-shirt from his jacket and handed it to her. Berniece held the garment in her hands. After a moment she rubbed the fabric against her face. Then she began to smile. "This one's easy. He's in the woods. He's cold and hungry and he's scared. I see a big rotted stump, about a hundred yards west of a rusty old tractor abandoned by a fence."

"I know where it is," Ben said in relief. "The tractor is on Julius Hinshaw's property. The man is his uncle from town. He must have decided to visit his nephew and become lost. I don't know how to thank you, Berniece."

"Don't bother," she said with a smile. "I get the feeling we're going to be seeing a lot of each other."

Ben smiled and kissed her on the cheek.

After the elderly uncle had been found and returned home, and after Ben had finished training his new dispatcher, he left the station. He halted the cruiser in his driveway and found himself thinking of raking his own yard. The rain gutters could use his attention as well. Not to mention the rotting frame on the picture window. Only since Lura had moved in with him had he begun to notice all the things that needed to be done.

There was no answer when he opened the front door and called for her. He walked into the kitchen and smelled a pot roast cooking. He sampled a stick of celery from a bowl on the counter and walked into the hall. "Lura, where are you?"

"Don't come in," she said to him through the bathroom door.

Ben paused and put his hand on the knob. "Why not?"

"Because I asked you not to."

"What if I said I had to go?"

"I'd say you can wait."

Ben remained outside the door. For no reason, Berniece's words and a vision of the razor blades on the bathroom shelf came to him. His palms grew moist. Ben had experienced bad dreams of his own since the night Annette Taylor killed her son. The old woman had gotten to him. She had scared him into worrying constantly about Lura. What she was thinking. What she was doing when Ben wasn't with her. How she was feeling.

"Lura," he said against the wood, "let me in."

"Ben, can't you—"

"Open the door, Lura."

"All right." She opened the door and stood back to put her hands on her hips. When Ben didn't say anything, just stared at her, she tossed the bottle of dye in the wastebasket and touched her glossy black hair.

"Well," she said. "How do you like it?"

Ben's mouth curved with sudden pleasure. She looked nineteen again.

"I love it," he said.